MAKE ME
BAD

USA TODAY BESTSELLING AUTHOR
R.S. GREY

Published: R.S. Grey 2019
authorrsgrey@gmail.com
Editing: Editing by C. Marie
Proofreading: JaVa Editing, Red Leaf Proofing
Cover Design: R.S. Grey
ISBN: 9781796441475

CHAPTER ONE
BEN

It's been quite a while since I threw a punch. The last time was in high school.

A part of me worries I've forgotten how to do it, but it seems intuitive: put some heat behind it, aim well, and be prepared for the consequences. Simple enough.

Normally, I don't find myself in situations like this: at a seedy bar on the wrong side of town, seconds away from losing my temper. I glance down at where my hand grips my drink. My knuckles are white. The glass is about to shatter into a million pieces. My palm will be a bloody mess.

My friend Andy notices. His hand lands on my shoulder in a gesture of solidarity. "C'mon, dude, ignore them. They're idiots."

Idiots is exactly right. At the table behind me, there are three guys I've known since we were kids. Usually, the only emotion I feel toward them is pity. If I grew up with a silver spoon in my mouth, they grew up with dirt stuffed in theirs. Since the days of little league and Pop Warner football, our paths have rarely crossed, but tonight, Andy wanted to get a drink at Murphy's. "It'll be fun," he said. "We've never been there. Maybe it has a cool atmosphere." So, here I am on a rickety barstool, drinking cheap beer and listening to these Three Stooges run their mouths.

It starts with low-hanging fruit.

"…pretty boy came to our side of town…"

"…thinks his shit don't stink…"

"…too good for us…"

I ignore them, drink, and watch the Rockets game on TV, but they're growing restless, getting impatient. They want a reaction, and the longer I sit here with my back to them, the more they dig for it.

"Hey Ben!" one of them shouts, trying to force me to pay attention.

I ignore them.

A low whistle follows and then another one speaks up. "Ben, we're talking to you."

I tell myself to keep my focus on the TV. The Rockets are up. I had a good day at the firm. My clients are happy. My beer is only half empty. Life is good.

"It's okay if he doesn't want to talk, guys." It's their ringleader piping in now—Mac. He's a big, burly guy with a thick scraggly beard. We played on the same little league team and he wasn't so bad then, but I remember his dad usually yelled at him a lot during the games. Guess the apple doesn't fall far from the tree. "He's probably sad about his mom."

His taunting words are a poison dart.

My vision tunnels and Andy turns on his barstool, jumping in before I can. "Hey, what's this about? Can't we all just watch the game? Let me buy you guys a round."

That's my best friend: level-headed, cool to a fault. He once sweet-talked his grade up from a 75 to a 93 on a law school paper. He still brags about it to this day.

The guys behind us laugh at his offer, and I finally turn to assess them over my shoulder. Mac meets my eye, and it's just as I suspected—he needs to lay off the fast food and find a dentist. He spits tobacco juice into a Styrofoam cup and sends a yellow-stained sneer my way.

I get it.

These guys are pissed at the world—high school dropouts, the outcasts of society—and we offered them a gift by stepping in here tonight. I'm everything they despise. To them, I'm the rich prick with my foot on their backs, holding them down. I'm the reason their lives suck. Maybe I would have let them take jabs at me all night just to ease their suffering a little bit, but the second they decided to bring my family into it, there was no going back. My dad and I have been through hell these last few years, and now that I think about it, I wouldn't mind taking out my anger on these guys. In fact, it sounds kind of nice.

I slide off my stool and shrug out of my suit jacket. It's new and I happen to like it enough to keep it clean. I toss it back onto my seat and then smile at the group while I roll up my sleeves.

"My friend offered you a drink," I say, my voice calm and even despite how hard my heart thunders in my chest.

The guy closest to me is wiry with oil-stained coveralls. I forget his name, but it's not important. He's leaning back and only two of his chair legs touch the ground. It's a cocky pose. He's daring gravity to get him.

He spits on the floor at my feet. "We don't want your fuckin' charity."

Andy frowns. "Now that's just not nice." He points down. "You got spit on his shoes. No one wants spit on their shoes, man."

Wiry guy makes a real show of hacking up more phlegm in this throat and then he takes careful aim at my feet again. To anyone else, it'd be enough to elicit a reaction, but I don't give a shit about this guy and his overproduction of saliva.

It's Mac who finally hits the target.

"Did you hear me, Ben?" Mac prods, sitting up to his full height. "I asked about your mom. She still fuckin' crazy? Oh, wait, that's right, I forgot she's—"

The rubber band inside me snaps. Without an ounce of hesitation, I step forward and kick the legs out from under wiry guy's chair.

Consequences be damned.

CHAPTER TWO
MADISON

Today is my 25th birthday and I'm standing in the middle of the children's section at the library while my coworkers serenade me. This is my official birthday party, the only one I'm going to get. I wish I were in Vegas at one of those clubs where the Kardashians have their birthdays. Strobe lights would be flashing, my dress would be killer, and I'd stumble upon a billionaire financier who just so happened to have the body of an NFL player in the hall on the way to the bathroom. I'd accidently trip and fall—*oops!*—right into his path. He'd fall too, for me, *instantly*. My life would forever be changed.

As it is, here in reality, there's a small cake and a few streamers hanging haphazardly from the ceiling. Most have already fallen to the ground, crunched beneath our shoes. To his credit, my friend Eli brought in a fancy fruit and cheese tray this morning, but there's really only a few blue cheese crumbles and sad melon left since we've been taking swipes from it all day.

"Happy birthday to you," he sings loudly, trying to carry the torch for the other two partygoers. He even waves his hands back and forth like an orchestra conductor as if that will energize them a bit. "Happy birthday to you. Happy birthday dear Madison—"

A lone voice breaks out from the pack. "Madeline…*er*…*Madison*."

Our intern, Katy, still doesn't know my name, and she's been here for six weeks. Also, she's currently texting.

Eli shoots her a glare and carries the song home for everyone. "Happy birthday to *youuuuuu*! Woo!" He claps uproariously. "Make a wish!"

My lone candle is seeping blue wax down onto the cake, which is homemade courtesy of Mrs. Allen. She's admittedly not a baker, but her heart was definitely in it, and she even wrote my name across the top in shaky white cursive. I love it.

I close my eyes and try to think of a wish right when Katy whispers to Eli.

"Do I *have* to be here? Like, am I still getting paid?"

All day, I've been carefully avoiding the urge to take stock of my life, a universal instinct on birthdays. I've stayed off of social media lest a stray engagement or birth announcement catch my attention. I've removed all temptation to text old flames (of which there are exactly 1.5) to see if they want to "catch up" by locking my phone in my desk drawer. Now, though, in the span of one millisecond, I'm struck with the quarter-life crisis I've so desperately been trying to fend off.

HOW IS THIS MY LIFE?!

I keep my eyes closed, tumbling through a wormhole of disbelief. *How did I get here?* As a preteen, I thought by the time I turned 25, my life would have really come together. I'd have a sleek red convertible, a three-story dream house, a hip-to-waist ratio under .75, and a boyfriend named Ken. Admittedly, I now see that was Barbie's future, not mine.

I blink one eye open, praying that, by some miracle, I've teleported myself to that club with the Kardashians and the billionaire, but unfortunately, my life is still the same. There are three people at my birthday party: Mrs. Allen, the 75-year-old library administrator; Katy, the uninterested intern;

and Eli, my best friend who works up in Fiction on the second floor.

We're quite the motley crew.

I lean forward and blow out my candle, not bothering to make a wish that won't come true anyway. "No, Katy, you can head home."

She grins and I can tell she barely stifles the urge to punch the air with glee. With a pop of her gum, she adds, "Is it cool if I take some cake for my boyfriend? He has a total sweet tooth."

That's cool. Her boyfriend likes sweets and my boyfriend doesn't exist. I grumble at her to take as much as she wants and then get to work slicing it. It feels good to stab something.

"What flavor is this, Mrs. Allen?" Eli asks, inspecting the strange, murky brown color of the cake sitting on his paper plate.

"Pumpernickel."

Makes sense. Why wouldn't you make someone's birthday cake out of rye bread? Vanilla? *Pah*. Too generic and delicious.

"But," she continues, "I didn't have any baking soda, so I just added an extra cup of flour."

Oh dear. I force down exactly one forkful, plaster on a large, appreciative smile, and am eternally grateful when Mrs. Allen flakes out soon after Katy with an excuse that her bunions are killing her. The second she turns, I spit the cake into a napkin and shudder from the taste.

"Oh my god, make it stop," I groan, dropping my head to Eli's bicep.

He pats my arm as if to say, *There, there.* "Wish I could, but birthdays are birthdays. We all have to endure them. Besides, this one isn't so bad. Remember when Jared left me on my 23rd and I got so drunk I cried on his front porch and then puked on his doormat? When he asked me about it the next day, I lied and told him some high school kids were going around town doing that as a prank."

"Yeah, that wasn't your best moment, but now you have Kevin and he's great."

His features immediately glaze over as he adopts a lovesick swoon. "True. He was worth the heartache. Which reminds me…"

He turns to me, his thick black-framed glasses barely hiding the guilt lurking behind them as his frown turns into a blatant please-don't-kill-me smile.

He's about to ditch me on my birthday.

"Don't hate me, but Kevin called after work. Apparently, he's had a terrible day and—" I must look pitiful because he cuts off his sentence, shakes his head, and reaches for his phone in the pocket of his jeans. "No. You know what? I'm just going to tell him I'll be home later. It's your birthday! We have movie plans!"

I reach out and rest my hand on his forearm. "No, you should go. Kevin needs you, and I'm sure it's important."

His brows scrunch together. "You sure? I really don't want to leave you—"

His phone rings and I know it's his fiancé because his face drops. I urge him to take the call and the second it connects, I can hear Kevin upset on the other end. He's a fireman. He does important work. I feel terrible, and I won't let Eli stay to help clean up the party. Besides, there's not much to do—most of the streamers have already been ground to dust. I gesture for him to go. *Get.* I'd kick his butt if I was flexible enough to reach it.

He shakes his head and mouths, "It's your birthday!" but I scoot around him and plant my hands against his shoulder blades so I can shove him toward the door. He turns back and covers the phone with his hand. "I'm sorry, Madison. I'll make it up to you. I promise!"

I stand at the door, watching him leave, thinking to myself how adorable he and Kevin are. They're both good-looking and in shape. They have a dog they dote on, and they frequent farmers markets and brunch spots. Their life is worthy of a magazine spread, and my life is maybe worthy of a footnote near the back, after the Sudoku puzzles and spot the difference pictures. My gaze catches on my reflection in the glass door.

Oh my god.

Surely that's not me.

This woman standing before me has a mustard stain on her blouse from her lunch. Her jeans are loose around her hips and a little too long. Her dark brown hair is a wild mess, going in every direction as if each strand is trying to jump ship.

I hold my hand up and my reflection does the same.

NO. Ugh. I whip around, turning my back on the terrifying image.

If you'd told me half an hour ago that my birthday party could get even sadder, I wouldn't have believed you.

It's already close to eight o'clock, but I don't rush with cleanup. There's no point. I tear down the streamers one at a time and toss them into the trash. The fruit and cheese tray goes next. I feel guilty throwing away Mrs. Allen's cake, so instead, I put it in Tupperware to take home. Just during the transfer process alone, I audibly gag three times. There's no way I'm eating another piece, but she doesn't need to know that.

After all evidence of the party is gone, I tidy up around the library, tucking away the toys in the toddler play area and

13

re-shelving the books that were left out on the tables. I straighten my name placard—*Madison Hart, Children's Librarian*—and then bend down to eye level to wipe away a microscopic smudge.

When all of my duties are done, I still can't muster up the will to leave, so I sit at my desk and play a few rounds of solitaire. The library is absolutely silent except for the clicking of my mouse. Lenny, the security guard, isn't even making his usual rounds.

When the cleaning crew comes in, toting their vacuums and mops, I know it's time for me to leave. I can't hide out here any longer. It's time to face facts: a three-game winning streak in solitaire is as exciting as my birthday is going to get.

I stand and grab my stuff. With my Tupperware, purse, birthday present from Eli (an early edition of *Pride and Prejudice*), and winter gear, I'm loaded down. I shuffle everything into one arm then lean down to turn off my computer monitor, pausing when I spot my blue birthday candle lying on the floor under my desk. It must have rolled off when I was cleaning up. I frown, overcome with pity for the candle, forgotten on the ground, and for me for never getting to make a real wish on it. It's silly, but I drop everything onto my desk and reach down to retrieve it.

There, all alone on the floor, I hold it up in front of my mouth, close my eyes, and make the only wish that comes to mind.

Please make this next year more exciting than the last twenty-five.

And then I blow.

———

I only live half a mile from the library, so I walk to and from work most days. When people ask me about it, I say I like the exercise, but really, I just don't have the money to blow on car payments and insurance. I'm saving every penny I earn. For what? I'm not sure.

It's late February, and even in Texas, there's a biting chill in the air. I wrap my arms around myself and burrow my face down into my coat as I trudge along the sidewalk.

It's darker outside than it usually is during my walk home. I probably shouldn't have stayed so late, but it's not like there's much to worry about. Our beach town has been growing fast in the last few years, but it's still small enough to feel safe even at times like this.

A car passes by and honks twice. I don't get a good look at who's driving, but chances are, we know each other. In Clifton Cove, everyone knows everyone. I'm about to wave when I realize I don't have a free arm to do it. I'm really loaded down.

Downtown is beautiful even at this time. It looks like something straight out of a Disney theme park. All the shops are styled in a similar way: shutters, flower boxes, and striped awnings. Each is painted in a coordinating bright shade that pops in contrast to their white front doors. The cobblestone street is lined with antique lamps that dimly light my way from one to another. I pass the candy shop and the post office, a fancy butcher shop I've never been into, and a toy store. All of them are closed at this hour, but I almost prefer it that way—no having to contend with milling tourists licking ice cream cones and posing for photos. I have the street to myself.

Another car passes and the wind picks up. My teeth chatter and a strange feeling winds its way up my spine. It almost feels as if I'm being followed. I glance over my shoulder, but the sidewalk is empty. Then I face forward once again and emit an ear-splitting scream as a man dressed in all black blocks my path. I have no time to react before he shoves me hard against the wall. Everything in my arms clatters to the ground. My early edition of *Pride and Prejudice* falls out of its gift bag and lands smack dab in a mud puddle. I guess I'm truly a book lover because that's the thing that is most concerning to me, not the fact that I'm now being held up at gunpoint.

"Turn around," the man growls gruffly before taking my arm and twisting it at a painful angle. I have no choice but to turn toward the toy store and let him crush my face against the pastel pink shutter. A teddy bear stares back at me through the window.

"Please let me go!" I scream in a panic.

"Scream again and I'll pull the trigger."

I know it's absolutely insane, but the thought that hits me right then is that I should have been much more specific with my birthday wish. Because, okay, yes, while this is technically "exciting", I was sort of hoping for something a little less dangerous. *Oh, wait!* I kick myself. I see what's happening now. This man isn't going to kill me. No, this is all a misunderstanding. Perhaps he's struggling to make ends meet and he needs money to buy food for his puppy or beloved box turtle. He only wants a few dollars, I'm sure.

"If you look in my wallet—"

"Shut up," he snaps, twisting my arm so hard I wince.

In the romance novels I read, this guy would be handsome. I'd convince him to leave his life of crime behind and we'd live together in perfect harmony. I chance a quick glance over my shoulder and see he's wearing a ski mask. The bone structure underneath doesn't look all that promising. Also, his black attire—which should be slimming—doesn't conceal the hefty paunch jutting out over his jeans. *Oh dear.* I really don't think he's a hunky criminal I'll be able to sway toward living a life of honor and integrity. This isn't going to turn out the way I want it to. As such, I have no choice but to try a different tactic.

"I have a lot of money in my purse. You can have it all! Also, that book on the ground is a priceless early edition of one of Jane Austen's most famous works. I think you'll really enjoy it. It's a little muddy now, but I can clean it for you and—"

He steps closer, and his breath is really atrocious as he spits out his next words. "I don't want your goddamn money or your book. Now shut up."

The only thing I can focus on now is the cold sharp pain from his gun digging into the side of my head.

CHAPTER THREE
B E N

The cop hands me back my phone and wallet, my watch, and my suit jacket. He's looking at me with annoyance and disdain, but I plaster on a fuck-you smile and make sure to thank him.

I've never been handcuffed before tonight. I've never sat in the back of a police cruiser and had my Miranda rights read to me. I've never stepped into a police station and been stripped of my belongings, shoved in front of a camera, and told to look up for a mug shot.

It's been an interesting evening to say the least.

Out of everyone involved in the fight, I was the only one to get arrested. Apparently, there were quite a few witnesses in the bar who claimed I was the only one to throw a punch, and while that technically isn't true seeing as I have the black eye to show for it, I *was* the first one to make a move by kicking that chair.

Andy tried to talk reason into the cops, but the moment they pulled up and saw me there in the middle of the chaos, I knew I was getting dragged down to the station. Just like with Mac, I'd handed the cops a gift by stepping out of line. The chief of police in Clifton Cove and my father don't get along. They haven't for years. It's more of the blue collar, white collar bullshit that divides our town. That's what happens when there's a wealth gap so wide there's no real middle ground between the haves and the have-nots. I don't even think there was an inciting incident, just years and years of prejudice on both sides muddying the waters.

I could have stopped the whole charade from the very beginning, but I went through the motions of letting them jerk me around. I didn't put up a fight when they shoved me into the back of the cruiser. I waited until they gave me my one phone call and instead of calling my dad, I called Judge Mathers. He was in bed, close to nodding off, but within the hour, I was a free man. Well, almost—I still have a shiny new misdemeanor on my record thanks to my plea of guilty.

That surprised everyone, including the judge. I could have easily had the charges dropped. My specialty might not be criminal law, but there is no way the assault charges against me would hold up in court.

I didn't try to get the charges dropped because I know that's what they all want—Mac, the police, the chief. I know they expect me to call in a few favors and weasel my way out of any real consequences, so instead, I'll suffer them. Gladly.

Outside the station, I start my walk home since my car's back at the bar. Andy's calling nonstop, trying to figure out what's going on. He must have alerted my dad as well, or maybe it was Judge Mathers, because he's calling too. I turn off my phone and pocket it, glad for the quiet.

Main Street is deserted, which is the way I prefer it. I shove my hands into my pockets and keep walking, wondering how long it'll take me to get home. My dad's house is closer, only a few blocks away. I could stop there for the night, but I'd have rather just slept in jail. He means well, but I just don't have the energy tonight. I turn left onto a side street so I can take a shortcut to my house then stop short when I hear a woman scream. At first, I think my mind is playing tricks on me, turning the howling wind into something more sinister, but there it is again, a muffled scream.

I jerk around and stand stock-still as I listen.

There's the sound of a car a few blocks away, a barking dog in the distance, the wind picking up again, but no more screams.

I shake my head, about to turn around and keep walking when I catch movement down near the toy store. I squint and try to make out what it is, but it's impossible to tell from this distance. It almost looks like two people, a taller man in black and someone else, mostly hidden.

"Hey!" I shout on a whim, no real plan in place.

I'm unarmed and my eye is swollen enough that I can't really see well out of it. I grab for my phone and shout that I'm calling the cops. Real macho stuff, I know.

The man in black shifts a little to the left and I see a small girl cowering there with a gun aimed at her head.

Fuck.

I take off toward them, sprinting. The man sees me and whips the gun around so it's aimed my way. He shoots and a bullet pings off a lamppost near my head. *Oh Jesus.* A smart man would run in the exact opposite direction. I'm not sure what that makes me.

"Get the fuck away from her!" I shout, adrenaline coursing through my body.

I have no idea what I'm going to do, but I don't think this guy does either because the closer I get to them, the more erratic his movements become. He tries to shove the girl down onto the ground and shouts at her not to move. She puts up a little fight, but he kicks her legs out from under her and she crashes down onto the sidewalk. I yell at him to get away from her again, and now I'm only a few feet away. He glances over his shoulder, looking for an escape route.

His gun fires again and the bullet whizzes past my ear.

He's got piss-poor aim.

He realizes there are only two options: fight or flight. I'm going to wrestle that gun out of his hand even if I get shot in the process, and maybe he can tell from my pace or my tattered appearance that I'm not really someone he wants to mess with at the moment because at the very last minute, he shoves away from her and takes off running.

I skid to a stop near the girl and watch him, debating what to do. I'm fast and I could probably catch him, but then the girl moans. I glance down and realize I shouldn't leave her. She's a child. What the hell was he going to do to her? And why was she out here alone at night?

"My back," she whimpers, and I jump into action, leaning down to gently pat down her spine, checking for injuries. The streetlamp doesn't offer much light, but it's enough to see that there's not any blood on her blue pea coat.

"Is your back hurt?"

She pushes my hand away and sits up, shaking her head. "No, not my back—my *book*."

"What?"

She swipes her brown hair out of her face and points at something behind me. I turn and spot an old book lying in the mud.

This girl was just held up at gunpoint and her first concern is a book?

"I bet it's ruined," she cries, sounding heartbroken at the prospect.

I'm completely confused. "Was he trying to rob you? Or…" I can't quite bring myself to say the other R word, but maybe I don't have to because she's still fully clothed, thank God.

"No," she says, getting to her feet so she can go retrieve the book. "I don't think so. I kept offering him money, but he didn't want it. He was mumbling a lot just before you ran over, saying stuff about 'teaching him a lesson'." She crouches down and cradles the book, trying to wipe off some of the dirt. "He must have been confused. He was probably on drugs or something."

I frown, aware that she hasn't really looked at me yet. She's so concerned with that damn book, and I think she must be in shock.

"Are you hurt?" I ask, pushing to my feet and hesitantly stepping toward her with my hands outstretched. I don't want to spook her.

She finally turns and looks up, the lamplight casting a hazy glow over half of her face and leaving the rest in shadow. There are tears staining her cheeks. At first, her small stature and long hair made her seem younger than she is, but now I see she's not a child at all.

For a few seconds, we stare at each other as she takes in my appearance, dragging her gaze down my rumpled suit and then back up to my face. She blinks and recognition settles into her bright hazel eyes, framed by thick black lashes and a few unshed tears. A deep frown settles on her lips just before her hand flies up to cover her mouth. "Oh my god, did he do that to your eye?"

Right, my eye—the one that's halfway swollen shut.

I actually chuckle. At this point, it's the only thing I can do. "No. If you can believe it, this happened in a different fight earlier tonight."

"Wow." Her brows arch in disbelief. "Ben Rosenberg, hardened street fighter. Who would have thought?"

I frown. "Sorry, I think you have the advantage. Do we know each other?"

She pushes to her feet and starts to gather up her things, which are scattered across the ground. I help her by picking up a crumpled gift bag and a Tupperware. Inside, there's some brown sludge that hardly looks fit for human consumption. Maybe it's not.

"Oh, no. We've never officially met. I'm pretty sure I would remember that." I glance back at her as I hand off the plastic container, trying to place her features, but the light is too low and she's too busy gathering her stuff to look at me. "Though there was a time last year when you were in front of me in the grocery store checkout line. I remember you bought roast beef. Is that weird?" She shakes her head and turns to me with a shrug. Then she holds out her hand, a small thing, and makes it clear she wants me to shake it. "I'm Madison."

"Madison," I repeat, a little dumbstruck. I wasn't expecting her to be attractive. Sure, her dark brown hair is kind of wild and her cheeks are bright red from the biting wind, but she has high cheekbones and beautiful eyes, even if they're a little sad. I realize I've said her name aloud two more times, and now I'm the one who looks like a weirdo even though she just admitted to stalking me at the grocery store.

"Yes," she says, nodding as she takes her bottom lip between her teeth. I think she's trying to keep from openly smiling at me, but I wish she'd just do it. I want to see her smile, even if it's at my expense. "*Mad-i-son*. Just like that. You've got the hang of it."

She's funny.

Her hand is still outstretched, hanging awkwardly between us, so I belatedly step forward to take it. My hand engulfs hers. She's ice cold and trembling. Of course, three minutes ago she was being held at gunpoint.

I only have her hand in mine for a brief moment before she jerks away and scans the ground again, confirming she has all her stuff.

"You're not hurt. Are you?" I ask. "You never answered me earlier."

She shakes her head even as her free hand reaches up to touch her hair. When she pulls it away, there's blood on her fingers. She sees me staring and clears her throat. "It's nothing, just a little cut from where he was holding the…"

Her sentence trails off, her gaze still on her bloody fingers, and I think she's going to pass out or throw up. Clearly, the shock is starting to wear off.

"We should call the cops." I got a decent enough look at the guy even with his mask on. I can recall his height and build and the direction he ran, at the very least.

"Oh, don't worry about that. I'll just tell my dad when I get home. Thank you for your help."

"You still live with your dad?" Jesus, I didn't think she was a kid, but maybe I'm wrong.

She must take my surprise for judgment because she lifts her chin proudly. "Yeah, it's just easier with rent and all that."

I feel like a jerk.

"Of course. Yeah, I get it. Is your dad's house close by?" I say, stuffing my hands in the pockets of my suit pants. Even with the residual adrenaline in my veins, the cold air is starting to get harder to ignore.

"Just a few blocks. Listen, I can't thank you enough for stepping in when you did. I'm not sure that guy would have hurt me, but still…" She shakes away the thought and glances up, her gaze meeting mine a bit unsteadily. "You probably saved my life, and for that, I'm eternally grateful."

With that, she nods just once then turns to walk away.

I scowl.

She's leaving? She thinks I'm going to let her walk home alone after all this? There's a good chance that guy is still in the area.

I watch her until she reaches the end of the block and is about to cross the street. Then she suddenly stops, turns, and glances back at me, worrying her lip between her teeth before she speaks. "Actually…I know you're probably busy what with all the street fighting and heroic deeds you have going on, but would you mind…maybe…walking me home?" Her brows scrunch together with her request and she speeds up her words, trying to rush out her reassurances. "It's really not that far, I promise. I could just call my dad to come pick me up, but—"

"Yes, of course."

I start to walk toward her, but then something catches my attention on the ground, and I squint, trying to discern if it's something she left behind on accident or if it's just a piece of trash.

"Oh," she says, seeing it.

"It's a birthday candle," I say quietly.

Huh. I bend down to retrieve it and when I glance back over, I see her cheeks burning bright red as she turns and pins her gaze across the street.

Of course, I should have thought of it earlier when I saw the crumpled gift bag.

"It's your birthday?"

She keeps her attention elsewhere, almost like she's embarrassed to admit it. "My twenty-fifth."

"What a way to spend a birthday…" I mumble under my breath.

I catch up to her and hold out the candle. She takes it and shoves it into her coat pocket like she wants to be rid of it.

26

"For what it's worth, happy birthday."

She laughs like it's the most preposterous thing I could have said, and we start to walk. I offer to carry some of her things, but she insists she doesn't need the help.

"So you'll have your dad call the police when you get home?"

For some reason, that question makes her smirk. "Sure, I'll have him call right away."

I don't know why she's being cavalier about this. Her life was just at stake. There's a criminal on the loose, and she's not calling the cops. *Why isn't she calling the cops?*

We turn a corner and keep walking past the manicured lawns and old Victorian mansions renowned around Clifton Cove. Real estate here is extremely expensive. Everyone wants to be within walking distance of the shops and restaurants, not to mention all the wealthy tourists who visit once and then decide they want to purchase a vacation home here. More than anything, they're the ones driving up demand.

If Madison grew up around here, she likely went to the same private school I did, which would explain why she knows who I am.

"Did you grow up in Clifton Cove?"

She nods. "Born and raised."

"And you went to Saint Andrews?"

I catch the moment her mouth lifts into a barely visible smirk. "No, Clifton High, and before you ask, I went to the public middle school and elementary school too." The question of how she knows who I am is poised on my tongue when she continues in a mocking tone, "Everyone knows who you are—your last name is on half the buildings around town. The Rosenbergs might as well be royalty."

As usual in life, my family's legacy precedes me.

"Madison!" someone shouts up ahead, grabbing our attention. "Where the hell have you been?!"

"Oh God," she hisses under her breath.

I glance up to see a man standing out on the porch of one of the homes a few yards away. It's small compared to the mansions around it, a modest one-story on a half-lot. In the driveway, two police cruisers are parked side by side, and I wonder if somehow Madison alerted her dad to what happened without me realizing it.

She picks up her pace and I'm forced to follow. She aims an apologetic frown in my direction, and I don't understand what it could possibly be for until I hear my name shouted from the porch. I look up to the large man in jeans and a white t-shirt, his gray hair trimmed in a short, military style. His face is contorted into an angry scowl and his eyes are locked right on me. Realization sets in.

"Ben Rosenberg, what the hell are you doin' with my daughter?"

The question is asked by the man I now recognize as Derrick Hart, Chief of Police in Clifton Cove and apparently, Madison's dad.

"Your last name is Hart?" I ask her.

She ignores me and glances up at her father. "Ben was just making sure I got home okay."

He grunts in disbelief. "Is that why you're a good two hours later than we expected you?"

I open my mouth, angry about the way he's talking to her, but Madison's gaze meets mine and she offers an infinitesimal shake of her head. I know I'd only make things worse for her by speaking up.

"It's a long story and Ben's gotta get home."

Her dad doesn't buy it. His eyes cut to me as he begins to walk down the stairs and down the front path. I've had a few run-ins with him over the years. Way back in high school, my friends and I could be arrogant assholes. We broke into public pools and raced our cars on deserted roads—typical kid shit. Since I turned eighteen, my record's been squeaky clean. He shouldn't be looking at me like he wants to pound me into dust.

His finger juts out accusingly. "I don't want you anywhere near my daughter. You got that?"

Madison steps between us and holds up her hand. "Dad, *seriously*. Stop."

I want to laugh. The situation couldn't be more wrong. I just saved his precious daughter from being held at gunpoint and now *I'm* the bad guy? The same prejudice Mac and his friends felt toward me at the bar lives inside Chief Hart, too. He thinks I'm a spoiled rich kid, here to fuck with him and his daughter, like I don't have more important shit to do with my time.

"I heard about the situation you got into earlier," he says, staring pointedly at my black eye and busted lip. "Why were you over on that side of town anyway? Lookin' for trouble?"

Madison steps right up to him, her hand hitting his chest. I shadow her, right there with her as if I'm worried he'll turn his anger on his daughter, but I have nothing to worry about. The second he glances down, that fire in his eyes is doused. His thick gray brows tilt up and he frowns with loving concern.

"Maddie, we've been waiting for you since dinner. Colten even helped me with the banana pudding. Did you already eat?"

She nods her head and pushes him back toward the house. "Yeah, but pudding sounds nice. C'mon, let's go inside."

He lets her push him away. Maybe she's got him wrapped around her finger, or maybe he feels bad because it's her birthday; either way, she saves me from getting my ass chewed some more.

Other than a small glance she aims over her shoulder, neither of them acknowledge me as they walk inside. I'm definitely not invited up for some of that pudding, though I could definitely go for a bowl or two. I stand there watching them go, convinced this is probably the last time I'll ever talk to Madison Hart. A pained feeling swells in my chest, and my hand hits my heart as if to soothe it.

Then the screen door slams shut and they disappear. I glance up at the sky and let out a laugh I've been saving all night, a big *Fuck you* to the universe for putting me through this fresh version of hell.

With a shake of my head, I turn and am about to head in the direction of my house when the screen door slams again and Madison runs back down the front path toward me.

"Wait!" She keeps running even though her dad is shouting at her from the door. She tells him to calm down. "I'll only be a second!"

Then she turns and she's right in front of me, head tilted back to get a good look at me. The wind sweeps up the loose hair around her face and here, with the light from her house, I can tell her eyes are more green than hazel, her smile's just as beguiling as I thought it would be, and her mouth is tempting enough to make me forget her dad is up on the porch watching us, probably loading his shotgun.

Something cold hits my chest and I glance down to see an ice pack.

I must look confused because she smiles and says, "For your eye."

CHAPTER FOUR
MADISON

"Was that Ben Rosenberg outside? What the hell was he doing here?"

I glance over my shoulder to see my brother leaning against the doorframe of the kitchen, still wearing his police uniform while he sips a beer. His brown hair is messy and he needs to shave, but he's still as handsome as ever. I want to pinch his cheeks.

"Yes." I arch a brow. "I was expecting you to come out there and start shouting too."

He shrugs and looks away as if guilty. "There were only a few seconds left in the fourth quarter and the Cowboys were tied with the Colts. Besides, it sounded like Dad was handling it just fine."

Ah, my dad, the big bad wolf. Not ten minutes ago, he was causing a big fuss out on the front porch, stomping his feet and pounding his chest. Now, he's sitting at the kitchen table with his nightly mug of decaf coffee and his half-finished crossword. His blue readers are perched on the end of his nose.

The big bad wolf is, in fact, a fraud. He's never so much as raised his voice at me, though maybe that's because I've never given him real cause. I never broke rules, skipped curfew, or dared to be bad in any way.

Still, just because he's usually a big teddy bear around me, I shouldn't have been surprised by his reaction to Ben. He was mean as hell to the few boys who've been courageous enough or stupid enough to try to get to know me over the years.

"You still haven't explained what you were doing with him," my dad says, adjusting his glasses so he can read the next clue. He's careful not to look up at me. It's like he's trying to make his inquiry seem casual, but we both know it's not.

"Yeah," my brother adds. "I heard he got into it over at Murphy's earlier. You aren't friends with him, are you, Maddie?"

I turn away from them and shrug. "No, we aren't friends. It's just…well…it's nothing. He saved my life. Oh, that reminds me—Dad, I need to report a crime. I got held up at gunpoint."

I pinch my eyes closed and brace myself for the worst of it. Just as I expected, the volume level in the kitchen hits an all-time high as the two of them circle around me. I wouldn't be surprised to find the walls quaking.

They shoot questions at me rapid-fire. They want to know every detail of what happened and how it happened and what did he look like and why exactly did I think it was a good idea to walk home alone at this time of night?

I answer them quietly and calmly as I stroll to the refrigerator and find the thing I'm looking for: banana pudding. It's my favorite. My dad makes it for me every year. I think with all the excitement, they've completely forgotten it's my birthday. I guess it makes sense, all things considered. I shove my brother out of the way and dig in the drawer of utensils for the biggest spoon I can find. The one I grab is technically meant for dishing out casseroles, and when I dip it into the bowl of banana pudding, I come up with half the contents. *Perfect.*

My dad's hand hits my shoulder. He's trying to get me to look up at him, but I can't.

I might be playing it cool on the outside, but underneath it all, I'm a complete mess, though not really for the reasons you would expect.

This has been the wildest night of my entire life. The birthday gods heard my wish and were like, *Hey, you heard the woman! She wants excitement! Let's ramp this shit up to an 11!* Examples of things that would have been appropriately exciting: having my shoe come untied; missing my turn and having to explore a new route home; or, I don't know, I could have stumbled upon a stray puppy and been forced to take care of him. (In the end, *he* takes cares of *me*.) Getting held up at gunpoint was seriously not what I had in mind.

The whole thing doesn't feel real, which is probably why I'm not crying or shaking or scared. I can look at the situation and logically see that my life was in danger. The man in the ski mask was deranged, nervous, and mumbling under his breath, and yet I'm not totally sure he wanted to do anything bad to me. Yes, sure, obviously you don't just hold a gun to someone's head for the fun of it, but he didn't take my money even when I offered it, and he didn't try to rip at my clothes. The whole thing just felt…off, almost like it wasn't happening to me. I know it makes me sound naive, but I'm not wholly convinced he would have hurt me even if Ben hadn't shown up.

Ben Rosenberg.

God. His name should always be accompanied by a long lusty sigh. Even now, my heart does a little flutter kick in my chest just thinking of him. I was actually grateful for his busted lip and swollen eye. Without them, I'm not sure I could have formed coherent thoughts. Even *with* them, my brain was only running at about 50%.

I'm *still* distracted by his looks—the one piercing brown eye that wasn't swollen, his hard cheekbones and defined jaw. Oh, and let's not forget his tall muscular frame poured into a navy suit with a few specks of blood dotting his shirt for good measure. I mean, Jesus, give a girl a break.

I dip my spoon back into the pudding aggressively.

Other than his haggard state, the only other factor I had going for me was that I was in total shock that he, out of EVERY person in Clifton Cove, was the one to appear on the dark street as my white knight. It was so shocking, in fact, that it enabled me to keep my wits about me on the walk home. It was like I wasn't convinced it was actually him. *Am I totally sure the guy didn't shoot me back there and this isn't all some weird purgatory I've fallen into?*

I'm still thinking about Ben later when we get home from the police station, after I've said every word I ever want to say about the incident, after they've cleaned up the small cut on my head and swabbed every inch of me for evidence. I'm finally able to sneak off upstairs and shower. I'm bone-weary and ready to pass out on any inanimate object that can support my weight, but my brain is wide awake, running through the conversation I had with Ben on our walk home. I try to remember if I sounded normal or not, charming or just weird.

It's not that I've never carried on a conversation with a cute man before. I have, *at least* twice. The reason it's such a big deal is because in Clifton Cove, Ben Rosenberg is a god, an urban legend, a man unto himself.

Let me put it another way. You know how people always have at least one story about a time they ran into a celebrity? *Once, on a flight home, I was seated ten rows back from Jennifer Aniston!* That kind of thing.

This night will be my celebrity story: *Once, Ben Rosenberg saved my life.*

There are quite a few reasons our paths have never crossed before today: he's six years older than me; he went to Saint Andrews and I went the public route; he went Ivy League for college and law school while I commuted to the state college 45 minutes from my house; oh, and I'm a total dweeb who spends her days at the library surrounded by books and her nights in her childhood bedroom surrounded by books while he probably has a very busy, very wild social life that includes a veritable buffet of sexual partners.

With that thought, I slam down my soap and step out of the shower. I wrap myself in a thick terrycloth robe and pad quietly to my room across the hall just in case my dad has any more questions he wants to ask me tonight. I care about catching the criminal and bringing him to justice. I really, really do, but right now, given the choice, I'd much rather dwell on Ben and the fact that more than likely, our paths won't ever cross again.

I throw myself onto my bed dramatically.

I'm an idiot.

I should have written my number on that ice pack.

CHAPTER FIVE
B E N

"Community service? Are you serious?"

"I don't have a choice."

"Are you doing this for chicks? Because, man, I know like four women who would cut their right arm off to sleep with you. I know because they made that perfectly clear to me the other night at Nick's barbecue. The last one gave me her number to give to you and I threw it in the grill out of spite. It's these goddamn cheekbones." Andy releases the bench press bar long enough to stroke my cheek goadingly. It tickles and I flinch, jerking away. "Do you sharpen them or what?"

I politely tell him to fuck off and he shrugs and looks away, bored. "I need a beer."

I finish my last rep and sit up, pointing out the obvious. "We're in the middle of working out."

He throws my towel at me. I drag it down my face then hang it around the back of my neck.

"Yeah, about that—why did I let you talk me into this? My whole shtick is that I'm kind of chubby but charming nonetheless. Women love it—well, the women who don't want you love it."

I shake my head, careful to ignore him. On a good day, Andy is unbearable. Most days, he's fucking ridiculous. He's the brother I never had, and we've been friends since kindergarten. We went to the same law school then followed through with our plan to move back to Clifton Cove after graduation and start our own firm. I could have easily taken

37

a position with my father, going for the easy hours and raking in the cash, but Andy and I had our own ideas. Besides, it's better this way. I don't like answering to anyone, not even Andy, which is why I own 51% of the firm and he owns 49%.

I glance over to the mirror to see him checking out one of the women across the gym. Arianna—he's been in love with her for as long as I can remember. She waves before I motion to him to come spot me again.

"When do you start?" he asks as I lie back and grab the bar.

"Friday, after work."

He looks crestfallen. "We're supposed to get drinks after work on Friday."

"Rain check."

He drops the bar and walks away.

"Andy!"

He ignores me. No doubt he's going over to talk to Arianna.

Out of the two of us, he's more easily distracted by the opposite sex. I'm pretty sure he loves women more than life itself, and it shows. On paper, Andy is more of a ladies' man. He dates. He Tinders. He swipes on every available app and prowls the gym every time we're here on the off chance his soul mate is within reach. Tonight, he's in luck. She's actually here.

As for me, I'm not really interested in dating at the moment. For the last few years, women have served a singular purpose in my life. I've been happy with nights spent with tourists I'll never see again. It's easier than the alternative: sleeping around with women in Clifton Cove. We all grew up together, and I've watched them become the debutantes their parents always wanted them to be. There's a mold they all adhere to, and while it's not a bad mold, it is a boring one. Even though I know it would make my dad happy to see me settle down, I can't seem to want a single one of them.

Just because I don't want to marry them doesn't mean I couldn't give in to temptation and accept the offers a few of them have made crystal clear since I returned from law school. That said, I adhere to the old adage *Don't shit where you eat.* Clifton Cove is small, and word travels fast.

I tell myself I'm not interested in dating and relationships because I have a lot on my plate with work. I enjoy burning the midnight oil, tearing through files and emails and prepping for meetings until my vision blurs from reading and my fingers ache from typing. I'm hungry for success even though it's all but destined for me, so love and women have naturally taken the back seat.

The truth is more complicated than that. After my mom entered a permanent facility, after we were sure her dementia would worsen, after she forgot my name, who I was, what I meant to her—something inside me split in two.

A more romantic person would say it was my heart, but I think it was my optimism, my hope for an easy, happy life. Watching a person suffer like that, enduring that suffering myself…I'm not sure I'm willing to take the risk again.

Then, for some insane reason, I think of Madison Hart.

Just thinking her name makes me frown, confused—no, *baffled.* She's impossible to forget, and believe me, I've tried. During the day, I can mostly put her out of my mind. Work and my social life keep me busy enough. Besides, we only had one brief, albeit crazy, encounter. The chances of our paths crossing again are slim to none. We don't run in the same circles. Her family despises me. And yet…at night, she keeps finding her way into my dreams.

The same few moments play out again and again. She's kneeling down on the sidewalk, underneath the streetlamp, just like that night. She's looking up at me and her eyes are so big and green, a swirling mess of a color that digs at something deep inside me. The green is so vibrant, the color of grass just after it rains, the color of life.

Sometimes I work up the courage to step closer and touch her. I cradle her cheek in my hand and she accepts the comfort so willingly. Other times, I jerk awake before I get the chance.

Either way, I'm frustrated in the morning.

————

It's been a few weeks since my arrest. My lip and eye have healed up, and other than a small scar beside my eyebrow, I'm good as new. Life has carried on as normal except for the misdemeanor charge hanging over my head. Much to the chagrin of my father and Judge Mathers, I stuck with my guilty plea and accepted my sentence: 100 hours of community service. After I'm done, I'll have the misdemeanor expunged from my record. It's silly that I'm going through with all this—I didn't assault Mac and his friends. We were all in there, throwing punches, taking our anger out on each other. Andy even had a few bruises to show for it, and he wore them proudly around the office before they faded. I swear he was a little sad to see them go.

I don't have to do the community service. Mac isn't going to know whether or not I weaseled out of my punishment. Hell, he probably assumes I did, but I'll know, and I guess, for some stupid reason, that matters.

Normally in situations like this, the courts would demand that the offender volunteer or pay restitution to the organization directly impacted by the crime itself. Since mine was a misdemeanor involving a simple assault, and since Judge Mather's heart wasn't really in it for the sentencing, he tossed a list of organizations at me and told me to pick one. I skipped over the soup kitchen, hospital, and retirement home. The last option on the list was the local library, a place I haven't set foot in since I was a kid.

I chose it on a whim and now here I am, ready to report for my first day. It's 5:00 PM on Friday and I've had a long week at the firm. Andy and I currently have more clients than we can handle. We've brought in four junior associates in the last two years, but somehow, the workload just keeps piling up. I could use a break, a night of just kicking back and shooting the shit with my friends, a real weekend where I'm not holed up at the office.

In truth, the last thing I need is another commitment on my plate, so now, more than ever, I'm kicking myself for getting into this mess. Was it really worth it to land that solid punch across Mac's face?

Yes. Yes, it was.

I park in the visitor's lot and hop out, glad I changed clothes before I left work. I'm not about to show up to volunteer in a suit.

It really has been a while since I've been here. Like I said, the firm has been keeping me busy, but I also avoid this place because it carries a lot of memories I'd rather not dwell on, like Saturdays with my mom, especially. I walk up the imposing staircase, past the statue of my great-great-great-grandfather cast in bronze, and then pull open the heavy door. Inside, there's a security guard perched at an ancient oak desk. When I ask him about a volunteer station, he looks at me like I'm from a different planet. Right. I'll find it myself.

Like most buildings around Clifton Cove, the library is ridiculously over the top for the function it serves. This isn't your standard one-story brick building with mismatched furniture and stained carpet from the 80s. The floors are marble. The walls are paneled and finished with crown molding. The ceilings stretch to heights usually reserved for churches, and the artwork hanging on the walls is no doubt on loan from various museums around the country.

The bronze guy outside—the original Mr. Rosenberg— endowed the city with the funds and oversaw the design and build of the library. Of all the buildings in the city that carry my last name, this one is my favorite.

I walk past the quiet study rooms, past two symmetrical staircases with wrought iron rails, past the magazines and periodicals. I'm looking around for some kind of help desk when a short guy wearing khaki pants and a blue gingham button-down walks right up to me like he's on a mission. Based on the fact that he's approaching me at all, I assume he's an employee who's seen me ambling around, obviously looking lost.

"Could you point me in the direction of—"

"Oh my *god*. Are you here for Madison?"

"What?"

He straightens his shoulders and shakes his head, affecting a gentler tone when he continues, "I just mean…after what happened…" His brows furrow in confusion behind his thick black-framed glasses. "Never mind, forget I said anything." His hand shoots out. "I'm Eli."

I accept his handshake. "Ben—"

"Rosenberg. Yes, I know." He drops my hand and steps back, frowning. "Are you here to check out library books? Because I looked and you don't even have a library card."

"Uhh…"

I look around, hoping to find some clues as to who this person is and why he seems to know so much about me. *Also, why did he bring up Madison?*

"And sure," he continues, pointing behind me, "that's your great-grandfather's statue out there, so technically all these books probably belong to you anyway, but still—"

"Eli! *Ahem*, Eli!"

I turn to see a short elderly woman holding a book outstretched toward the guy talking my ear off.

"Eli," she says, tone stern, chin raised. "This book has a tear right down the first page. I think it's only fair that I get to keep it—for free."

I turn back in time to see Eli roll his eyes. "That's the fifth book this month. Mrs. Taylor, if you keep tearing up our books, we're going to cut up your library card."

She harrumphs and then turns away, nose in the air.

Eli shakes his head in distaste. "Criminals…"

What in the hell have I gotten myself into?

"Actually, I'm just looking for the volunteer desk," I offer, hoping to end this odd exchange as soon as possible.

Eli glances back at me, brows suddenly perked up with interest. "Volunteer desk, huh? Well why didn't you say so? It's downstairs, right by the children's section. You can't miss it."

I narrow my eyes in speculation. He looks entirely too pleased to be sending me downstairs, but I shake off the feeling. Maybe they're just really in need of volunteers.

I thank him and head in the direction he's pointing, but I don't make it very far before I remember what he said. I frown as I try to recall his exact words. *Are you here for Madison?*

"Hey wait," I call out to him as I turn around. "You know Madison?"

He smirks. "You could say that."

Then, before I can ask anything more, he turns and walks away.

I'm thinking over what his cryptic words could possibly mean as I walk down the stairs and into the area of the library that's been designed with children in mind. There are colorful art installations hanging from ceilings, rows of computers, a section of bean bags and tiny chairs, and stacks upon stacks of books. Oversized stuffed animals sit on top of the shelves, and whereas the areas upstairs were quiet, down here, the atmosphere is alive and happy. A toddler runs right into my path and I have to stop on a dime to keep from toppling him over. His mom runs after him and shouts a quick thank you to me before she catches up and whisks him off the ground into her arms. He laughs like it's the funniest game he's ever played, and I'm smiling like an idiot before I realize and wipe it off.

I scan the area and spot a sign hanging from the ceiling that points me in the direction of the help desk. Surely someone there will be able to tell me where the hell I'm supposed to be. Of course, no one is currently manning it. There's a small bell sitting near the edge, so I ding it once and wait, hands in my pockets, eyes scanning the room.

After a few moments, I realize with the noise level down here, it'd probably be hard for someone to hear the bell, so I try again, dinging it twice this time.

"I'm coming! *I'm coming!*" a feminine voice calls out.

I catch movement to my right and look over just in time to see a brunette pop out from behind one of the shelves with a dozen children's books piled in her arms. She blows a few strands of hair out of her face and then announces in an annoyed voice, "Eli, if that's you—"

Then her green eyes glance up and her sentence cuts off sharply when she sees it's me.

CHAPTER SIX
MADISON

Well, it turns out, I'm a witch. It's the only possible explanation for the turn of events currently taking place in my life. There I was, just a few moments ago, re-shelving books and daydreaming about Ben Rosenberg, as I've often done in the weeks since I last saw him. I was lost in thought trying to recall the exact shade of his eyes—*amber or more of a pale honey?*—when the bell rang at my desk and low and behold, here he is, in the library, waiting for me.

I must have conjured him up out of thin air, and I did an excellent job recreating him from memory. He's wearing dark jeans and a gray crewneck t-shirt. His brown hair is shorter than it was the last time I saw him and styled like he came straight from the office. He looks severe, daunting, beautiful. He's not smiling. No, in fact, he looks sort of annoyed, I think. His features—the strong brow, sharp cheekbones, and pronounced jaw—are so easily swayed to look menacing. I could faint from the sheer shock of seeing him again, but I square my shoulders and try to affect a cool, calm exterior.

"Ben Rosenberg. Come to take the library back from us once and for all?" I quip as I round the corner and start to walk toward him. I take a very quick, very thorough stock of my appearance, trying to visualize how I look to him in this moment. My jersey dress is a pale shade of blue, long-sleeved and knee-length. The top is fitted across my chest, but the skirt flows around my hips and thighs. All in all, it's more comfortable than cute, as is much of my wardrobe. My hair is in a loose braid, and damn it all to hell, would it have killed me to apply a little makeup before work this morning? A swipe of daring lipstick? Some false eyelashes? A smoky eye? I want to turn back around and pinch my cheeks—or better yet, slap them—in the hopes that I'll appear youthful and glowing rather than tired and overworked.

"Retake the library? Eli did mention something about all these books belonging to me."

Oh good, his tone is hard and emotionless. Maybe he's trying to seem as unflustered by our reunion as I am—or, you know, maybe he actually is unflustered.

I step closer and drop the children's books onto my desk, working up the courage to glance up at him. He really is tall. If I had to look up at him for long, I'd get a crick in my neck. "He was exaggerating. They belong to the city." I frown. "At least I think they do. Now, what can I do for you?"

His eyes assess me coolly for a moment. Ah yes, they're amber, and so intimidating my palms are sweating. He takes me in from top to toes, and I swear if I dug deep enough, I'd find a hint of appreciation behind his gaze, but I can't be certain. He's so much more in control of his features than I am. If I ever found myself across from him at a poker table, I'd lose my entire life savings.

"I'm here to volunteer my services."

My eyes widen and my cheeks burn red hot. It sounds like a sexy euphemism: *his services*. I immediately imagine him kissing his way across my body, burning a path down my skin. This jersey dress would be so simple to rip right in two. Then my brain kicks in and I realize the true meaning of his words. Of course he catches my reaction and seems mildly amused by it.

I clear my throat and finger the top book on the stack on my desk. "Why? Er—" I clear my throat. "Why are you wanting to volunteer here?"

"Court-ordered community service. It's mandatory thanks to that fight I got into a few weeks ago. You remember?"

"Ah, right." I glance back up at him. Do I remember? I have every second of that night permanently ingrained in my memory. His words, his appearance. I remember the swollen eye and red, busted lip. His lips are fine now—in tiptop shape, in fact. I'm staring at them as I say dumbly, "Your eye has healed up nicely."

His fingers reach up to touch the corner of his eye and I'm forced to look there, at the bright amber hue and black lashes.

I'm aware that one of us should speak soon. We can't just continue to stare at each other like this, so I give myself a mental kick and paste on a weak smile. "Shame you didn't scar—could have given you some major street cred."

Then I plop myself down in my desk chair and click my mouse three times, trying to wake up my computer. I want to show him that I'm a busy gal. I have work things to attend to: emails, and conference calls, and mergers, and financial documents. *Oh right, I'm a children's librarian.* A child screams a few feet away and I'm reminded that I'm about as intimidating as a church mouse. The things on my agenda for today include things like Princess Story Time and Toddler Play Hour.

I still make a real show of typing a bunch of meaningless gibberish on my keyboard, just in case, but then my computer doesn't feel like playing along. It locks me out because I've entered the wrong login password too many times. A loud, angry noise blares like an alarm and I frown at the stupid thing.

"Computer on the fritz?" he asks, and when I glance up, I see he's wearing the barest hint of a smirk. My stomach flips upside down like an amusement park ride. This won't work. He can't stay here, lingering, giving me hope where there is none.

"It's fine. Anyway, sorry to disappoint you, but the only place we need volunteers is down here, in the children's department. I don't think you're quite cut out for it. Baby talk, screaming toddlers, poopy pants…" I scrunch my nose so he gets the idea.

He looks out into the distance as if surveying the landscape for all the possibilities I just outlined. He doesn't look as deterred as I would have thought.

"Really…lots of poop," I add, trying—for some insane reason—to convince him to leave. I think it's because of how I feel in this moment: so totally out of control. I know I'm making a fool of myself and yet I can't stop doing it. I want him to take a step back. Better yet, I want him to take ten steps back. I'd come to terms with the fact that I probably wouldn't see him again any time soon. I reasoned with myself that it was for the best. What could possibly come from spending time around Ben Rosenberg other than one-sided feelings and a whole hell of a lot of heartache?

Then I realize I have one more solid reason why it's not a good idea for him to volunteer here, with me.

"Besides, I'm supposed to stay away from you. Bad news, apparently. Are you, Ben?"

"What?"

"Bad news?"

He looks like I'm confusing the hell out of him, and maybe I am.

I pick the books up off my desk and start walking back toward the stacks. He's forced to follow if he wants to continue the conversation.

"Why would you think that?"

I glance at him over my shoulder. I swear he was looking at my butt, but I can't be sure. "My dad warned me about you. He said you and your family think you're entitled to anything and everything in Clifton Cove, even the people."

"It sounds like your dad doesn't know me very well." His words are bitten out in annoyance.

I feel bad now, for hurting his feelings, for assuming he's one way when maybe he's the exact opposite. We're between the tall stacks now. I've unintentionally hidden us away. It feels like there's not a soul in sight. I press the books to my chest and turn my gaze up to him. He's watching me with his brows furrowed and his mouth tugged into a sharp line.

"I didn't mean to offend you. I'm sorry if I did."

He doesn't reply.

My heart rate picks up and I wish we weren't so alone right now. There are a dozen kids down here—would it be so hard for one of them to run over in our direction and kill the tension building up between us? Maybe produce one of those poopy pants I warned him about?

I'm trying to come up with a solution for our problems. He needs to volunteer here to fulfill his community service requirement, and I need him as far away from me as possible. One of us is going to end up having to concede, and it'll likely be me. I've never been great at standing my ground, but maybe there's something I can get out of this after all.

My birthday flashes back into my mind, that lonely moment when I was staring at my reflection in the glass, the wish I made underneath my desk.

Inspiration strikes and I run with it before my brain has time to decide if it's a good idea or a bad one. Chances are, it's the latter.

"Here's the thing: I'll let you volunteer here if you do something for me."

His eyes narrow suspiciously. "What?"

"No, forget it."

"What is it?"

"It's stupid."

"Madison, say it."

His tone is hard and his words are so commanding, I suddenly blurt out, "I want you to help me change."

"Change?" His gaze drops to my dress like I mean it in the literal sense rather than the figurative. "How?"

I'm going to have to be more specific, and being more specific means putting more of myself out there for him to judge and ridicule. There's no way I'll finish explaining my request without him laughing himself right on out of this library.

But, if I'm not honest, nothing will change. This year will be the same as the year before that and the year before that. In eleven months, I'll be standing in this exact room, blowing out candles on a crummy ol' birthday cake courtesy of Mrs. Allen. Eli will be off honeymooning with Kevin and Katy will be gone, replaced by some new bored intern desperately wishing they could go home.

So, I take a deep breath and speak the truth, the whole truth, and nothing but the truth, so help me God.

"I want you to, y'know…help make me…*different*."

"Different?"

Right, yes. What does different mean? I've spent my entire life in this exact role: the good girl. The rule-follower. The curfew-keeper.

"I want you to help make me bad."

I squeeze my eyes shut.

There. I've said it.

"I'm sorry, I couldn't hear that. You were covering your mouth with your hand."

Oh right. Oops.

He leans forward and forcibly lowers my hand. We're touching and my skin is on FIRE and maybe he realizes it because he lets go. It's too late, though; I can still feel his warmth there, and on a whim, I make a fist as if to try to keep his cooties on me for as long as possible.

"Madison," he says.

My name is a spell on his lips and I'm sick of being the good girl, sick of always staying in my lane and taking the easy way out of things. One second, I'm standing in front of Ben Rosenberg, too scared to be honest for fear of what he'll think of me. Then the next, I'm throwing caution to the wind and shouting, "Make me bad!"

I heave a sigh as if I've just lifted a million-pound boulder off my chest, and *wow I'm still at work and I definitely just caused a ruckus. Jesus, what have I done? Make me bad?! What does that even mean!?*

A mom with a small child stomps over between the shelves and looks at me in horror.

"…is the name of the book I was telling you about," I mumble. "New York Times bestseller, great storyline." I smile really widely at her to throw her off my scent, but she still leans down for her daughter's hand and drags her away.

Ben, meanwhile, is looking at me like he's never looked at me before, like he's interested in what's going on inside my head. I hope he finds out because I'd like to know too.

Then, the edge of his mouth tips up and this…*this* is the last image I want to see before I die of embarrassment: Ben

Rosenberg smirking at me—Ben Rosenberg with his perfect jaw-to-cheekbone-to-brow ratio, with his rich person arrogance and his cocky posture. *Be still my loins.*

"What do you mean, 'make you bad'?"

He's barely stifling his smile. I know it.

I roll my eyes and return to my duties of shelving books. "When you say it, it sounds stupid. It's just part of my birthday resolution. I want to make this year different, more exciting. I have things I want to achieve, but I think I'm too chicken to actually do them on my own. That's where you come in."

"Why me?"

"Because, Ben…" Now I'm the one smirking, the one stepping closer and tilting my chin up to stare into those amber eyes. "You're bad news, remember? The perfect partner in crime. You'll be like Virgil guiding me through hell."

He props an elbow on the shelf beside him, addressing me with equal levels of curiosity and amusement. "So what are we talking about here? Eating grapes at the grocery store before we pay for them? Jaywalking?"

I tilt my head back and forth, mocking him. "Oh, yes, *ha ha.*" Then suddenly, I'm as serious as a heart attack. "No, real stuff. I want to get my first tattoo. I want to go to a party—one where people are making bad decisions and I might too."

His eyes narrow on me, and I swallow and look away.

There's another thing—something pivotal—that I'm leaving out. I've only ever admitted it to Eli, and he's never judged me for it. *No,* I curse myself. *It's not something to be ashamed about.* It's not like I'm some kind of old spinster just because at the ripe old age of twenty-five…

"Also, youshouldknowI'veneverhadsex."

I say the words so fast it's like they come out in one lump sum, just a pile of syllables that don't add up to much, but leave it to a guy to hear the letters s-e-x said in succession and figure out exactly what I meant.

Ben coughs, but it sounds more like a strained choke. "That's part of it? You want to change that too?" he asks, hoping for clarification.

I nod, and then because he looks like I've just demanded that he strip me down right here and do me against one of the bookshelves, *and* because he looks absolutely horrified at the prospect, I find it important to clarify. "I'm not asking *you* to change that. Oh my gosh, *NO*. That's…" I shake my head, letting that sentence die on my lips. "But you probably have a hot friend or something. I don't know—we'll get to that later. I just thought you should know *everything* before you make your decision."

He should be turning on his heel and bolting out of the nearest emergency exit. I've just laid it all out there for him, all the awkward bits of me that, in normal circumstances, I'd rather die than reveal. In a way, it makes sense. It's much harder to share dirty secrets with family and friends, people in your close circle, people you'll have to be around for the next fifty years. Ben Rosenberg is so far out of my league, out of the realm of possibilities, that somehow, my secrets are safe with him.

I glance up and try to discern what he's thinking. Are we about to shake on this and call it a deal or am I going to have to find some other person to push me out of my comfort zone? I fidget and wrinkle my nose, brush a few stray pieces of hair away from my face, thinking, very hard, about turning and walking away from him without another word. I'll go my way. He'll go his. We'll never see each other again. In time, I'll be able to convince myself this whole afternoon was some horrible nightmare.

"When do we start?"

I blink twice as his question sinks in, and then hope blooms on my face. *He's going to do it?!* His features don't change. He's as hard and unyielding as I've ever seen him. If he thinks it's awkward that I've just discussed my virginity with him, he doesn't let it show.

I clear my throat and try to sound nonchalant as I reply, "Next Saturday. You come volunteer in the morning and—"

"No." He shakes his head just once. "Too much time for you to chicken out. Tonight, my friend's having a party. Jake Larson—you know him?"

My eyes widen. "He's friends with my brother."

"Is that a problem?" he asks, boldly.

My heart pounds wildly.

"No, you're right. There's no problem."

CHAPTER SEVEN
B E N

I'm still not wholly convinced this isn't one big joke. What are the odds I'd end up stumbling upon Madison in the library and she'd tug me between two bookshelves then beg me to help make her into a bad girl? It can't be real, any of it. It's nearly pornographic. Her, in that dress, the pale blue color setting off her bright eyes and flushed skin and generous lips...and hell, I was still recovering from the shock of seeing her again when she launched into her master plan, or rather, her ultimatum: if I didn't help her, she wasn't going to let me volunteer here. It's hot air. I could go around her. She has a boss. I could find a way to volunteer pretty easily, I'm sure of it. Still, I like her gumption, not to mention the fact that there's no way I'm going to say no to her. Why the fuck would I? It's not like she's asking me to move mountains. In fact, she's requesting the exact opposite.

Make her bad.

Jesus.

I'm losing my head.

I've been out of high school for over a decade and here I stand, feeling like I'm eighteen again. This whole thing feels wrong. She's the innocent little librarian and I'm apparently the last man on earth her father wants her to be talking to. I guess everyone has a little rebel inside them.

"What time is his party?" she asks, glancing down at her hands.

I want to smile, but I don't. Something tells me she wouldn't appreciate being the butt of a joke right now. I can tell she's nervous around me. She meets my eyes every now and then, but it's fleeting. She's fidgety, shifting back and forth on her feet. Maybe she doesn't want to get caught slacking on the job, or maybe she doesn't want to get caught between these shelves with me. Either way, she's blushing and her heart is racing. I know it.

"People should get there around 8:00," I explain.

Her brows shoot up. "I'm usually in bed with a good book by like 8:15."

The corner of my mouth hitches up. "Backing out already?"

Her head tips up and her gaze locks on mine. My taunt has finally forced her to show a little pride.

"*No,*" she emphasizes with a steely tone.

I nod. "Right. Then I'll pick you up on my way."

Her eyes widen in alarm. "That's probably not a good idea, considering…" She shakes her head. "I'll just have my brother take me. I'm sure he's going."

Fine. Makes sense. I'll still see her there.

After we agree, our conversation shifts to volunteering. She walks me through the children's area, explaining the basics. It's not exactly rocket science, which is good because I barely listen to a word she says. I'm still hung up on her revelation. *Virgin.* Madison Hart is a virgin. How is that possible? Was she homeschooled? No. Kept under lock and key? Not likely. Hidden away from every man in the entire world? If her dad had anything to do with it, yes.

There's no way around it—she's a knockout. I even try to look at her objectively, stripping away the details I've come to know: the girl-next-door charm, the enigmatic appeal. Are there men who don't like large green eyes? Guys who aren't into dark brown hair and fair skin? Maybe, but that means they're idiots or blind. Those are the only two options. I guess some might prefer obvious beauty, the done-up sex dolls, but Madison *is* obviously beautiful, just not conventionally beautiful. There's a difference.

"Ben, are you listening?" she asks as leads me through a doorway.

"Yeah."

No, I am not listening. I'm staring at her profile and thinking about how I'm going to navigate this mission she's just thrust upon me. I keep waiting for her to break character, crack up, and tell me she's been teasing me all along, but she doesn't.

We're back in the storage room now and it's a complete mess. Apparently, she's been asking her intern to come down and rearrange some of the boxes for a while, but she hasn't gotten around to it, so that means the task now falls to me. It's my first duty as a volunteer.

"The boxes are kind of heavy," she laments before glancing over at my arms. Her brows lift before she jerks her attention back to the boxes. "But I guess that won't be a problem for you."

Her phone rings at her desk and she has to run to answer it. She tells me to come find her if I have any questions, but like I said, this isn't groundbreaking stuff. The boxes are labeled and easy enough to lift onto the shelves.

I'm left back there by myself, alone with my thoughts. It's probably for the best. I have some things on my mind anyway.

On the surface, it might seem like I have a schoolboy crush on Madison. I obviously find her attractive. Her personality, while a little different, has a strange appeal. I like her honesty and openness. There's no cool facade to her. She is who she is and it's a refreshing thing to encounter in an age when everyone's so obsessed with filters and false appearances.

The dreams I've been having about her would further confirm my crush, but then I remind myself that they probably don't mean what I think they do. That night a few weeks ago was a harrowing experience for the both of us. I came to her defense when she was in a life-threatening situation. Obviously, it had some kind of impact on me.

The alternative—that I'm dreaming about her because I'm harboring feelings—is out of the question now.

By revealing her birthday resolution, by laying every bit of herself on the line for me, she effectively stamped out any potential there was for us. I might not be a complete gentleman, but I'm also not such an asshole that I'd pursue and toy with the emotions of a girl like her. She's innocent, and not just when it comes to matters of the bedroom. I can't believe how honest she was with me, a perfect stranger. I could use that honesty against her. A lesser man probably would.

It suddenly feels like I'm her confidant, her accomplice in a daring mission. She wants to change her life and check things off her bucket list. Some might find it a little ridiculous, childish even. To me, it's daring. So many people wake up and repeat the same things day in and day out. How many have the courage to shake things up? To reject the safety of their routine? I haven't stepped out of my comfort zone in years, and maybe I need this as much as she does.

Even all of that aside, the final nail in the Ben and Madison coffin was hammered home when she openly rejected the idea of sleeping with me and then followed it up by casually mentioning the idea of doing so with one of my friends.

The thought stings a bit, so I shove it aside and get to work moving boxes.

I'm down there for two hours, tidying the place up. When I'm done, the closet is ten times more organized than it was when I found it. Madison can hardly believe her eyes when she comes down to see it. Eli's with her, and I could hear them talking and laughing out in the hall. Apparently, they're good friends, not just work colleagues, and I wonder why in the world he hasn't tried dating her—or maybe he has? Maybe he's stuck in the friend zone?

Madison steps inside and spins in a circle with her arms outstretched. "Oh my gosh, Ben! You're amazing! There's so much room in here now!"

Eli swoops in and grabs her hands, spinning her around and around. I watch from the doorway, curious about their friendship. They seem so comfortable with one another. He wraps one arm around her back then dips her low and she goes with it, trusting him completely. Her dress slides up her creamy thigh just enough to catch my attention, but then he yanks her back up to stand and they switch.

"Okay, do me! Do me!" Eli says, forcing her arm around his back.

I chuckle then, wondering if he might not be interested in Madison the same way I am.

"Eli and his boyfriend have been taking ballroom dancing lessons," Madison explains to me over her shoulder.

"I'm better at it than he is," he confirms proudly.

"Is that one of the things on your list? Dance lessons?" I ask, watching Madison as she's forced to use both of her arms to pick Eli back up from his courageous dip. His head nearly collided with the ground.

Eli glances between us with a frown as he straightens his shirt. "What list?"

Madison clears her throat and waves her hand. "Oh, I just gave Ben a list of things to do on his first day of volunteering—clean up down here, reorganize the shelves, that kind of thing." She turns to me and her voice takes on a joking lilt. "*Ha ha*, no, Ben. No dancing is required of library volunteers."

Her lie further confirms my suspicion—I really am her only confidant. Not even Eli knows what she's up to. He nods, buying the terrible lie, but when Madison looks my way again, I arch a brow.

Her cheeks burn red before she looks away.

I like knowing her secrets.

I like seeing how flustered she is now, scared I'll reveal everything. I won't, of course, because where's the fun in that?

We stay down there for a little while. I ask how long they've been friends and learn they both sought out jobs at the library right after college. Eli says Madison is great with the kids, patient and enthusiastic. She beams under his praise and then waves it off. "Anyone would do the same. It really is a fun job."

No, not everyone would do the same.

"So you'll be with us for the next few weeks, Ben?" Eli asks, giving me a quick once-over.

I nod. "Just until I fulfill my community service requirement."

"Ben's a hardened criminal," Madison quips. "Didn't you know?"

Eli feigns a damsel-in-distress faint. "As if you weren't making us all suffer enough already."

I smile and catch Madison's gaze on me. She's been studying me, stealing glances when she doesn't think I

62

notice. The fact that I've caught her sends her into a near tailspin.

"Right, well, the library is closing soon and I still need to go finish a few things," she says, making a move to exit the room.

I step into her path and glance down at the top of her head. Good thing I don't have any plans to kiss her because if I did, she'd need a step ladder.

"So we're still on for tonight?"

She doesn't meet my eyes as she nods, confirming she'll be at the party.

I don't actually think she'll show.

———

"I need you on wingman duty tonight," Andy says, rubbing his hands together like he's got a plan. "I'm finally gonna go for it with Arianna. I'm not fully convinced she's *into* me, into me, but I have it figured out. I just need you to stand there and not say a word. I mean, truly don't say a word. Act like a bump on a log, and that'll give me the chance to charm her with my witty conversation skills."

"Can't. I invited someone."

We're standing in Jake's kitchen later that night. He has a new condo out on the beach. It's nice, modern, not quite my style, but I can see the appeal. The entire back wall is made of glass panels that slide open, and if the weather wasn't so cold, I'm sure he'd have them pushed to the side so people could mingle out on the deck. As it is, most everyone's in the living room, except for me and Andy. He dragged me into the kitchen to go over his master plan.

"What? Who'd you invite?"

"Madison Ha—"

He jerks back from the kitchen island, hands flying to grip either side of his head like I've just admitted to murder. "NO. Tell me, for the love of God, you didn't."

I don't think I've ever seen his brown eyes so wide. His reaction seems a little over the top.

"What? Why is that a problem?"

He starts listing things off with his fingers. "Umm, her dad's the police chief. Her brother—also a gun-toting police officer, *who by the way*—hates your fucking guts."

Eyes narrowed in thought, I ask, "How do you know her brother hates me?"

He starts to pace, hands digging into his hair. "What do you mean? Everyone knows that. You stole his girlfriend back in high school, remember? Kylie, Kira—something like that. She didn't live here long, but you plucked her away from him like it was the easiest thing you've ever done, not to mention we totally messed with the public school kids any chance we could get. Remember the parking lot incident? The bonfire? The dog poop!?"

He can't be serious. That stuff happened over a decade ago. "That's water under the bridge."

His eyes widen once again like he's trying to instill some panic in me. "Is it? 'Cause it seems more like a building tidal wave."

"Andy, Madison and I are just friends," I insist.

"Oh okay," he mocks, like he doesn't believe me for one second. "Then tell me right now you don't think she's hot."

I scowl. "How do you know she is?"

"It's common knowledge! Where have you *been?* Madison Hart is hot as shit, but with that dad and brother, you'd have to be a psycho to date her. No man in his right mind would touch that girl with a ten-foot pole."

I reach for my beer, tip it in his direction as a silent cheers, and then turn for the living room. His warnings are useless. I'm not trying to date Madison, and I've come to terms with that. We're just going to be friends. I swallow that thought like a bitter pill and chase it with my beer.

In the living room, I'm amazed to find that even more people have arrived. I don't know what Jake was thinking. There have to be a hundred people in here. It makes sense, I guess. Jake grew up living in the rough part of town until his mom remarried, and then he transferred to Saint Andrews for high school. As a result, he knows everyone, and tonight, he's invited them.

Of course there are a few new additions, boyfriend and girlfriends, recent transplants to our small town, but there's still a good chance that if I turn in any direction, my gaze will catch on someone I know pretty damn well. Even though I'm hanging off to the side, near the kitchen, trying to stay out of the madness, it still finds me.

I wasn't always antisocial. It's just that in recent years, with all the changes that have taken place in my life, it feels phony to put on a fake smile and shoot the shit. I'd rather sip my beer in peace. Usually Andy's around and he talks enough for the both of us, but he must still be pissed about me refusing to be his wingman because he's left me to fend for myself out here.

"How's the firm, Ben?" someone asks.

Growing.

"Are you still renovating that house?" someone else wonders.

Finished it a year ago.

"How's your mom?"

Dead. Thanks for asking.

65

Of course I don't say that. I wait for realization to hit, for their faces to crumple, and then I let them off the hook by asking them a stupid question about their life. *Oh cool, you have two kids now? Tell me more about potty training.*

It's never-ending.

Finally, Andy takes pity on me.

"How many people have asked about your mom?" he asks, cutting through the crowd to get to me.

"Five."

"Why are people such idiots?" he asks, scanning the party, no doubt looking for Arianna. "Is your girl here yet?"

"She's not my girl, and no."

I've been staring at the door, watching it like a hawk. I'm worried I'm going to bore a hole through it soon. Not that I've been incessantly checking my watch or anything, but it's already close to 9:00. There's no way she's coming. I knew I should have picked her up and brought her myself.

"All right, c'mon," Andy says, clapping me on the back and trying to drag me through the crowd. "There's a poker game starting up in the dining room. With that mean mug of yours, you'll come out on top for sure."

I don't have a chance to reply because we get sucked into a swell of people. It's partly my fault for keeping my distance from everyone. I haven't been out at a party this big in a while, and everyone's curious to talk to me and catch up. There's a weird kind of celebrity surrounding me and my family in this town. Growing up, I loved and abused the power. What teenage guy wouldn't? Now, I could do without it.

There is no way we're going to make it to the poker game. More than likely, my entire night will be filled with small talk, and if that's not hell, I don't know what is. I contemplate stealing the beer from the woman currently

66

blocking my path to the dining room. Becky is her name. She and her friend are flirting with me, but all I want is her beer. I'm eyeing it, and like a schmuck, I realize a little too late that she's holding it level with her breasts. She thinks I'm staring at her cleavage. *Shit.*

I'm in a bad mood. Because of Madison. Because she's not here and she told me she would be.

The noise level increases in the room even more. Becky's friend elbows her in the side and angles her head toward the door. I follow their gaze just in time to see Colten Hart walk in with a case of beer in hand. He's with a few of his buddies from the police force, guys I recognize from around town. Then he steps aside and reveals a small brunette standing behind him in a pale blue dress.

She didn't change after work, but she took her hair down. It's a wild mess, hanging in loose curls down her back. A few strands fall across her face and when she reaches up to push them behind her ear, my gut clenches.

"Is that Colten's little sister?" Becky asks, curious.

"No way," her friend replies. "She never comes to this stuff."

She laughs. "Colten must have felt bad for her."

I nearly snarl before I catch myself.

Madison is finally here and looking like an angel.

An angel, I remind myself, who's decided to fall.

CHAPTER EIGHT
MADISON

I haven't seen Ben yet, but I know he's here, and just the thought sends a shiver down my spine. He's probably too busy to realize I just walked in the door. Chances are there are enough beautiful women flocked around him to keep him occupied. At this very moment he could be off somewhere with a woman, doing things with her—*to her*—things I've only dreamed about. Or, I tell myself, letting hope flap its wings inside me, he could be watching me right now. He could find me as beautiful and mysterious as I find him, but let's get real—that's highly unlikely. If he has seen me arrive, he's probably assessing my appearance and wondering why the hell I didn't change out of this silly dress or bother to fix my makeup or maybe, I don't know, run a freaking brush through my hair. The truth is, it was hard work convincing my brother to bring me. I wasn't going to make it even worse by strapping myself into a tight dress and sliding on five-inch heels.

Colten came over to eat dinner at the house after I got home from the library. Though I normally try to cook healthy options for my dad, I decided tonight it was better to strategize. I prepared lasagna and fresh garlic bread. I made sure there was a chilled beer waiting for each of them on the table. Also, I pulled Scrabble off the shelf in the hall closet— Colten's game of choice. We hadn't been playing for long when he warned us that he wouldn't be able to stay too late because he had plans. I'd known that moment was coming. I'd thought about it nonstop during dinner. It was why the lasagna was slightly burned and why I was losing so badly at Scrabble (a game I usually won handily).

If I wanted Colten to take me with him to the party, I had to be careful and play it just right.

For starters, I had to sound casual when I asked him where he was headed. Still, he knew right away that something was up. I don't usually ask about his social life. Even though he's only a few years older than me, we don't ever go out together. He never invites me, and I've never been brave enough to ask for an invite.

Until now.

"Jake's party?" I asked, rearranging my Scrabble tiles.

"How'd you know about that?" he asked, frowning.

I tried to seem as if I was concentrating hard on the strategy of the game rather than the strategy of my reply. "My friend at work mentioned it."

I even added a half-hearted shrug for emphasis.

He seemed skeptical. "Eli?"

"No, someone else. Anyway, I was thinking of going."

He and my dad studied me intently from across the table. This cavalier suggestion that I would attend the party wasn't just out of character for me, it was as if aliens had infiltrated my body and were now using me as a human proxy.

"Think that's a good idea, kiddo?" my dad asked, sipping his coffee.

I ground my teeth together in annoyance. "Why wouldn't it be?"

Colten played his turn and then replied, "Dad's right. That sort of scene isn't the right place for you, Maddie. I'll take you another time. Hey, Cassie is getting a few people together to go to the Astros game next weekend. Want to come with us?"

A baseball game, really? Was he also going to buy me a little stuffed animal and some ice cream too? He was casting me aside. They both were. I was used to them handling me with kid gloves since they'd done it my whole life, but surely this was taking it too far.

"I'd like to go to the party," I said, glancing up at Colten and making sure my features didn't seem overly eager. "It could be fun."

He and my dad exchanged a worried glance. They were about to forbid me from going, as if I still had to abide by their rules at twenty-five years old.

"I'm going, Colten," I said, suddenly shooting to my feet and accidentally knocking my hip into the table. My Scrabble tiles went flying and my dad's coffee lapped over the edge of his mug. My cheeks burned with embarrassment. I hadn't caused a scene on purpose, but it still left me looking like a petulant child.

"Fine, Maddie. I'll take you, but we're only going to stay for a little while. I have an early shift tomorrow."

I should have told him that didn't matter. *I* didn't have work in the morning. *I* could stay at the party as long as I wanted, but I was getting my way, and I didn't think I needed to push my luck.

I have a complicated relationship with my family. My mom passed away soon after I was born from hypertrophic cardiomyopathy, which is a fancy name for a heart problem no one even knew about, so it's only ever been the three of us: my dad, Colten, and me. My brother was already six when I was born, and he was fiercely protective even then. Apparently, when we would go to the playground as kids, he'd hold my hand and help me up the stairs and down the slide. He wouldn't let bigger kids get within ten feet of me and always made sure everyone knew he was my big brother, there to defend me if anyone got in my way.

In my eyes, I had an idyllic childhood. My dad took Colten and me fishing and camping and hiking. I was outside most of summer and by the end, when school would start up again, I'd have calloused feet, a smattering of freckles across my cheeks, and a few new scars to show off to my friends.

Looking back, I'm not sure when my relationship with them became stifling, but I can see the wrong turns I took. I didn't move out when I was eighteen. I stayed home and commuted to college. After I got my degree, Dad had just had a mild stroke. It was nothing major, but I didn't feel comfortable leaving him alone in the house, so I stayed. My dad hasn't had another stroke in three years, but I still live in my childhood bedroom. I'm under my dad's thumb and Colten's protective shield. They mean well. They love me as fiercely as I love them, but it can't continue like this.

Something has to change, starting tonight.

―――

The party is a little more packed than I expected it to be. Full of beautiful people dressed to the nines, the house is also a lot nicer than I expected. When I heard it was a house party, I pictured plastic red cups and beer pong in someone's dingy basement. I forget sometimes how high the wealth soars in Clifton Cove. Jake's house looks like he pulled it right out of the pages of Architectural Digest. It's metal and glass and hard lines, all designed to showcase the breathtaking views of the water. The sun has already set, but the moon is high and full enough to illuminate the lapping waves crashing on the shore a few yards beyond his house.

He's done well for himself. My brother told me on the way over that Jake manages a hedge fund. With that on top of his family money, it seems he'll never want for anything in life. I wonder what that would feel like.

We're still hovering near the door. My brother, while not exactly touching me, is still making it perfectly clear that he wants me to stay by his side. I might as well have a collar around my neck. He keeps glancing over at me, making sure I'm doing okay. We're standing in a circle of his friends as they talk about things I really don't care about. Someone offers me a drink, and Colten chastises him.

His friend laughs. "Last I checked, she's not a little kid anymore, Colt."

My brother shrugs off his remark and turns to me, giving in. "You want something to drink, Maddie? I'll get it for you."

I look down at the beer in his hand and scrunch my nose. I don't drink alcohol all that often, but I know enough to pass on the cheap stuff. A few of the women are carrying around flutes of champagne. It feels wildly ridiculous in a setting like this, but then I realize maybe it fits perfectly and the only thing out of place is me.

"I'll take some champagne," I say, smiling.

Colten's friend, Ryan, jumps into action. "I'll go get you some, Madison."

"Just bring the bottle," Colten demands, catching my eye once again. "Never let a guy fix you a drink unless you watch him do it, even Ryan."

"I heard that, you asshole," Ryan shouts over his shoulder.

Colten and his friends lapse back into talk about the Astros' early season, and I give myself the first opportunity to glance around the party and look for Ben. I'm disappointed he hasn't approached me yet. I wanted him to be pacing at the door, wild with anxiety over whether or not I'd make an appearance tonight.

Of course that's not the case. It doesn't take me long to find him. All I have to do is follow the line of adoring fans, the sycophants waiting anxiously for their turn to talk to the king.

He's dangerously attractive tonight in a white shirt underneath an army green fatigue jacket. His dark jeans and brown suede boots are so effortlessly cool. Of course the whole outfit only works so well because of his tall frame and broad shoulders. His thick hair is styled back away from his face, and his features are more severe than they've ever seemed before. I study him intently, realizing I've never had the chance to observe him like this. He has a face for fury, an underlying arrogance that could cut straight through you if he wanted it to. His only saving grace is the light amber color of his eyes. They soften him. A little.

His circle of friends makes up the epicenter of the party. While the women here are all beautifully made up, the ones surrounding him are the glitziest of the bunch. Their dresses are daring and hug their tantalizing figures perfectly. I watch two of them edge closer to him, vying for his attention at the exact moment his gaze finally lifts to meet mine. He doesn't look surprised in the least. In fact, it's like he's been aware I was watching him this whole time. If I had any sense, I'd look away now, but it's like he has me on the end of his hook, caught.

One of his brows rises gently. There's no smile or wave to accompany it.

I turn away right when Ryan returns with the bottle of champagne and uncorks it ceremoniously in the middle of our group. Everyone cheers and I know Ben is still glancing over here, watching—or maybe I'm just hoping he is. Ryan pours a hefty amount of champagne into a plastic cup for me. I guess I don't seem fancy enough for a crystal flute.

"Cheers to Madison and Colt," he says, and another friend chimes in, "He finally let her out of the house for a change!"

Everyone laughs good-naturedly, even Colten. I make a show of smiling even though it hurts to be the butt of the joke. We tap our cups and glasses together and then I take a gulp of champagne, aware of how badly in need of the liquid courage I am. Colten's hand hits my arm and his reproaching glare sends a fissure of annoyance through me.

"Slow down, sis," he says, loudly enough for our entire group to hear.

A few people chuckle and poke fun at how protective he is, but my patience is dwindling fast. I only came to this party because Ben asked me to, but there's no way Colten will let me out of his sight long enough to actually have a chance to talk to him. Even if I did break free, there's no way I'd be able to fight my way through his horde of admirers—not that I'd even want to. Maybe he only invited me here tonight out of courtesy, or worse…*pity*. I think back to the way I unloaded my life on him in the library. I rambled on, forcing an ultimatum upon a man I hardly know. My cheeks are two hot flames. I can't believe I did that. At the time, it felt daring, like I was finally taking control and steering things in the direction of my choosing. Now, it feels silly, *pathetic*. What kind of person enlists a total stranger to help her lose her virginity?

Oh my god. The entire idea of it slams into me like a Mack truck. I need to sit down or throw up. I glance around, trying to find a piece of furniture within reach in case I need it, but Jake's taken everything out of the living room so there's more space for people to gather.

I'm stuck standing unless I want to try to lean against that fancy modern sculpture of a hand over near the fireplace. Where are the folding chairs?! The card tables covered in plastic tablecloths?

I tug on Colten's arm. "I'm going to use the bathroom," I announce, not waiting for him to protest before I break away from the group and turn down a side hallway. The line is ten people deep and I don't actually have to go, so there's no point in standing there. Besides, if I'm gone that long, Colten will assume I've been abducted.

I start down another hallway that looks promising, telling myself I have a good five minutes before I have to return to my overbearing chaperone. I pass a bedroom and a home gym. At the end of the hall, I peek past a doorway and am inspecting the inside of a library that makes my heart pitter patter with jealousy when a cool, hard voice speaks behind me.

"The library's off limits."

I turn and jump out of my skin, my free hand flying to my chest. I manage to save most of my champagne from landing on Jake's polished black wood floors by absorbing it all into the front of my dress. Wonderful. I can see the outline of my lacy bra.

Ben is standing a few feet away, somehow here in this hallway with me even though he belongs back there in the crowded living room. The overhead light is off, a deterrent meant to keep people out of this area of the condo. I didn't heed the warning, and apparently, Ben didn't either. Without the lights, he's half cast in shadow, watching me. We're alone, and that knowledge sends my heart into a race I'm not sure it'll win.

"I wasn't going to go in," I say hurriedly, embarrassed to have been caught snooping.

Ben is still standing there, the very edge of his lips barely lifted. His cheek wants to dimple, but he won't let it.

"Shame," he says before stepping forward, grabbing my hand, and tugging me inside. My body whirls after him. The door slams closed behind us. I stand stock-still near the entrance of the room while Ben continues inside, his hand releasing mine, leaving it cold and bereft. The sound of his boots against the wood floor is the only noise beyond the waves crashing against the shore. Like in the hallway, the lights are off, but with the large windows, the moonlight is enough to illuminate Ben as he wanders over to peruse Jake's collection of books.

I watch him with bated breath. It's comical that I thought we were alone a moment ago in the hallway because now we truly are.

I reach for the door handle behind me. "My brother—"

He glances at me over his shoulder, wearing a bored expression. "Is currently in the middle of a conversation with Norah Adler. She's doing it as a favor to me."

My eyes widen. "Why would you do that?"

He goes back to browsing the rows of books, his finger trailing along the spines as he replies, "Because your brother wasn't going to let me talk to you. I had to get creative."

The admission sends a thrill ricocheting through me. He wanted to talk to me. He wants me here. Then a realization hits me. I frown, worried for Colten. "You shouldn't have done that. He really likes Norah."

Ben nods, not at all shocked by the revelation. "It's exactly why I asked her to occupy him. Anyone else and he might not be distracted enough to forget his role."

"His role?"

"Playing the protective big brother," he says, finally turning his attention fully to me. His face looks menacing even as he glances down at my champagne-stained dress. I wonder if he feels bad for scaring me. If so, he doesn't apologize. "Want me to find you a towel?"

I shake my head. It's no use now, but I still wipe aimlessly at my dress with my hand, highly aware that the light blue color is all but sheer now that it's drenched. I pull it away from my chest as if trying to air it out and then look back up to find him watching me.

We're half a room apart, and I think I prefer it that way.

His head tips to the side. "I've been wondering, does your brother know about your big life plans?"

I nearly choke. "No. Of course not. He and my dad like things just the way they are. If they had it their way, I'd never leave the house, would never walk outside or experience anything that wasn't perfectly…wholesome."

He smiles then, appreciating my honesty. "So what you're hoping to achieve this year is too devious to tell your brother about. Interesting."

He's not moving and yet it feels like he's circling around me like a snake, squeezing me tighter…and tighter. Soon, there'll be no air left.

"You're on the right track then," he continues. "You made it to the party, and you snuck off into a room that's not really intended for guests." His brows arch. "What are you going to do now?"

Umm, congratulate myself on the achievement and call it a day? If I booked it home, I could still be safely tucked in bed before ten.

I can't say that, obviously, so instead I deflect by answering his question with one of my own.

"What would *you* do? If you were me, if you wanted to be bad…"

He moves then, heading for the tufted leather couch sitting against the wall underneath a framed black and white abstract painting. He turns and sits down, stretching his long legs out in front of him so they're crossed at the ankles.

"There's the obvious choice. Normally, if I'm alone with a woman at a party, there's no real question about what we're about to do."

One of his arms gets propped on the back of the couch. He's the picture of easy confidence when our eyes meet again.

I resist the urge to stuff my fist into my mouth and bite down. Still, my insides flip and then clench tight. My bottom lip is tucked between my teeth before I realize what I'm doing and release it on an exhale. I'm lucky I didn't draw blood.

His sinister smile stays in place as he continues, "But, since that's not on the agenda for tonight, we'll have to think of something else."

Not on the agenda, of course. Why would it be? I'm just standing here looking as if I've entered a wet t-shirt contest. If I was more of a woman and he was less of a man, we'd be on the floor, tumbling around like two wild animals.

I try not to take offense at the fact that sex and anything pertaining to it has been so easily wiped off the table. Am I so unattractive that the very thought of sleeping with me sends him running in the other direction? Maybe it's just that I'm not in his league, or perhaps not even on his radar.

In a way, it's liberating having him reaffirm what I already suspected. I don't have to be so serious about this. Sure, I'm alone with an attractive man, but I don't have to worry about impressing him. He's shut the door on that subject—locked it, in fact, and thrown away the key.

I finally move freely, stepping over to inspect the books that have been calling my name since I first poked my head into the room. Jake's collection isn't too shabby, but it's obviously curated. Every title is here to impress rather than to be enjoyed. I know, because nearly all of the spines are perfect. None of these books have been cracked, torn through, *devoured*.

"You could steal one of them," Ben suggests.

I glance over my shoulder at him with a wry smile. "Why stop there? Let's take his TV too."

He laughs and shakes his head. "It's just a thought. You want to be bad, but this location is sort of limiting."

I nod, continuing to peruse the shelf as he continues, his voice slightly more goading than it was a moment ago.

"I suppose if you don't want to take something, you could leave something instead."

His words are as tantalizing as the meaning behind them. I freeze with my finger resting on the spine of *The Divine Comedy*. How fitting considering my Virgil is sitting right behind me.

Without turning to him, I ask, "Like what?"

"A token."

I might be innocent in some ways, but I'm not so naive that I miss his meaning. I have so few things with me, no purse and no phone. I didn't think I'd need them since I was coming with Colten. I have my mostly empty cup of champagne and the clothes on my back, a hair tie around one wrist. None of those things qualify as a token, though. No, a token is something compelling, a part of yourself. The first thing I think of is my *unmentionables*, the things I've never taken off in the presence of a man before. I cringe considering I can't even refer to them directly in my own thoughts.

Your lacy panties, Madison. That's what he wants me to leave behind.

My hand trembles on the book. I yank it away at the same moment I work up the courage to peek over at Ben. My mouth is hidden against my shoulder, but his is stretched into a mocking smile.

"I'm kidding."

His amusement strikes a nerve inside me. He thinks I'm too chicken to do it.

"Close your eyes."

His smile drops and mine widens tenfold.

"I *said*…close your eyes."

He shakes his head in disbelief and lets his head fall back against the couch. Then he does as he's told. I have an unobstructed view of his neck pulled taut, his Adam's apple bobbing when he swallows. It's slightly unnerving to see a man like him in such a vulnerable position.

"I don't hear clothes being removed," he mocks.

I resist the urge to throw a book at him. With his eyes closed, it'd probably hit its target.

I sigh and then glance down at my dress, assessing the hem with fresh eyes. It reaches my knees. I'm going to be fine. No one will notice that I'm sans-panties when I walk back out into the living room. If anything, they'll be too preoccupied with the fact that I apparently haven't mastered the use of a cup yet.

"Can I open my eyes now?" he asks as soon as my hands reach up under my dress.

I panic. "No!"

"What are you doing?"

"Taking my panties off!"

He makes an inaudible sound and then throws his arm over his eyes like he needs extra reinforcement to keep himself from looking. *Interesting*. Just because he doesn't want me doesn't mean he wouldn't be a little curious to see what I have to offer. That thought thrills me even though it shouldn't. I truly need a boyfriend.

"Hurry up," he says, rudely.

"*Okay*! I'm doing it." My fingers hook on either side of my panties and I slide the lacy material down my thighs. If I'd known I would be leaving them behind, I would have worn one of my oversized cotton pairs, my period panties— the ones I put on when I've just about given up on life.

I push the silky material past my thighs and knees then step out of the panties as quickly as possible. I yank the *The Divine Comedy* off the shelf, stuff them inside, and whip the book closed with a loud clap.

When I glance behind me, Ben's eyes are on me. Maybe he heard me close the book and knew it was safe to look...or maybe he was watching me the whole time. I'm too scared to ask.

"He'll never find it," he points out, standing up to walk over to me. "I don't think he's read a single one of these books."

"You're right," I say, gloating. "It's the perfect crime."

He laughs and suddenly, there are voices out in the hallway, bits of conversation filtering into the room.

"She said she was just going to the bathroom," Colten says, his voice angry and accusatory.

"I'm sure she's fine," Jake reassures him. "She's probably just—"

I don't catch the rest of his sentence because Ben's hand grabs my arm and yanks me across the room. There's a niche carved out near the fireplace, mostly hidden from the door.

There, Ben pushes me up against the wall and covers my body with his just as the door opens.

I'm holding my breath. My heart pounds against his chest like it would rather be in his body than mine. He still has his hand wrapped around my forearm but now it's squashed between us, the backs of his fingers grazing the side of my breast.

My lips part and Ben presses his other hand over my mouth, apparently worried I was about to give us away. And *oh god*, maybe I was. His skin is on my parted lips. His scent is wrapped around me and it's the first thing I take in when I finally remember to breathe, him and his exotic blend of spice and sandalwood. Having him press me against this wall and cover my mouth with his hand is as erotic as a first kiss, *more* so considering every guy I've been with has treated me like a porcelain doll.

His eyes implore me to keep quiet and then he turns his head, trying to listen.

"She's not in here," Jake says, sounding annoyed at having been forced on this wild goose chase.

"I've called her ten times," Colten snaps, and then I hear the faint sound of a phone ringing through his speaker before my voicemail kicks in. "*Hi, this is Madison! I can't come to the phone right now, but if you need me, leave a message!*"

Ben's looking down at me again with mischief in his eyes.

He likes that he just heard my voicemail, likes the trick we're playing on my brother.

To him this is all a big game, and that's okay. It'll hurt less when I eventually fall in love with him if I know there's absolutely no hope he feels the same, and I *am* going to fall in love. I'm falling at this moment, with his piercing amber eyes locked on mine and my lips pressed to his palm.

My breasts heave and brush against his chest with every breath, his smile slowly fading into something more sinister. His expression is one I've never seen him wear. I swear it's carnal.

"She's probably back in the living room, looking for you," Jake says. "C'mon, man."

Colt groans then the sound of their footsteps echoes down the hall. They left the door open. We're alone again, but we have to be quiet.

Ben removes his hand slowly and I breathe deeply, but he doesn't move. His hips have left no room between me and the wall. I wouldn't be surprised to find he's flattened me like a pancake. If he wanted to cage me in, he could. His body would completely eclipse mine. My dress is hiked up to the middle of my thigh and his dark jeans feel like sandpaper against my skin. Abrasive. Raw. He follows my gaze down to where our bodies are touching and we must remember at the exact same time that I'm no longer wearing panties because he steps back and I leap to the side as if to get away from him, which is ludicrous because he's already getting away from me.

He wipes a hand down his face, brushing his jaw like it's giving him pain.

My cheeks are so red, I'm fairly certain they'll stay that way permanently.

"Mission one: accomplished," I quip, trying to lighten the mood. Jesus, I need to reach behind him and pop that window open, air this place out a little—or better yet, throw myself out of it.

Where do we go from here?

I can't think of one witty or interesting thing to say. My nerves are still frayed from where he was touching me. I need a moment of silence for Ben and the fact that his glorious body was just touching mine, but there's no time for that because he's telling me to go first, to leave.

He sounds gruff, and I hate that I'm disappointed.

I should have realized—he wants to go back to the party. He has friends to attend to, women to kiss.

He lifts his chin toward the door. "I'll hang back until the coast is clear."

I nod and brush past him to exit. I try to rack my brain for some sendoff, some way to make this night as memorable for him as it was for me, but I come up empty. All I manage is a lingering glance over my shoulder before I turn the corner and flee.

CHAPTER NINE
BEN

It's late and I should go straight to bed, but I'm not tired. I left while the party was still in full swing, but by the time I made it back out to the living room, Madison was gone and Andy was busy trying to woo Arianna. I pulled an ol' Irish goodbye and headed home.

Now, I walk into my kitchen and flip on the light. I don't use this room as often as I should, especially considering how much money I put into it during the renovation. An interior designer picked out all the countertops and finishes, assuring me my wife would love every detail.

Wife.

My stomach clenches at the thought and I swear my house has never felt quieter or more isolating.

I pull open my pantry door, looking for a late-night snack, and settle on the best comfort food of them all: sugary cereal. I pour myself a bowl, sit down at the oversized marble island, and try to ignore the hard object poking me in the ribs. I eat a few bites before I cave and reach into the inner lining of my jacket, feeling for *The Divine Comedy.*

Yeah, I stole it.

I guess I'm more of a criminal than I thought. First a misdemeanor, and now petty theft.

I slide it onto the counter in front of me and take another bite of cereal, staring at it. I didn't steal it because I want her panties. I'm not going to take them out and do weird shit with them; I just couldn't leave them in Jake's house. They don't belong to him.

Her book choice was interesting—I'll give her that much. She compared me to Virgil the other day, and I suppose she's continuing the inside joke. I wonder, though, if I open it on a whim, will my finger land on the circle of hell designed for thieves or the one reserved for lustful sinners? Apparently, I'm both.

I can't believe I pulled her into that library. That was stupid, reckless. Her brother could have found us. Worse, I could have acted on the all-consuming urge I had to kiss her while he was in the room, when I was pressed up against her and her dress was nearly see-through, when I watched her wet her bottom lip and then take it between her teeth. Her green eyes were staring up at me with such sincere openness. I could have seen the outline of her soul if I'd looked hard enough. Every emotion was right there, brimming on the surface. She was afraid to get caught, but more than that, she was excited. Every part of her was begging for a kiss.

Maybe I should have done it.

No.

I jerk the thought out of my head. I've moved on from my attraction to Madison. I'm not in her life for that. I finish my last bite of cereal and load my bowl into the dishwasher. After, I slam it closed a little harder than necessary and am about to switch off the kitchen light when I turn back and swipe the book off the island.

I have to see the color at least.

Just that.

They're pale blue and lacy.

Fuck.

———

I'm not on the schedule at the library again until next Saturday. I know because I have an email waiting for me when I arrive at work first thing on Monday morning. It's short and to the point.

From: MadisonHart@RosenbergLibrary.com
To: BenRosenberg@RosenbergSteinLaw.com
Subject: Volunteering

Hi Ben,

If it works for you, I'll need you at the library this Saturday at 8:00 AM. You'll be helping with toddler story time.

See you then,
Madison Hart
Children's Librarian, Rosenberg Library

Below all of that is a phone number. On a whim, I text it.

Ben: Hey, this is Ben. I just got your email. Saturday morning is fine.

She texts back right away.

Madison: Oh, great!

Madison: Also, maybe I should clarify that this is my personal phone number, not my work number.

Another text pops up right after that one.

Madison: I can get you the number to my work
phone at the library if you'd rather have that?

Why in the world would I want that?

Ben: This is fine.

A little bubble pops up to show she's typing a reply. It
disappears. Then another one pops up in its place. It
disappears too. She's obviously overthinking whatever she's
about to tell me. If she were here in person, I'd shake her and
tell her to spit it out.

Finally, a new message appears.

Madison: Okay, great. I just didn't want to make
things too personal if you'd rather leave them
professional.

Another text immediately follows that one.

Madison: I feel like I'm not coming across well via
text. Does my tone seem weird to you?

Andy walks into my office then with a cup of coffee in
hand. He's whistling under his breath, much too happy to be
in the office this early on a Monday morning.

"Who're you texting?" he asks once he sees my phone
in my hand.

"I'm not texting. I'm checking my emails."

"Okay, first of all, you're smiling, so I know you're
lying. Second of all, why would you check your emails on

your phone when you're sitting at your desk with your computer right in front of you?"

I glare at him and make a point of dropping my phone, turning my attention to my computer, and going straight to my email.

"Do you need something?" I ask brusquely.

He helps himself to the seat across from my desk usually reserved for clients, crosses one ankle over his knee, and gets comfortable. He's smiling at me. His blond hair's a little disheveled. His socks are brightly colored and striped. He's getting on my last nerve.

I want to tell him to get out of my office, but he speaks up first. "I wanted to check in and see how things went on Friday. You left early."

My phone vibrates and we both stare at it.

"Need to get that?" he asks, eyebrows raised tauntingly.

"It's fine," I say, turning back to my computer.

He sips his coffee, eyes narrowed on the window behind my head as if he's just enjoying the morning sunrise.

He has work to do. We both do.

My phone vibrates again, a reminder that I didn't open the last text message.

Andy clears his throat and with a near growl, I grab the phone like I'm angry at it.

Madison: You know what? Forget I said all of that. Ha ha. Also, I'll stop texting you now. You're probably very busy at work.

I fire back a quick response.

Ben: I texted you first, remember? Also, I don't have a client meeting until 9:00 AM.

I'm staring down, waiting for the little dots to pop up again. She clearly doesn't subscribe to the standard rules of texting as evidenced by the fact that she texted me three times in a row before I replied. Now, nothing.

The dots don't appear. I lock my phone, unlock it, open my texts again. Nothing new has come through.

Then something finally does.

Andy: Hi.

I resist the urge to laugh. I really do hate the guy.

When I glance up at him, he's smiling over his cup of coffee, phone in hand, pleased with himself.

"Anything you'd like to share?" he asks, feigning innocence.

"Nothing."

"I saw you disappear with Madison at the party."

I open my desk drawer, drop my phone inside, and then slam it closed. "I was in the bathroom."

"For thirty minutes?"

I shrug. "Bad fish."

"We live on the coast—there's no such thing."

"Andy, I'm not going to talk to you about her."

"Oh I know. I'm just over here wondering why that is."

I'm saved from having to reply to him when my secretary, Mrs. Cromwell, walks in with an armful of files.

I work straight through the morning and then meet my dad for lunch at the club. I don't see him as often as I should, especially considering how close we live to one another. I think it's easier for both of us to have some distance. The last few years have been hard, and I don't think either of us has quite adjusted to the reality of our situation: it's just the two of us now.

He met my mom when they were teenagers and they got married young. She was with him through college and law school, and she helped him build his practice to what it is today. He's one of the top litigators in the state and has no plans to retire any time soon.

We look a lot alike, and though his hair has turned gray and he wears glasses now that his eyesight isn't as sharp as it used to be, he's still a handsome guy. He could date if he wanted to, but I know he won't.

"Tell me something good," he says after we finish our meals and the waiters are clearing our plates.

I lean back in my chair. "The firm's really taking off. I think we'll need to hire—"

He laughs and the skin around his eyes crinkles. "Outside of work, son."

Right. That's all we talked about through lunch.

I wipe my mouth with the linen napkin and fold it neatly across the table, stalling. "The house has really come together. The landscape architect you recommended put the finishing touches on the back yard last week, and with the pool, it'll be a nice spot for entertaining."

I'm not sure he means for me to see his disappointment, but it's there in his subtle frown, in the way he nods but doesn't offer a reply.

He scoots his chair back from the table after signing the bill, and we walk in silence toward the door. Once we're outside, standing shoulder to shoulder, waiting for the valet to bring around our cars, he speaks about the subject we usually do our best to tiptoe around.

"I've been hoping you'd come to terms with your mom's passing on your own, but it occurs to me that I might have failed you in that department."

We're both staring out at the manicured golf course, unwilling to turn and meet the other's eyes. We don't talk about this, at least not often. If he's bringing it up, it's with a hell of a lot of courage.

"I was with her for 47 years, Ben. The suffering there at the end was only for a short while. Ask me if I regret the 47 years because of how it ended. Go ahead."

It's too hard to swallow past the lump in my throat, much less speak.

"The answer's no. I don't regret a single damn day. If you want to keep your focus on that firm and that house, that's all right. It's your life, your *only* life, and you get to choose how you spend it. I just don't want you to get to my age one day and regret…" He pauses and scratches his chin, buying himself time. "Oh, I don't know. I'm rambling, aren't I? Look, there's my car. You'll be free of me soon enough. Forget I brought it up, all right?"

He claps my shoulder twice and then steps forward to greet the valet. I catch his boisterous laugh and the few words they exchange, but my attention is still on the horizon.

It's your life, your only life, and you get to choose how you spend it.

I reach into the pocket of my pants and pull out my phone.

CHAPTER TEN
MADISON

I honestly didn't expect to hear from Ben again. After the strange way we ended things on Friday, I sort of expected him to cancel his volunteer assignment at the library and avoid me at all costs. My email to him was my way of casually putting the ball in his court. *Are we going to steer clear of each other from now on? Pretend we don't know each other? Or is the "make me bad" plan still on?*

So, you can imagine my utter shock when I saw his text message pop up on my phone first thing this morning. *Hey, this is Ben. I just got your email. Saturday morning is fine.* It felt strange and thrilling and wonderful and I replied quickly because I was so excited, but now in hindsight, I realize I should have waited and played it cool.

His text was kind of curt, impersonal. One reply from me would have sufficed, but no, I had to let my fingers fly and send off half a dozen rambling messages before common sense finally kicked in and I nearly flung my phone at the wall. Reading our conversation back to myself only made matters worse. None of my texts make any sense. *I asked him about my tone?! If he wanted my work number?!*

He probably exchanges texts with actual supermodels, and I couldn't manage to think of a single witty one-liner or teasing innuendo? I am deeply ashamed.

My solution to all of this is to just stop texting him altogether and shove my phone out of sight in my desk drawer. Well, kind of.

The pattern goes like this: I put a few books away, check my phone. Help a mom and her son find age-appropriate chapter books, check my phone. Set up for mommy-and-me story time, check my phone. I think I've checked it so many times, I've worn down the home button. It's getting a little ridiculous, so when Eli comes down to retrieve me for our lunch break, I leave my phone behind and go without it. It's nice, liberating. I sit in the restaurant and focus on my meal. Sure, my knees are bouncing under the table, and I seriously consider stealing Eli's phone, logging into my iCloud, and checking my text messages—but I don't! And that counts for something.

Fortunately for me, Eli doesn't notice how weird I'm acting or the fact that my knee has bumped into his approximately 37 times. He has a lot on his plate. He and Kevin are trying to work with an adoption agency, and they're hitting every single roadblock imaginable. The whole process is way more expensive than they realized. I feel terrible. He has actual problems. Even still, on our way back to the library, he finally remembers to ask me about Jake's party.

"Was it fun?"

Keep it short, I tell myself.

Then, I proceed to tell him every single detail down to the brand of champagne I spilled on myself.

"Did your brother flip out when you disappeared?"

I let my head fall back against the seat and groan. "*God*, that was a fiasco."

The minute Colten found me at the party, he yanked me right on out of there and insisted we go straight home. It didn't matter that I had a pretty good lie for where I'd been for the past half-hour. First, I told him I'd accidently spilled my drink on my dress and being too embarrassed to go back into the party, I'd gone down to the beach to have some time to myself. I thought that'd put the matter to rest, but it had the exact opposite effect. Colten told me in excruciating detail all the reasons that was a bad idea. Some guy from the party could have followed me out there. I could have bumped into a stranger on the beach and been _____. Fill in the blank with some kind of horrible thing: raped, stabbed, shot, kidnapped. I tried to point out that even though I recently had something bad happen to me, the crime rate in Clifton Cove is ridiculously low and the odds of me stumbling upon someone who wanted to do me any harm *again* are slim to none. He didn't want to hear it, though. He told me I needed to take my safety more seriously. They haven't found the guy yet. It wasn't a joke.

Even worse, he got my dad involved.

The two of them rambled on about how I need to take extra precautions while the police investigate my case. I wanted to throw my hands up and tell them the truth: I was inside the house the whole time! Yup! I was inside, throwing myself at a guy you both hate who at best thinks I'm a weirdo and at worst thinks I'm pitiful. Now leave me alone!

After the incident, I'm not grounded per se because I'm a twenty-five-year-old woman and I did nothing wrong, but I did get an *I'm disappointed in you* glare from my father at the breakfast table the next morning. To break the ice, after I scrambled us some egg whites, I pushed a deck of cards toward him and suggested a few rounds of two-person Spades. By 10:00 AM, we were back to normal.

Let's hope it goes as easily with Colten.

He's coming over for dinner tonight.

I texted him earlier today, just to say hey, and he never responded. He's still upset with me, and it's probably because he knows I lied to him. I *hate* lying to him, but there was no way around it!

I can't tell him where I was. I'm not ready for this illicit friendship with Ben Rosenberg to end, especially because when I return from lunch with Eli and all but leap at my desk drawer, I have a new text message from Mr. Off-Limits himself waiting for me.

Ben: I've been trying to think of what your next task should be...

I nibble on my bottom lip and reread it twice before the library phone rings and I remember I have actual work to do. Time gets away from me as the afternoon continues. The library is always the busiest after school lets out for the day. Families rush in to tackle homework and tutoring. Children run around, getting out their pre-dinner jitters. I'm pulled in one direction after another, trying to inform as many parents as possible about our spring literacy program. Children who read 100 books before May get to choose one thing from the prize cabinet: stickers, yo-yos, puzzles, board books. It's cheap stuff, but it's the idea behind it that's so exciting, not to mention the little bonus I'll receive if I get enough families to sign up. Needless to say, I shove books onto anyone I cross paths with.

During all of this, I don't forget about Ben's text message. Ha. No, no. A case of amnesia could not erase his words from my brain. The reason I don't reply is because I don't have a witty response, and I've yet to find the time to think of one. I run straight from work to the grocery store to pick up some last-minute items for dinner. I had to stay a little late to manage the chaos, and of course, the checkout lines are insane because it's Monday and apparently everyone needs groceries on Monday.

I make it home twenty minutes before Colten is due to come over and my father warns me he's working the night shift, so I'll have to hurry if I don't want to make him late.

My dad carries in the groceries and I unload them, noticing his pill case on the counter. I'm unpacking the milk and yogurt when I ask if he's taken his blood thinner yet.

"Yes."

"Statin?"

"*Yes.*"

"What about your aspirin?"

"All right, kid, you got me. I forgot the aspirin."

I send him a searing gaze over my shoulder and he throws his hands up as if to say, *What are ya gonna do?*

"I'll take it in a second. Now what are you going to make? I took that lunch you made me to work and those tater tots tasted off."

"They should—they're cauliflower tots."

He reacts as if I've just admitted to poisoning him. Then he spots the pasta I'm unloading and his complaints increase tenfold. "What's this? Looks like a science experiment gone wrong."

"It's veggie pasta."

"Oh no. Now you've really done it."

His ensuing groan is deep and heartfelt, but I'm not swayed.

I yank it out of his hand and shoo him away from the stove. "I'll still cover it in spaghetti sauce and ground turkey. You said last week that you couldn't even taste the difference."

"I was humoring you!" he shouts from the other room as he flips on the football game.

This is our routine: I try to fix healthy food for a father who would rather fill his arteries with cheeseburgers and French fries, and he protests every step of the way. I'd be shocked if he ever sat down for dinner and actually wanted to eat what I made him.

Colten's usually better about not complaining. He's a fit guy, after all, so he enjoys my healthier options. This meal is his favorite, and it's no coincidence that I've chosen to make it tonight. I'm still trying to get back in his good graces, which yes, I'll admit is absolutely ridiculous because I really didn't do anything wrong, but that's the problem with our family. We're a screwed-up bunch. We don't have the normal brother-sister-dad dynamic. I see them almost every day. We're in each other's business. We bother and poke and pester because we care, and I'm not going to throw in the towel just because Colten's a little overbearing. I'm going to push back, gently, and see if I can't carve out some newfound freedom for myself. I'll have to do it slowly. In fact, I should probably carve with a spoon rather than a shovel.

I've thought a lot about what I would do with more freedom. For one, I'd move out. I told Ben I couldn't move out because of what rent would cost, but that was a lie…kind of. I have some money saved up, more so now that my student loans are paid off. I could probably find a one-bedroom apartment. I check my savings account a lot, dream about taking the leap. Actually, the last time I checked, I'd even have enough for a down payment on a very shabby, very rundown house if I played my cards right.

I laugh sardonically. The idea that I would ever do something as insane as purchasing a house is too crazy to even consider. I'm the girl who still lives at home, who hangs out with her dad on Friday nights. I'm the bookworm, the person easily forgotten by everyone outside of her own family.

The back door opens and Colten steps in wearing his uniform, looking very sharp and snazzy. He sees me at the stove and smiles gently. I'm surprised. I was ready for another stern talking to, but it appears he's ready to make peace after all.

"Hey Colt."

He lifts his chin in greeting. "Whatcha cookin'?"

I hold up the veggie pasta. "Your favorite. It'll be ready soon. Dad's in there watching the game."

That's all we say to each other, no apologies or drawn-out explanations, but I know things are back to normal now.

I put the pasta on to boil and am browning the turkey when I realize I still haven't texted Ben back. I have a few minutes to spare, so I retrieve my phone from my purse, open my texts, and reread his words.

He wants to continue.

Sure, I've technically forced him into this role as the devil on my shoulder, but if he didn't want to do it, he wouldn't be suggesting another task. My heart leaps in my chest at the prospect that the second mission could be anything as wild as the first one. I took my panties off in front of him. I stuffed them into one of Jake's books! I let him hide me away in a corner, his body and scent and touch all but stealing the life right out of me. I've been thinking a lot about that moment when our bodies were pressed together, when I let his hand graze the edge of my breast. I think about it most at night, when I'm alone in bed. Last night, I unbuttoned my pajama top and ran my hand across my stomach and then…lower.

My stomach dips from the memories then Colten walks back into the kitchen. I jerk forward for the wooden spoon and get busy mixing the pasta.

He looks at me like I'm weird. "What are you doing?"

I wave my phone. "Just looking up the recipe to make sure I'm doing it right."

He frowns as he opens the fridge and reaches in for an apple. "Haven't you made it a dozen times?"

"Yeah," I say, staring at the boiling water and waiting for inspiration to strike. "But…well…sometimes I salt the water and sometimes I don't. I forgot which way I like it."

Lame. Bad. *Very unconvincing, Madison.*

He levels me with one more skeptical glare then turns back for the living room without another word. I hear him take a big bite of the apple and then I sag against the counter.

I wasn't doing anything wrong, I tell myself.

I wasn't fantasizing about Ben with my brother and dad in the next room. I was *thinking* about fantasizing about Ben. There's a big difference!

Still, I decide there's no point in texting him back now. I wait until Colten's gone and the leftovers have been put away. I'm cleaning the dishes when my dad walks in with his adult softball league shirt on. I forgot he has a game tonight. It means I'll have the whole house to myself for the next few hours. I let him kiss me on the head and wish him luck before he walks out the door. Then, with speed usually reserved for X-Men and dudes running from the cops, I dart across the kitchen for my phone. My hands are still covered in suds. I can't even unlock the screen.

"Gahrrrr," I grumble impatiently, wrenching the towel from where it hangs on the stove and drying my hands as quickly as possible. I toss it over my shoulder. It lands on the ground. I'm typing out a text as fast as my little fingers can tip-tap-type on my iPhone.

> Madison: Okay, I know what I want to do. Are you free tonight?

My hand is shaking so much, my phone screen is blurry. I can't even read my own words. Why did I text him? Oh my god, he has friends. He's probably at a dinner party or like a fancy fashion show. I don't know—how do rich people spend their time? I'm pacing now, chewing on a nail, angry at myself, angry at Ben for turning me into this version of myself. Everything is dark and abysmal. I hate my phone and whoever invented texting. Mr. Apple, Elon Musk—they all suck. I bite my lip and resist the urge to shove the offending device down the disposal, and then it vibrates and *it's him!* He's replied and my whole world is bright and beautiful again. Butterflies float around my head like a halo.

> Ben: I'm still up at the office, but I'm leaving soon. What do you have in mind?

Oh my GOD.
This is my moment. I have to take life by the balls, and then because that sounds gross, I decide to take life by the hand, but forcefully.

> Madison: Great. Come pick me up. I'll tell you where we're going then.

I have no idea what he means by "leaving soon". It could be ten minutes, could be an hour, so I rush upstairs and yank my dress off as I go. I won't repeat the same mistakes I made over the weekend. I'm not going to wear the same boring dress I wore all day at work. I pick out a pair of jeans and a short, flowy white peasant top. When I move, it exposes the barest hint of my midriff. It's probably the sexiest thing I own, which is a little sad now that I think about it. I should at least have some kind of black leather dress that suctions to my skin hidden away in a glass box with a label that reads *Break in case of emergency*.

I slide on some brown leather boots I splurged on last year when Anthropologie was having a sale and then I step into my bathroom. My hair is in a braid, so I shake it out and assess the damage. The long brown waves still have a little volume left in them. It's kind of a wild mess, but it'll have to do. I don't have time to become a hair wizard—for all I know, Ben's only five minutes away.

I pull out my makeup, eternally grateful that I let Eli talk me into getting some new products at Sephora last summer. I had no idea what contouring or highlighting was before that day. I still know *very* little about it, but the enthusiastic employee taught me the bare minimum for what I need to do to make my green eyes pop and my skin a little more flawless.

Who am I kidding? I have to wipe off my eye shadow four times before it looks halfway decent, but when I step back and look at myself in the mirror, I'm kind of impressed. My eyes seem even bigger than usual. My lips are a soft pink. My cheekbones are accentuated. Most important of all, I still look like me, just a little…sexier.

My phone buzzes on my bed and I leap into action, answering it as I run down the stairs. I'm at the door, yanking on a jacket when I realize I forgot to say hello.

"Madison?" Ben says on the other end of the line. "You there?"

I laugh and pause, remembering to breathe for the first time in what feels like forever.

I hold the phone up to my ear. "Hey, sorry."

I can see him through the window in the foyer. He's sitting at the curb in a sleek black SUV.

"I'm outside."

"Okay," I say, forcing myself to lie. "I'll be right out, I just need another few minutes."

"Take your time."

He hangs up and I stay right where I am, willing my heart to slow its wild pace just a little. This is going to be a big night. I'm about to get into Ben Rosenberg's car, and just the idea of it feels wrong. My dad didn't ask me what I was doing tonight, so I'm not deceiving him by going out. I'm allowed to leave the house. I just never do, so it feels strange. I heave a sigh, reach for the door handle, and step outside to begin an adventure I'll likely never forget.

Ben gets out and rounds the front of the SUV to meet me at the passenger side door as I walk down the front path. I have a sudden urge to walk in the exact opposite direction. My confidence has left the building. He didn't change after work, but he took off his suit jacket and rolled up his sleeves. If he was wearing a tie, he's not anymore.

He's as out of my league as he's ever been. Handsome, confident, and poised, he moves like he's never spent a single day wishing he were in someone else's body.

How did we get here? I wonder as he pulls the door open and then watches me walk the last few yards toward him. When I get close, he tips his head.

"Madison."

I bite down on my smile and tip my head right back at him before I step up into his car. Black leather seats warm my tush. *Ah, rich people really do know how to live.*

He closes the door behind me and I watch him circle back to the driver's side. He hops in with the confident grace of a panther then turns to me, one hand casually draped over the steering wheel.

"Where to?"

CHAPTER ELEVEN

B E N

"Funny. This is a first for me too."

"You've never been inside a tattoo shop?" she asks.

I'm staring up at the wall covered in intricate designs when I shake my head.

"Hey, if you're a walk-in, you'll have to come back," a grizzly voice says behind us. I turn and assess the guy behind the counter. He's probably in his mid-thirties, black concert tee, jeans, buzzed hair, colorful half-sleeve on his right arm. "One of my artists is out sick and the rest are booked solid."

Madison's smile falls. "Crap. I didn't even think about scheduling an appointment."

She turns to me with brows tugged together, her bottom lip sticking out just a little. I don't like her expression. I also don't like the idea of our night getting cut short.

"Do you tattoo?" I ask the guy.

He crosses his arms over his chest and aims a disdainful glance at me. "This is my shop."

Good—he won't fuck up her skin.

"I'll pay you five times your normal rate if you can shuffle some things around. The tattoo she wants won't take long."

I actually have no idea how long it'll take. I'm just assuming at this point, but I think it's fair to guess Madison doesn't have anything too crazy in mind for her first tattoo. I glance over to her and she nods, mouth agape.

The guy considers my offer for a second, frowning. He's annoyed, but not so annoyed that he won't do it.

With a sigh, he turns for his office. "Yeah, fine. Give me a second."

Madison walks over, tilting her head to whisper, "You didn't have to do that. It'll probably be ridiculously expensive now."

"So what? You're about to permanently ink your body—at least now you're in good hands."

A few minutes later, the owner introduces himself as Paul and leads us toward the back. He takes more of an interest in Madison than me, walking beside her and asking her how she heard about his shop. There's music playing loudly overhead and a constant whirring of needles as we pass other artists at work. Paul has his own private room—perks of owning the place, I guess—and once we're inside, Madison describes what she wants.

"Really, just an outline of a rose."

My heart lurches in my chest.

"Small," she continues, "and I mean small—*microscopic* even."

Paul chuckles.

"Here, I have an image saved on my phone."

He steps over to where she's sitting and she holds it up for him to see. I'm still wondering if I heard her right. *She said rose, didn't she?*

"Okay, so more geometric than organic," he says, nodding in understanding.

"Exactly. It's almost like a stripped-down version of a rose. Someone else might not realize what it is at first glance."

"And no stem?" She nods and he steps back. "Right. I got it. Let me sketch something and I'll be back in a second."

When he leaves the room, he closes the door behind him and Madison glances over to me, brows raised.

"So I guess I'm really doing this," she says, her mouth hitched up in a nervous half-smile.

"Why a rose?" I ask through a clenched jaw. My nerves are all pulled taut. I feel like a live wire.

She doesn't notice, too self-conscious about her choice of tattoo. She thinks I'm judging her.

"I don't know," she says, blushing. "It's supposed to be a tattoo in memory of my mom, which is…I don't know, probably idiotic because I didn't even know her. I'm not even sure she liked roses all that much, but I just thought—"

"My mom's name was Rose," I blurt out, appreciating the air that rushes into my lungs right after.

Her eyes widen in shock. "Really?" Then realization hits her as she remembers. "Oh right, Rose Rosenberg." She all but whispers the name, as if she's conjuring a ghost.

"What a name, right?" I say, trying to lighten the mood. "She always joked that she must have really loved my dad to marry him and take that name."

Madison looks down at her hands as she twiddles her thumbs. "I don't know…I kind of like it." Then she jerks up and her eyes lock with mine. Under the fluorescent lights, she should look washed out, but instead she's lit up—fair skin, red cheeks, bright green eyes. "I don't have to get it, Ben."

I push off the wall I've been leaning against and walk toward her, hand outstretched. "Let me see your phone."

She fumbles for it and holds it out to me. It's like she thinks I'm angry with her for wanting to get a tattoo of a rose, but it's actually the exact opposite.

"It's a cool design. Where are you wanting to get it?"

"Left butt cheek."

I blink, my face a mask of horror, and it takes me a solid three seconds to realize she's completely joking.

"Ben, I'm *kidding*. I'm thinking I want it along my ribs, somewhere I can hide it."

"From your family?"

She smirks. "From the world. This tattoo is just for me."

And for me.

I'm the only one who will know it's there. Me…and Paul.

When he returns with the finished design and Madison happily approves, he walks her through the steps of what to expect and then tells her she'll have to go sans shirt and bra.

Her eyes widen. I guess she didn't think that far ahead.

Paul senses her discomfort and produces a paper drape and some micropore tape.

"It's fine if you'd rather cover up, but I don't want you fidgeting around while I'm trying to tattoo. Just put the drape on so it's open in the back, and leave your left arm out. Your boyfriend can tape it down along your breast so I'll only have access to the skin along your rib, where you want the tattoo."

"Oh he's not—"

"That's fine. Got it." I step forward and take the tape from him before Madison can protest. Paul shakes his head at me like I'm a jealous boyfriend. Little does he know, I'm just jealous. I don't get any of the perks that come with the second word.

When Paul leaves the room again, Madison is glaring at me suspiciously.

I shrug. "It's either this or no drape at all. I'll turn around while you get situated."

She laughs as I turn to face the door.

"This is hilarious. It's like I'm doing it on purpose—continuously undressing around you, that is." Her voice lowers. "I swear this wasn't my intention."

I close my eyes, pinch the bridge of my nose, and will her to hurry up. I hear her slipping her shirt over her head and then unhooking her bra. *Jesus.* I imagine the entire thing in excruciating detail. My mind fills in the gaps with a fantasy, and now I'm wishing I'd just gone straight home after work.

"Where should I put…"

She's wondering where she should put her clothes. Who the fuck cares?! Put them on your head. Throw them on the ground. Just do…*something.*

"The table, Madison," I snap impatiently. "Just put them on the table."

"Oh, okay," she says with a shaky breath. The paper drape whips open and it rustles loudly as she tries to finagle it in place. "I think I've got it. Here, come tape."

I turn and she's sitting on the edge of the table with her feet dangling over one side. The thin blue material covers her, but I can still see the outline of her breasts. I tilt my neck side to side, willing the tension to leave my shoulders. She's staring down at where her hand is holding the drape in place then her gaze slowly drifts to me and she waits, patiently, with her green swirling eyes and her soft pink lips…

I need to move. My legs need to propel me toward the table, the table on which a beautiful woman sits, nearly naked.

Blood is rushing south.

My dick assumes it's go-time.

"Turn around," I say brusquely, both to give my body time to control itself and so I can actually reach the spot where I need to tape.

She gives me an odd look and then props her feet up on the table, angling her exposed side and back toward me. She has a delicate spine. Small waist. Fair skin that looks silky to the touch.

Angrily, I step forward and yank off some tape, leaning down to press it against her skin and the drape. I'm not gentle, by any means, and Madison tells me so.

"Good thing you're not the one giving me the tattoo."

Yes. Good thing.

I do a bang-up job with that tape. I use half the roll. Paul won't see the barest hint of Madison's breasts. Also, she'll probably have to wear the drape for the rest of her life because it's permanently attached to her skin now. I step back, proud, before Paul reenters the room.

"All set?"

I chuck the tape at him. Unfortunately, it doesn't smack him in the head like I want it to.

"All set."

―――――

I was already aware that Madison is a talker in normal circumstances, but in instances of high stress—like now—she's a veritable chatterbox. Paul's moments away from getting started. He's assured her we'll only be here thirty minutes, forty-five tops. Madison is lying on her side with her head resting on her right arm so Paul can access the area of skin along the edge of her ribs. I'm sitting on a stool near her head, out of Paul's way but close enough that I can see what he's doing.

I steal quick, intense glances at her bare back. I wished I'd taped the other side of the drape to her skin as well. It pools on the table, exposing all of her trim back down to the top of her jeans. Her hair splays out across the table. It shouldn't be sensual, but it is. All of this is, even as she describes her job at the library to Paul. She's outlined the various programs they offer and her favorite children's authors, and now she's in the middle of explaining a spring reading initiative when Paul interrupts to tell her he's going to start.

"Oh god, really? Okay. Did the needle just get louder or is that just me? Did I already tell you guys I don't like needles?"

Twice.

Her eyes jerk up to me. "Will you hold my hand?"

Paul glances to me. "Actually, try drawing on her hand. The movement will distract her from the pain more, but don't tickle her. If she flinches, I'll mess up."

She lets out a nervous laugh. "Oh god, I thought he was going to say, *If she flinches, I'll kill her.*"

Wow. Her brain has left the building. She's a mess. I reach for her hand and rest it on my knee. Her body is still angled where Paul needs it, but now I have better access to her palm. I spread it flat, amazed by how small it is. How can a human adult have hands this small? This soft?

"Your hand is really warm," she says, half delirious with nerves. Our eyes are locked when Paul begins.

"If you need me to take a break, let me know."

"Ah!" she yelps as soon as the needle meets skin.

"Is it too painful?" he asks, but her eyes are still on me.

I tilt my head in question. "Going to chicken out so soon? What about your list?"

She bites her bottom lip and shakes her head. Paul continues.

Her eyes pinch closed and her palm tries to curl in on itself, but I flatten it back out and think of some way to distract her. It shouldn't be that hard, but *she's* distracting *me*. We're touching, holding hands, almost. Her skin feels good against mine. I hadn't thought my hands were all that calloused from the gym and the odd jobs I did around my house during the remodel, but compared to hers, they're rough.

She winces and I remember my duty: distract *her*.

"Try to tell me what word I'm spelling out."

She blinks her eyes open. "What?"

I start to draw letters against her palm with the pad of my finger to show her what I mean: M-A-D-I...

"Madison," she guesses. The edge of her mouth hitches and I know I've got her.

I smile and start again, focusing my attention on her hand. Now that she's watching me, I can't think of a single word. I'm just drawing aimlessly on her palm. It's cathartic. I trace her lifelines and wonder what pieces of her future they hold, if any. I wonder if the tugging in my chest is from the pizza Andy and I split at lunch or if I'm completely ignoring an obvious truth standing (or rather, lying) right in front of me.

She scrunches her nose. "I didn't catch any of that. Were those letters?"

I clear my throat. "Let me try again."

B-E-N.

She laughs. "Creative."

W-A-S.

"Oh my gosh. Tell me you aren't—"

H-E-R-E.

Paul glances up, watching Madison laugh with an appreciative gleam in his eye. "How long have you two been together?"

Our mouths open at the same time as if we're both about to rush out a reply and tidy up this situation before it becomes any more awkward, but then seconds ticks by. More. Neither of us says a word. Maybe we want to avoid the sitcom trope of speaking over one another and telling conflicting stories. *A week! A month!* Or maybe neither of us is in a hurry to correct him. We both close our mouths and I watch as Madison's eyes soften and her lips curl into a tempting smirk. She's daring me to play along.

"A year next month," she lies confidently.

My brow arches. A year? That's quite a serious relationship.

Paul wipes her tattoo, cleaning the skin, and then continues. "Going to do anything special for your anniversary?"

This time, there's no pause as Madison launches into her answer.

"Ben is taking me to Europe. I've never been. We're skipping the cliché parts though—no Eiffel Tower and Vatican for us." I smirk. *Oh really?* "We're going to Italy, to this little fishing village right on the coast." I'm impressed. "You can only get there by train, and there's a bed and breakfast owned by an English couple. It's a real hidden gem."

"How'd you guys hear about it?" Paul asks.

I tip my head. *Yes, Madison, how did we hear about it?*

"My friend Eli stayed there a few summers back. He said if I only take one trip in my whole entire life, that's where I should go. Vernazza."

"Sounds like it'll be romantic," Paul says, casting me a glance that makes it clear he thinks I'm a lucky guy.

Her tattoo doesn't take much longer after that, not that it matters. With Madison carrying the conversation for the three of us and her hand still in mine, I draw random doodles on her skin, enjoying myself more than I should. She talks about the most boring stuff, like the library cataloging system, and yet I'm riveted, completely and utterly transfixed.

I'm so disturbed by how I feel that I'm quiet on the drive home. Annoyed, even.

Madison notices.

"Do you not like the tattoo? I thought it looked really cool before he covered it."

I glance over to her briefly before I put my attention back on the road. "No, I like it."

She nods and taps her hands on her knees. "I wasn't too much of a wimp, was I? In the beginning, I really thought I was going to cry, but I held it together."

"You did fine."

"Paul was nice, right? And it was cool of him to just charge the normal rate."

I hum half-heartedly as I put on my blinker and take a left. We're only a few minutes from her house now, just a couple more turns and she'll have to get out. I ease my foot off the gas just a bit to slow my speed.

"Okay, I give—did I do something?" Madison asks suddenly, turning toward me.

"No."

"It's just that you seem a little standoffish. If you're annoyed that I told him we were together…" She forces a laugh. "That was just a joke."

"I'm not annoyed. I'm thinking."

"About what?" she pushes.

I'm not used to women like her. Madison wears her emotions right on her sleeve and expects me to do the same. Most women would back off and give me space for fear that

I'd push them away, but Madison's not scared of that. Hell, sometimes I don't think she's scared of anything.

Maybe it's time I try for a little courage too.

"So you've thought of all these items for your bucket list, right?"

"Not really. I mean, I had a few things, like my tattoo—"

"And having sex for the first time," I press, if only because I don't have that much longer with her in my car and this courageous streak might be fleeting.

She looks away, out the windshield. "Yes. That too."

"Well, is finding a boyfriend on your list? Or does that not matter to you?"

I know if I looked at her, her cheeks would be red. I purposely keep my gaze on the road.

She laughs lightly, but it sounds a little strained. "Oh sure, I mean, in an ideal world, I'd find a boyfriend this year. Hell, I'd find the love of my life and we'd get married and live happily ever after, but I have to be realistic. That probably won't happen."

The girlish notion makes me laugh, but then she jerks in her seat and faces the window. Maybe I shouldn't have laughed.

"So you've thought a lot about it, huh?" I press.

"Yup," she says, her voice sounding colder now. "I even think I know someone who might be a good fit for me—wait. Pull over here so my dad doesn't see us." She's pointing to the curb up ahead. "I can just walk the rest of the way."

I jerk the wheel to the right and hit the brake a little too hard. Maybe I'm annoyed that she doesn't want her dad to see her with me, or maybe I'm angry at the idea of her with another guy. *Who's to fuckin' say?*

I put the car in park and finally turn to look at her.

She's staring down at her lap, fidgeting with the hem of her white top. I can see the barest hint of skin between it and the top of her baggy jeans. I think of how easily those pants would peel down her hips. I jerk my gaze elsewhere.

"Who?" My jaw is locked so tight the word barely makes it out of my mouth.

"What?"

"Who do you have in mind?"

"Oh…well, I was thinking maybe Andy. *Or*—" she amends hurriedly, "someone like Andy."

I laugh. Her answer came straight out of left field, so much so that she has to be joking.

My brows shoot up and I lean in, just to ensure I'm hearing her right. "Andy? As in *my friend*, Andy?"

She's nibbling on her bottom lip. "He's not really my type per se, but he's so nice. Well, I don't personally *know* if he's nice, but everyone says he is, and most importantly, he's not too intimidating, unlike—" She clears her throat and stops short. We both know who she was referring to anyway. It's hilarious considering I've just spent the last hour drawing fucking hearts on her palm.

"So you want a nice guy," I press, sounding like an asshole even to my own ears.

"Nice," she concurs.

"In bed? You want a nice guy in bed?"

"*Ben*."

"What, Madison? A second ago you were pushing me to open up to you, and now I'm just requesting you do the same. If you think you want a nice guy, I'll set you up with Andy."

"Fine," she snaps. "Thank you. That would be great. I'm going to get out now."

She turns to me, and her eyes could put emeralds to shame.

She wants a nice guy. Not me.

"Awesome," I mock, angry.

"Good night," she bites out, *angrier.*

Then she gets out and slams the door.

———

The next morning at the firm, I find Andy in his office. He's sitting behind his desk, sipping his coffee, oblivious to my wrath. I barely slept last night. Visions of him and Madison replayed in my head until I eventually tossed my blankets aside and headed for the gym. I did an intense workout. I forced myself to engage the flirtatious blonde near the water fountain and accepted her business card when she offered it. Sure, I might have tossed it out in the locker room, but still, I should feel invigorated. Instead, I feel twice as annoyed as I did last night. I'm a pot that's been on simmer for far too long.

"Andy." I knock hard on his doorframe. I wouldn't be surprised to find the wood had splintered. "Mind if I come in?"

"Oh, sure." He grins like the nice guy he is.

Suddenly, I hate him.

"How'd ya sleep, bud?" I ask, fingering the items on his shelves. He has framed photos of his family on a ski trip, a little drawing from one of his nieces—nice guy shit.

"Great, actually. I just bought a new mattress and it's really improved—"

"Glad to hear it."

"Uh…"

"Listen, Madison wants me to set her up with you."

He's so shocked, he spits his coffee all over his monitor and keyboard. Shame.

"*Jesus*, warn a dude next time."

No, actually, I don't think I will.

"So anyway, consider it."

"Wow. I don't have to consider it." He's dabbing a napkin over his damp computer. "I accept, *obviously*. She's way out of my league. Let's go to the gym after work. Think I can get a six pack in one day?"

My gaze jerks to him. My heart lurches in my chest. My hands fist at my sides. "So you're going to do it?"

"Of course," he says, leaning forward, basically foaming at the mouth. "Have you *seen* her?"

I step toward his desk, sizing him up. *Do I have it in me to kill my best friend?* At this moment, maybe.

I look around for something sharp at the precise moment he bursts out laughing. His hand hits his chest and he's really letting himself go. I've never seen someone laugh so heartily. "Oh man, I can't keep it up. You should see your face right now—you want to slam my head against my desk." He pinches his eyes shut like the hilarity is just too much. "Jesus, do you love her or what?"

I reach down and shuffle the papers on his desk, inspect some accolade he won at some point, and then stare past his head out the window with my hands stuffed in my front pockets.

"So I'll tell her you're not interested?"

"Uh, yeah—tell her I'd prefer to keep my balls intact, thank you very much."

CHAPTER TWELVE
MADISON

"Do you think there's good service in here?" I ask, holding my phone up toward the ceiling to see if I can manage to wrangle another bar or two from the cell tower.

Eli shrugs. "I've never had a problem."

He pops another Cheeto in his mouth and munches like the world isn't a bleak and desolate place. Ben didn't text me after our weird sort-of argument in his car. Nothing the day after, either. Oh, and you guessed it, a big fat nada for yesterday and today. It's Friday. There's been a black hole of doom between the last time I talked to Ben and this moment I'm in right now.

Life has continued on at an alarmingly normal pace. I wake up, don a comfortable dress or old jeans, throw myself into work at the library, and then head home to serve my dad and brother in whatever manner they see fit. *Oh god, that sounds bad.* It's not their fault. I've taken it upon myself to cook dinner because I want it to be marginally healthy, and I never accept help when they offer to clean up because it's faster if I just do it myself. My dad can manage his medications on his own, but sometimes I like to make sure he has everything right, just as a precaution. I'm not trying to paint myself out as some kind of Cinderella here. I'm not. I have a good life.

A GOOD LIFE, I remind myself, looking around me.

Like right now, I'm in the break room at the library eating a ham and cheese sandwich on a warm baguette. It's delicious. Eli is sitting across the table regaling me with

121

stories from a trivia night he went to with Kevin and some of their couple friends. I'm genuinely entertained. I'm not at all bitter that I was not invited because I do not qualify as a couple. I'm just Madison, party of one.

Mrs. Allen has tried her hand at baking again and there's a nice deflated *thing* sitting on the break room counter, waiting for us to devour it. It could be a cheesecake or it could be a door stopper. Either way, *yum*.

Katy (my glorious intern, Katy!), has arrived at work nearly on time all week and has even kind of listened when I've given her tasks. Sure, yesterday I found her sexting with her boyfriend down in the storage room (I know because she *bragged* about it), but that's nothing a quick Clorox wipe to my brain can't take care of.

Things are looking very good. My tattoo is healing surprisingly well, and even if that's the craziest thing I do before my 26th birthday rolls around, I've decided I'm still calling this year a win.

I'm a wild child.

A rebel without a cause.

Ben Shmen, if you ask me.

A phone somewhere in the Western Hemisphere vibrates and I lurch forward to check my screen as if my life depends on it.

Eli notices. "Are you still hoping he'll text you?"

I decide to throw him off my scent by seeming overly confused. "To whom are you referring?"

Eli knows everything. He knows I snuck off with Ben at the party, knows I slipped out of my panties in response to a dare he delivered. He knows that while I was getting a tattoo permanently inked onto my skin, Ben was cradling my palm and permanently inscribing doodles onto my soul. He knows I pushed Ben to set me up with Andy as a way to make it seem like I wasn't a total loser. *I have options. See?! Maybe your friend wants me.* God, it's so pathetic I want to let my face fall onto my sandwich. I'm really not good at this stuff.

"Look at me," Eli insists.

I look at his shirt.

"Look at me."

I glance at a point on the wall just over his shoulder, eyes narrowed.

"*Madison*, look at me."

I finally force myself to meet his gaze and it's just as I feared: intense. He looks like my dad when he's about to impart some wisdom to me. Oh god, he even puts down his Cheeto. This must be serious.

"Please don't fall for Ben. I don't want to be harsh, but I feel like you need to hear the truth. He's not the guy for you, Maddie." A knife thrusts itself right into my stomach—a rusty one with a dull blade. "You need someone less...I don't know. Someone a little bit more attainable, you know?" He bends his head to try to catch my eye because the second he spoke my gaze jerked down to the table. He reaches out for my hand. "It's better if you two just stay friends. *C'mon*...Ben Rosenberg? That's not the guy you want for your first time. Believe me. Need I remind you about Patrick?"

I shake my head. "No, you're right. Jesus, did you have to say it that way though?"

"It's better, I swear, like ripping off a Band-Aid. I could have totally tiptoed around it and built up your hopes about him, but then what? You don't need someone telling you to go for it with a guy like him. That has disaster and heartbreak written all over it."

"I know."

They're the only words I can muster because there are tears burning the corners of my eyes and my throat is closing up tight.

I hate that Eli is right about this.

I hate that I'm such a cliché. How many of us are out there roaming the earth waiting for Ben Rosenberg to text us? We should form a support group. Make t-shirts. Cry on each other's shoulders while we stare lovingly at life-size cutouts of him.

I should feel embarrassed to be a card-carrying member of this group, but I'm not. Maybe it's okay to be a cliché, to reach for something that might be unattainable. I know how it feels to have lived twenty-five years with a safety net. I know how it feels to stand on the sidelines and watch other, seemingly more deserving girls get the guy.

The whole point of my birthday wish was that I want this year to be different. The funny thing is, if someone asked me now, in this moment, if I would proceed forward knowing there's a good chance Ben will ruin me, ruin my life, leave me heartbroken and sad, I'd still press down on the gas and take the leap, if only to see what happens.

Who cares if I go *SPLAT* against the ground? I have the rest of my life to recover. I'll be old and weary, rocking back and forth on my front porch, dreaming of the time I almost, *nearly* got Ben Rosenberg. And yes, even in old age, I'll still be wearing the support group t-shirt, threadbare and all.

———

It's Saturday and Ben is scheduled to volunteer this morning. I hardly slept, I was so anxious to see him again. I hop out of bed with so much enthusiasm I'm liable to break out in song. I put on a long-sleeved white sweater dress and my brown leather boots. I tell myself I'm not really doing my hair, just curling it a little. This makeup is really what I normally do for any ol' workday, just…jazzed up a little. It's Saturday, after all! Everyone wants to feel pretty on Saturdays!

I'm in the auditorium setting up for toddler story time when I hear the door open behind me. The library doesn't open for another hour. It could be Lenny, the security guard, checking in on me, but he prefers to keep to himself. He's into watching sports on a little TV at his desk. Sometimes, when his team surges ahead from behind, his whoop of joy carries through the whole building.

Besides, I know it's not Lenny. I know it the same way I know the sky is blue and the earth is round and day follows night. It's Ben. It's Ben walking up behind me and I need to turn to address him now or things are going to get awkward.

I glance over my shoulder, picking a spot on the wall behind us. It assures I don't make a total fool of myself. "Morning. There's coffee and bagels over there."

I point to the side table where I carefully arranged breakfast for us. Now that I'm seeing it from his perspective, it looks a little intense. There are five different types of bagels. Two kinds of spreads. The napkins are fanned.

He smiles. "Oh, I brought bagels too."

I muster up the courage to look at him, and sure enough, he has a brown paper bag of his own—but that's not the sight I get hung up on. God, *Ben*. He's wearing a pair of dark jeans and a black t-shirt. His hair is mussed up a bit, not quite as perfect as he wears it during the week. His jaw is clean-shaven.

Oh, I'm gawking. He notices, but thankfully, he saves my dignity by holding up the bag.

"But these are special," he says, waving them. "*Apology* bagels."

His mouth is on the brink of a smile.

"Oh really?"

"For Monday."

I swallow, not wanting to delve into all that again. I turn back to the task at hand and shake my head. "Oh, it's no problem. It was my fault too for suggesting the stuff about Andy. That was—"

He steps up behind me. "I reached out to him like you asked."

I squeeze my eyes closed, wishing we could just skip over this whole conversation.

"Sorry, Madison, he—"

"No, it's fine."

Why are tears gathering in my eyes?

"He's hung up on Arianna."

"I get it. I mean, c'mon—Andy and I weren't going to date."

My self-deprecating laugh hurts.

For some insane reason, this feels like a rejection, even though I know with all my heart that's not the case. I don't want Andy, but now I know Andy doesn't want me, and that hurts because why *doesn't* Andy want me? I'm not so bad!

"You two weren't the right fit," Ben says, like he's trying to ease my suffering.

If he wants to ease my suffering, he should try putting that paper bag over his head. Cover up some of that charm. Now *that* would ease my suffering.

"What kind of bagels did you get?" he asks, changing the subject.

"Variety pack. You?"

"Same. Madison?"

"Uh huh?"

His hand hits my shoulder. "There's a nice guy out there for you. It's just not Andy."

He sounds so confident, I actually believe him.

Wow this is embarrassing. I wonder what Andy told him when he brought all this up. If he laughed, I'll die right here and now.

"Want to eat?" he says gently. He's scared I'm going to shatter. I refuse to give in to the urge. Instead, I wrap up my hurt as carefully as possible, trying to compartmentalize the pain so I can focus on this moment. I don't want him to see me like this: pathetic and sad and lonely. So, I take a deep breath and shrug. The smile I aim at him is halfway genuine.

"Sure."

We eat bagels on the floor of the multipurpose room like it's a grand picnic. He tells me about his job, why he likes being a lawyer, the thrill of growing his business. I listen intently, not because I care at all about legal proceedings but because of how compelling he is when he talks about his career. Am I this passionate about children's books? Hilariously enough, I think I am.

After we scarf down as many bagels as we can handle, we finish setting up for a jungle-themed story time. When the kids arrive with their parents, Ben helps me pass out paper masks that turn the kiddos into ferocious lions, tigers, and snakes. Everyone sits in a semicircle and I stand at the front holding up a book, projecting my voice so everyone can hear me. Ben leans against the wall, watching me with a smile, especially when I go for it with the animal sounds. Apparently, I make a very compelling elephant. He tells me so as we're cleaning up.

One second, he's half complimenting, half teasing me, and then the next, he turns and asks casually, "Want to get lunch?"

I hide my shock and offer a casual shrug. "Oh…yeah. That'd be fun."

And we do get lunch. We order sandwiches to-go at a deli down the street and we take them to the park. It's our second picnic of the day, but this time, we've really mastered it. We pick a nice shady spot and Ben unwraps our food. We replay all the funny moments of the morning while we eat, and when I'm done, I lie back on the grass, staring up at the underbelly of the oak tree stretched over us.

I can feel Ben watching me from where he sits a few feet away. I'm wondering what's on his mind a moment before he tells me.

"I feel bad the setup with Andy didn't work out."

My stomach squeezes tight. I keep my attention on the tree as I hum a noncommittal reply. *Please, do we have to talk about this again? Anything else, I beg you.*

"Did you really like him?"

I still can't find words, so I shake my head.

"If you're willing to take another chance on love," he continues, a bit teasingly, "I could find you someone else. Just tell me what you're looking for in a potential boyfriend and we'll go from there."

I pop up on my elbows, surprised. "Like physically?"

He smirks. "Sure."

I'm skeptical. "Why do you want to know?"

He wipes his hands clean of sandwich crumbs and then bends one knee up to his chest so he can prop his arms on it. He's the poster child for relaxed confidence. "Because if you want me to set you up with someone, I should know what to look out for, don't you think?"

"Oh, right."

I lie back down as I think so I can almost pretend he's not there, listening to me. I can be as honest as I want to be, and right now, the truth seems to want to spill right out of me.

I think of Ben and how to describe what I like about him, how he makes me feel. I can't just tell him: *you*. Find someone exactly like you. Find someone who happens to have all the indefinable qualities you have. So, instead, I dig deep and try to think of why I'm so drawn to him.

"I want to feel exhilarated in his presence," I start. "Like I'm grateful just to be near him."

He laughs. "That sounds nice, but I need something a little more tangible."

I close my eyes, imagining him. "Right. Okay, how about this? I'd like him to have brown hair. I've always been into guys with brown hair. And tall. Yes, he should be tall."

"Easy enough."

"I think I want him to be funny, but not so funny that he always tries to be the center of attention. That could get annoying."

"Marginally funny, got it."

"Good dresser. No cargo pants." I shudder at the thought.

"Does he have to be well-off?"

"Eh, doesn't matter. I just want him to have a job, any job."

"What about the teenager who was making our sandwiches earlier? He seemed into you. When you went to the bathroom, he asked me for your number."

"Hilarious."

"Okay. Keeping going."

"He has to enjoy reading."

"That's a given."

"And it'd be nice if he got along with my family."

He hums then, as if deciding something. "So that rules me out."

I sit up like I've just been zapped back to life. My eyes are wide open. "What do you mean, 'rules you out'?"

Was he considering himself an option?!

He's looking away, eyes narrowed as he watches a group of kids playing frisbee. For a second, I think he's not going to respond to me, but he finally speaks. His profile is all I've got, so I stare, wholly absorbed. "Have you ever thought about what could happen between us if we weren't in this town? If you weren't the daughter of the police chief and I wasn't a Rosenberg?"

"What do you mean?"

He shakes his head, reaching down for an acorn so he can dismantle it and toss away the pieces. "Forget it."

Forget it?! Yeah right! I want to reach over and yank those thoughts straight out of his head. I want to squeeze those chiseled cheeks between my hands, get within an inch of his face, and demand he tell me the truth, but the tone of his voice and his narrowed gaze warn me off of pushing him on the subject. I don't think I'll like the answer, but still, I have to know...

"Can I ask you something?"

Even if we'll never be anything more than what we are in this moment, I'm curious about one thing.

"What?" he says, tilting his head so the sun catches his eyes. My stomach swoops.

He has that effect on me with just one glance—imagine what it would be like if he got close enough to kiss me. I suppose I'll never find out.

"I'm just wondering, if we were in that scenario you just mentioned…just two normal people going about our life. Maybe we meet on the streets of New York or in some coffee shop in Seattle." I'm picking at grass while I speak. "If you weren't the last man on earth my dad would ever want me to date and I somehow caught your eye, would you find me…attractive?"

He chuckles then and shakes his head. "I can't believe you even have to ask."

That's all he gives me. No affirmation one way or the other, no piercing gaze locked with mine confirming I'm the most beautiful woman he's ever laid eyes on.

I want to demand more, but I don't get the chance.

"Heads up!" someone shouts from across the grassy field just before a bright yellow frisbee flies into my peripheral vision. I yelp as hard plastic collides with my forehead.

———

"It's not so bad," Mrs. Allen assures me at the library on Monday. "I can hardly see it."

"That's because you're not wearing your glasses."

"Oh." She reaches for the beaded lanyard around her neck, positions her glasses in place, and then gasps. "Oh dear! We need to get you to a doctor!" She reaches for the phone. "Let me call 911."

I hold down the receiver.

"I've already been to the doctor, remember? I just told you all about it."

Ben took me on Saturday even after I insisted I was fine. It was a waste of time. The doctor just confirmed that I knew

131

where I was and then poked and prodded my head a little. It hurt, but I would live. He prescribed ice and rest.

The strangest part about the whole ordeal isn't the fact that I now look like I have two heads; it's the way Ben has acted about the whole thing. He insisted I see the doctor and wouldn't hear of dropping me off around the block from my dad's house afterward.

He nearly snapped at me when I fought him on it.

"I'm taking you home, Madison. Jesus, you could have a concussion."

I held the ice pack to my head and kept my mouth shut. If he wanted to deal with my dad, so be it. Turned out, I was worrying for nothing—my dad wasn't home. Ben pulled up to our empty driveway and shot out of his car to open my door before I could. He wanted to carry me up the front walk, but when I insisted I could do it on my own, he resorted to toting me along like a wounded soldier. My feet barely touched the ground. At the door, he took the keys out of my hand and unlocked it, pushing it open for me.

I stepped inside and he hovered there, toeing the line.

"Do you think you have enough ice packs?" he asked, brows furrowed in concern.

I gestured to the one currently in use on my head and the two others the doctor had given me that would promptly get placed in the freezer.

"Do you have some medicine to take for the headache? The doctor said you could."

"Yes. Lots."

His eyes widened. "Don't overdo it."

"Ben," I said, stepping forward and patting his chest to get him to calm down, but then my hand sort of had a mind of its own because his chest was unreal, like a living, breathing brick wall. I pat, pat, patted it, and he didn't even tell me to stop because I think he assumed my injury had really set in. I wasn't in control of my actions. I could have declared my love for him right there and he would have blinked and told me to go lie down.

"How many times a week do you work out?"

He shook his head and stepped past me. "That's it. C'mon, I'm going to help you get set up so you can rest."

"Ben! Oh my god, you have to get out. What if my dad comes home?!"

I leaped in front of him as he tried to walk down the hall to the kitchen, my ice pack forgotten on the ground. I propped two hands on his chest, dug my heels in, and then pushed him with all my might. Nothing. I groaned and tried again. Worse—*he* moved *me* aside.

"Where's your room?" he asked, walking away from me.

"Not there! That's the kitchen!"

I was freaking out, scared my dad would stroll in any minute. What would he think if he found me alone with Ben in the house? Oh dear god, I wasn't prepared to find out.

"My room is up this way!" I shouted, hoping if I was extra compliant, I'd satisfy him enough that he'd leave.

I took the stairs two at a time and pushed the door open at the end of the hall. There she was in all her glory, my childhood-bedroom-turned-adult-hideout.

Sure, I updated my comforter from the zebra print to a nice neutral blue a few years back, but the bed itself is still baby pink, and the ceilings are still bordered by a thin row of colorful daisies. I've been meaning to do something about all those old posters on the wall, but it was too late because Ben was there, right behind me, staring at them and judging my love for the Backstreet Boys.

Or maybe not. He swept his gaze across the space with near indifference until his attention settled on my bed. Did it meet his standards? Did he sleep with women on queen-sized mattresses or was his lovemaking so rambunctious that only king-sized would do?

"C'mon. Take your shoes off," he said, pushing me toward my unmade bed.

"Huh, I always thought my first time would be more romantic than this."

My attempt at humor was lost on him.

"Sit down. Socks too." He pushed me down to sit on the edge and kneeled to peel off my boots and socks. In the process, his finger pad ran along the bottom of my foot and goose bumps bloomed down my spine.

"I take back what I just said about this not being romantic—*that* was downright erotic. Put my socks back on and take them off again."

His mouth stayed right smack dab between a smile and a frown. He wasn't going to give in to my delirium.

"Lie back," he insisted, pushing to stand and lifting my legs up onto the bed for me.

I had a bump on my head, but to him, it was like my entire body had stopped working. I wasn't even trying to play it up as a terrible injury or anything; he'd come to that conclusion all on his own. I think it was because he blamed himself for the frisbee hitting me in the first place, as if he should have been standing guard like a sentry or something.

"Do you want anything from downstairs?" he asked, moving to the door. "I'm going to get you some water."

"You don't have to tend to me. I'm fine, I swear."

After ignoring me, he returned five minutes later with some water, a bottle of Advil, an apple, and a bag of pretzels. He must have raided my bathroom cabinet and the pantry.

"Are you feeling okay?" he asked, passing me a pill and the water.

I downed it and smiled, tugging the blankets to my chin. "Peachy. How do I look?"

I fluttered my lashes and he frowned. "You'll heal up. Do you want me to stay? I could find a show or—" His gaze swept to the paperback on my nightstand. "Read to you."

My hand reached out for his arm, gripping it so tightly I likely cut off circulation. He had to stop. Was he trying to send me to an early grave?

"I'm fine. I promise."

He nodded and stood up. His hand got dragged through his hair for the hundredth time since the frisbee smacked into my skull. "Right. Well, I'm only a phone call away if you need something."

"All right, when my glass of water gets low, I'll give you a call," I teased.

He finally cracked a hint of a smile and then bent down to gently brush the side of my forehead. "I'm sorry our picnic ended this way."

Not sorrier than me.

Sunday, Ben texted me twice, once in the morning—just before my dad noticed my bump and I had to feed him a lie about how I'd tripped at the library—and once at night to check in on me and make sure I hadn't taken a turn for the worse. He thought I was on my deathbed. From an errant frisbee. My life is just not that interesting, sorry dude.

Back in the library on Monday morning, Mrs. Allen says since I won't let her call the police (she means an ambulance), she has a great olive oil I can rub on my head to help it heal quicker.

"Do you mean an essential oil?"

"They're the same, I think. This one's extra virgin."

Oh good, extra virgin—just like me.

Then she leaves me alone at my desk with Katy. We just had a new shipment of board books arrive and we're adding them to the library's system. Obviously, by that, I mean I'm adding them and Katy is mostly scrolling through Instagram.

She cracks up at something, ignoring me when I ask her to hand me a book.

"Katy."

Nothing.

I try again. "Katy."

She groans like I'm a pain in her ass, and I recall the conversation I had with my boss earlier where I tried to insist Katy be fired or moved to a different department far, far away from me. "No can do," was his response. Apparently, we get a small grant from the city for taking on interns like her and I'm the only dummy willing to put up with her.

She finally reaches for a book and holds it out to me without looking. It's not even remotely within my reach. I have to stand up and bend over to grab it. When I do, I resist the urge to smack her with it just as her gaze lands on something other than her phone. It's a first. There's either a celebrity or a zombie in her line of sight, and I pray it's the latter. At least then I'd be rid of her.

"*Jeez*. Who's the hunk?"

I glance up to see Ben walking into the library. His presence is like a solid punch to the gut. Oof. His suit is black. Oof. His face is sharp and mean-looking and worthy of being carved into stone. *Oof.*

He spots me right away and his expression eases a bit until he notices the nice bruise on my forehead. His brows tug together again, and I blanch. I should have worn a hat. I tried on a dozen: fedora, beanie, scarf tied around my forehead. In the end, I settled on acceptance. This is me, world, bruise and all.

Katy jumps to her feet and pushes in front of me so she looks like the person on duty behind the desk. Her phone is forgotten on her chair. I'm shocked. I could have sworn it was surgically attached to her hand.

When he steps within earshot, she leans forward, exposing cleavage. "Hi! I'm Katy! How can I help you? Do you need a library card? Schedule of events? We have an adult book club that I know you'd love. A man like you enjoys a good thriller—I can tell."

Ben frowns at her and doesn't reply. Then his gaze shifts to me as I step around the desk toward him.

"Katy, go down into the storage room and lock yourself inside."

"What?"

"I said, go down to the storage room and push the boxes to the side, the ones we need to break down and recycle."

"But I was going to…"

Her sentence drifts off as she realizes no one is paying attention to her. My head is tilted back so I can look at Ben. He steps toward me and, without a word, holds up his hand. I wince, afraid he's about to touch my bruise, but he stops short, his fingers a few inches from my forehead, then he lets his hand drop.

Katy stomps off while muttering about a hostile work environment.

"That's quite the bruise you've got there," he says, sliding one of his hands into his pocket and holding up a grocery bag in the other. "I brought you some stuff."

I peer inside, a little confused by the contents.

"That's an ice pack I saw at the grocery store last night," he explains. "It seems like it might be a little better than the ones the doctor gave you."

"Oh."

"And, this…" he says, producing a faded navy baseball hat. "Is my favorite hat. In case you wanted a hat. I don't know, you don't need it. The bruise doesn't detract from—" He shrugs. "Anyway, I thought you might like it."

I take it from him and stare at it like it's a foreign object from Mars.

"I know it looks old, but I washed it recently. Well, last month—"

He reaches over to take it back and I yank it away from his grasp, cradling it against my chest. If he wants it, he's going to have to pry it from my cold, dead fingers.

His head tips to the side and my eyes narrow teasingly.

His mouth tugs into a smile and I poke him in the chest.

He grabs my hand and holds it for a second, as if to keep it away from him, but it feels more like he's ensuring I can't pull it back.

We're not speaking, but we're communicating loud and clear.

"What kind of law do you practice again?" I ask, perusing his suit.

He squeezes my hand and then lets it drop. "Corporate."

"Pity. You look like you should be putting criminals behind bars. Very intimidating today, like you'll bite."

He half-smiles and his dimple softens the effect, just barely.

"Anyway, thank you for this stuff. That was really thoughtful, but it's not necessary. I'm good as new and wondering when I'm going to check off another item on my list."

His attention catches on my bruise again. "Don't you think we should take the week off?"

A week off means a week without him, and the prospect sounds as if someone's suggesting I go a week without air. I envision myself on the ground, writhing in pain.

"I'm fine, really. Look." I put his hat on and adjust it so I can see. It's a little big, which is good because that means it doesn't touch my bruise. "All better."

He flicks the brim playfully.

Over his shoulder, my gaze catches on one of the library's patrons, grumpy Mrs. Taylor. She usually stays up on the ground level harassing Eli, but he's out for the day, dealing with some adoption things, which means she has her sights set on me. Lovely. She walks straight to the desk, which I'm standing right by, and rings the bell three times in quick succession.

"I'm right here, Mrs. Taylor."

"Yes, well, you weren't officially at your post. Are you done smiling at your young man there? Because my tax dollars aren't paying for you to cavort around the library with handsome gentlemen."

"*Cavort*," Ben repeats under his breath, highly amused.

I sigh and turn to face her fully, giving her my undivided attention.

"What can I do for you, Mrs. Taylor?"

"Yes, well, first of all, is that tattered baseball hat part of your uniform? It's very unbecoming." I stare at her blankly so she's forced to move on. "Right, more importantly, I've lodged a complaint about this in the past, but it seems no one cared to remedy the situation." She holds up an issue of *National Geographic*. "There are women in here with *bare breasts*."

A chuckle escapes Ben before he can stifle it.

I, however, keep my expression solemn and serious. Mrs. Taylor is a tiny elderly terrorist. This will end sooner if I give in to her demands. "Yes, Mrs. Taylor. I'm aware of that."

Her eyes widen in horror. "So then you knowingly allow this crude material to be circulated in a public library?" She leans forward and hisses. "There are *children* in here." Then she straightens back to her full height—a solid two feet, five inches—and flips open the magazine to the offending page. "Now, all I'm asking is that you go in and cover up the pornographic images. I have scrapbooking supplies and a hot glue gun in my car if needed."

While I try hard the rest of the day to scrub this entire conversation from my memory, Ben, of course, can't let it go. To him, it's deeply amusing.

Later that night, while I'm in bed, icing my head, he sends me a text.

Ben: Cav · ort: apply oneself enthusiastically to sexual or disreputable pursuits.

Ben: Seems we didn't take the week off after all. See you Saturday.

CHAPTER THIRTEEN

MADISON

Ben is scheduled to volunteer with me this morning and before he even arrives, I know it will be one of the highlights of my life. Today, we're doing a Jane Austen themed story time. If you think I didn't intentionally plan that, you really don't know me at all. I rented costumes from the local theater company and ensured Ben was prepared to go the extra mile.

> Madison: Today will interesting. Fair warning— there are costumes.

> Ben: No problem. Those animal masks were fun. The kids loved them.

Ha ha ha. He thinks I don't have a full Mr. Darcy lookalike costume for him. How cute. When he arrives, I usher him into the storage room and present the idea.

"We both have to do it," I say, sounding really annoyed by the fact that I have to wear a gorgeous blue silk dress with a full petticoat and prance around like a princess. Ugh, the worst, am I right?

He laughs and shakes his head. "No."

Just one simple word, clipped out with a sharp tone.

No.

"But the kids will love it!"

"Yeah, no."

I sigh then look down and fidget with my hands, seeming innocent. "Well, I really didn't want to have to do this, but…seeing as I'm in control of your community service hours, I'd hate to have to contact the judge and tell him you aren't cooperating."

I'm completely talking out of my ass. Judge? Cooperating? What does that even mean? I don't have a direct line to the courthouse. I just want to leverage what small amount of control I have over Ben and force him into this costume for my own amusement. Sure, some would say that's an abuse of power. I say what's the point of having power if you don't abuse it a little?

Ten minutes later, Ben steps out of the storage room, and I swear to God, I have a heart attack. I've seen every period film in existence, every one of Jane Austen's movie adaptions: the Kiera Knightly version of *Pride and Prejudice*, the Colin Firth version of *Pride and Prejudice*, the Gwyneth Paltrow version of *Emma* (a personal favorite), etc., etc. So, when I say Ben looks like the hottest version of Mr. Darcy I've ever seen, believe me, he does. Tall. Dark. Handsome. *Pissed*. I'm positive I'm having real heart palpitations.

"Oh dear," I lament, shaking my head. "It's too good. The moms won't leave you alone."

He gives me a broody look, and OH MY GOD, is he doing it on purpose?! He *is* Mr. Darcy!

"Where's your dress?" he asks, clearly annoyed.

He's fidgeting with his tailored black jacket. It's a little too small, which means his biceps are in danger of busting through the seams. I have to lean against a wall to support myself.

"In there. I'll change. Just…stay out here in case I need your help with it."

I've read enough historical fiction novels to know how to slip into one of these oversized dresses. The thing is, the women in the novels usually have a lady's maid to assist them in tightening the corset. I only have myself, and I can't quite reach the laces.

I'm wearing a thin cotton chemise underneath, so it's not as if I should be nervous for Ben to come in and help me. Still, I hesitate for a good long while, attempting to do it myself but failing.

He knocks on the door. "What are you doing in there? Did a box of books just tumble to the floor?"

Yes, I just bumped into a shelf while jumping around, trying to reach the corset loops. Books are scattered everywhere. I can't do this on my own.

I groan and fling the door open.

"Come in—*quick*."

His eyes are wide. I glance down in embarrassment. *Please tell me my boobs are put away.* Thankfully, I'm mostly covered up. The top of my chest and shoulders are bare in the traditional style of dresses like this, but I'm not so indecent that he has to look at me like that.

Women go to clubs in less clothing than this.

I spin around and explain what I need him to do.

"Just lace it up and tighten the corset," I say, like we do this sort of thing together every day.

He steps forward, brows furrowed, and then pushes my long hair over my shoulder.

"This dress is ridiculous. There's so much material you won't be able to walk."

I blush. Not quite the reaction I was hoping for. Usually in my historical novels, when the handsome duke stumbles upon the fair lady in her evening gown, he's so beside himself, he feels an all-consuming urge to seduce her *that* instant. We should be tumbling against the shelves, knockings things off, ferociously kissing like we're two animals in heat.

In reality, Ben grumbles under his breath as he tightens the laces. I can feel the heat of his touch through the chemise. He cinches the garment too much. I can hardly breathe.

"Are you almost done?" I ask. My voice sounds like it came out of a mouse.

"Not if you don't stand still."

His hands grip my waist and he squeezes.

Apparently, I'm fidgeting. Hot. Bothered.

He ties the laces together at the bottom and steps back.

I turn around and hold out my arms. "What do you think?"

He clears his throat, glances away, and when he looks back, his gaze is narrowed. "I think it's a little much for a toddler story time."

I glance down and laughter erupts out of me. "Oh jeez."

My breasts have been pushed up and forced together to form a tantalizing amount of cleavage. Even *I'm* slightly turned on by the sight. I look like a serving wench. I yank the chemise higher, covering my décolletage and transforming the look into something a bit more modest.

"How about now?" I ask, peering up at him from beneath my lashes.

He grunts and rolls his neck. He's truly annoyed with me. "It's fine."

I smile then and reach out to poke him in the chest. "Relax, will you? This is supposed to be fun."

"Fun? Try torture."

I bristle at his remark. Fine. If he wants to turn this day into something sour, I won't stop him. I am, however, in a kickass gown, and I intend to enjoy every minute of it. I roll my eyes then make a move to walk around him and leave the storage room.

His hand juts out to stop me. His fingers wrap around my arm.

"You look…" He clears his throat and looks away. "The dress is fine."

THE DRESS IS FINE?!

"Wow, you have such a way with words."

He smirks then, finally letting go of his annoyance.

"The dress is very…*blue*."

I throw my hands up and walk out. He trails after me, calling down the hall.

"I've got it now—it's *poofy*! How's that? Better?"

As retribution, I force him into a more prominent role during story time. He has to read a children's version of *Sense and Sensibility* aloud in the front of the kids while I stand to the side. Every mom in attendance sends me a silent thank you. I've never seen them quite so riveted to a children's book before. It is a cute book, but that's definitely not what they care about. When he's done, a few of them linger, asking Ben about the book and where they can get it. Then the questions turn a tad more personal.

"…is that your costume…"

"…oh, it's just a rental?"

"…how long do you have it for…"

I titter as I clean up, appreciating every minute of his torture.

He gets the last laugh, though, because I was very excited to go out to lunch with him just like we did last Saturday. Unfortunately, he already made plans with his dad. Through a Herculean effort, I make it seem like that's totally fine. Cool.

I have other stuff to do too!

145

I don't, of course. I never do. But, it's Saturday afternoon, and I have a plan. It's not a good plan, and it entails a little bit of lying, but I'll be sure to atone for it later in life just in case the big man upstairs has any issues with my methods. Oh, I know what I'll do: if I see a turtle trying to cross the street, I'll stop and help it, no questions asked. Sins begone.

The first part of my evil genius plan is confirming that Eli and Kevin are both free for the night. Eli says they have plans to stay in and binge the TV show *YOU* on Netflix, but I spoil the ending for him so he's forced to do my bidding.

Eli: Are you kidding me?!

Whatever, I'll save two turtles now.

Madison: This will be fun, I swear!

Then, I send Ben a text. I start out by making a little small talk, nothing too intense.

Madison: How was lunch with your dad?

Ben: Good. I told him about the costumes and showed him the picture you forced me to take...

Madison: Ha! What'd he say?

Ben: He said he wants to meet the woman who convinced me to wear that.

My heart flutters and I press my phone to my chest before I realize what I'm doing and jerk it away. *Keep it together, Hart!*

Madison: Sounds like a fun afternoon. Listen...I need a favor. Please tell me you don't have any plans tonight.

Ben: I was going to watch the Astros game at Andy's with some friends.

Madison: Oh...all right. It's just that Eli and Kevin invited me to go bowling with them, but they want to play as teams and I can't find a plus-one this last minute.

LIE. LIE. LIE. I could have an entire month and still wouldn't be able to find a guy to accompany me to the bowling alley. I'd be better off looking there. *Hey, you, crusty old man with a smoker's cough—be my partner?*

Ben: That sounds fun, but Andy will be annoyed if I cancel.

Madison: Invite him! Tell him to bring that girl he likes. Arianna?

Do I sound desperate?
I wish I could erase that exclamation mark.

Ben: Okay. What time are you guys headed to the bowling alley?

Madison: 8ish.

Though the bowling alley is public enough that I could run into Colten, I know he's working tonight. Plus, I don't think he and his friends go bowling all that often. It's the perfect place to hide in plain sight.

Now begins part two of my master plan. I have to come up with some way to transform myself into someone irresistible, someone Ben will trip over himself to talk to, someone he can't help but fall for. It should be easy, and I have a few hours. How long can a total makeover really take?

I ask Eli when he and Kevin arrive to pick me up at 5:00 PM.

"I thought we were going bowling," Eli says, confused.

"We are, just later. Right now, I'd like to do something I've only ever seen in movies, something I've desperately wanted to do since I grew boobs."

I give him the short version and when I'm done, he frowns.

"Oh, so you're just assuming that because I prefer to sleep with men that I also happen to know a thing or two about fashion? That for the last three years I've been dying to strip you out of those hideous jeans and burn them on the spot? That I have several outfits saved to a secret Pinterest board entitled 'Sexy Madison' in the event that you ever wanted me to dress you? Well friend, you are in luck. Let's go. The mall is still open for another few hours."

———

At 7:55 PM, we pull up in front of the bowling alley. Eli and Kevin unbuckle their seatbelts and reach for their door handles, but I jump forward and grab their shoulders.

"Wait! Don't get out yet!"

"Why?" Kevin asks, glancing at me over his shoulder.

"Because…"

Oh right, I haven't exactly filled them in on the rest of my plan. Eli assumed I wanted this makeover for myself, just to feel good and update my look. I didn't correct him, but now I have to.

"We have to wait a few minutes, just to be sure Ben and his friends are here already. They'll be bowling with us."

Eli jerks around. "Are you serious? Is that why we did all this?" He waves his hand over my getup. "For *Ben*?"

I puff out air like that's a crazy idea. "No, it's for me. I wanted some new clothes." And sleek hair and killer makeup.

"Maddie…"

I dart my gaze out the window, trying to fend off his pity. I don't want it. I don't want Eli to think Ben is out of my league. Because he's right.

He sighs. "I just think this is a bad idea—"

"No. Listen," I say, turning to him with my chin raised and conviction in my words. "You think he's going to break my heart and maybe he is, but you have to let me experience this on my own. I know what I'm doing, I swear."

Kevin reaches out to touch Eli's shoulder. "She's right. I was way out of your league and look, we're madly in love."

Eli's frown softens. "Oh, ha ha, very funny. I just don't want her to get hurt."

"Well '*her*' knows what she's doing," I quip just as Ben's black SUV pulls into a parking space in the row in front of us.

I duck for cover, of course.

"That's him!" I hiss. "Is he looking over here?"

"No, you're good. There's a lamppost blocking his view. Plus, he's talking to his friends."

Oh good. I sit back up and fix my hair as I watch him, Andy, and Arianna walk toward the front entrance. They're so beautiful, they look like a pack of vampires. Arianna is svelte and long-legged with short blonde hair. Her outfit is so damn cool! She's wearing black jeans and an off-the-shoulder red sweater. The boxy fit would make me look shapeless, but she looks hip! Trendy!

Then I remember we aren't so shabby either. Kevin's really cute, blond and tall and tan. He's the surfer boy to Eli's handsome bookworm, and I look pretty dang good myself—fancy, even, though I'm not wearing anything more than jeans and a black shirt. The jeans are new, though, and they fit me like a glove. The long-sleeved black top is tight, like a second skin, and the U-neck dips down to reveal the perfect amount of cleavage. It doesn't hurt that my bra is accentuating every curve I have. My hair is sleek and straight thanks to the salon Eli and Kevin took me to, and they did my makeup there, too. A woman chatted my ear off as she swiped on all sorts of fun things—bronzer, blush, eyeshadow. I let her do whatever she wanted and when that chair spun around, I was completely struck silent by my own appearance. Some people really are miracle workers.

We wait exactly ten minutes before we get out of the car and follow Ben inside the bowling alley. I'm not really *trying* to make an entrance, it just happens that way. I think it's largely by accident. Kevin and Eli hold the doors open for me. I step inside right when the music changes from upbeat pop to something slow and sultry, a song that would fit perfectly in my dirty dreams. An employee passing in front of me accidentally drops a WET FLOOR sign and it clatters to the ground, drawing the attention of everyone nearby. The final touch comes from the fan overhead, placed there to keep the heat in and the cold air out. I look like I'm in the middle of a photo shoot. *Hello, Gigi? You're fired. There's a new supermodel in town.*

Ben is standing a few yards away, talking to Andy and Arianna. He stops midsentence when he sees me. If I were talking, I'd have paused too. Mussed brown hair. Sharp amber eyes. Cool jacket. Dark jeans. The guy knows how to dress, and it probably didn't take him three hours to get ready like it took me. His gaze meets mine and his brows shoot up a smidge. It's an acknowledgment of my new look, possibly the only one I'll get.

"Sorry about that," says the employee in front of me, the one who dropped the sign. He waves the thing in front of my face. "Guess we need a warning for the sign too."

I frown. "What?"

He blanches, stumbling over his words. "Oh, j-just…the sign is supposed to caution people about a slippery floor, but the sign slipped out of my hand, so…"

I laugh because that's actually pretty funny.

His face lights up. We're having a moment. I mean, he's like 17, but I can still tell from his appreciative gaze that he thinks I look hot, and that's something.

Ben steps up behind him and the kid turns to look up at him, eyes widening in fear. Ben sends him a scathing glare.

"Madison, we already paid for the lane," Ben says, all but dismissing the guy. *Tell me he's not really jealous of a 17-year-old?! Amazing.* "You guys just need to grab shoes."

Oh right. Boo. I hadn't considered that my cool vibe would be thrown off by clunky clown shoes.

I guess Ben will look silly too, but oh, what's that? He looks just as hot? Figures.

When he finishes lacing his up, he kneels down in front of me and holds out his hand.

I give him a high five and he glares at me as if he's annoyed. He's not. His eyes are crinkled in the corners.

"Shoe," he says, and I slap one into his hand so he can lace it for me.

"I'm not an invalid. My head is all healed up, in case you didn't notice."

"I noticed," he says, yanking hard on the laces.

I smile. "This is the second time you've laced me up today. You're getting really good at it."

He huffs out a short breath just as Andy and Arianna come sit down on the bench beside us.

Andy waves his shoes in the air. "Can you lace me up too while you're down there, Benny boy?"

The glare Ben delivers should singe Andy's ass to the bench. I take the opportunity to reach over and introduce myself to Arianna. "I don't think we've formally met. I'm Madison."

She smiles and accepts my handshake. "Hey, yeah, I saw you at Jake's party the other week, right? You were there with your brother?"

Memories flash through my mind like a highlight reel: panties, book, dark corners, Ben's hard body pressed against mine.

"Oh, um, yes." *Wow, is that my voice breaking?* "I was there."

When I look back at Ben, he's smiling at the floor.

"So are you two dating?" she asks, pointing between Ben and me.

"Dating?" The word drops out of my mouth like a hefty stone.

"Nah, Madison's looking for a nice guy," Ben replies with an edge to his tone.

My eyes narrow teasingly. "Or at least someone who knows how to properly tie shoes. You did it so tight, I can't feel my feet."

Eli and Kevin join us and we continue introductions. Turns out, Arianna and Kevin already know each other. Their parents are friends, and just like that, the group seems to mesh a lot more organically than I thought it would. Andy's talkative enough for everyone, and the bowling alley has placed us in the lane against the wall, which I'm grateful for because I'm not really that great at bowling and I worry about errant balls accidentally taking out small children.

Ben's quiet as we all stand around the old-school computer, deciding on rules and teams. Arianna and Eli are arguing about the merits of putting up gutter guards. I glance at Ben out of the corner of my eye and catch him dragging his gaze down my legs. He turns away, quickly. It's almost so fast I don't catch it.

"What do you think, Maddie?"

I think this outfit is doing exactly what I wanted it to.

"Maddie," Eli says impatiently, waving his hand in front of my face.

I blink. "What?"

"Gutter guards?"

"Sure. I'm not trying to kill anyone tonight."

So, it's decided, we'll use the bumpers, and the teams form naturally. Of course, Eli and Kevin will pair up, Arianna and Andy, and me and Ben. I go to pick my ball and feel his presence behind me. I go for the lightest option, and he has to bend down to grab one of the heavier ones.

"Bright pink," he teases, motioning toward my selection. "I think that's for kids."

I stick my fingers in the holes and hold it up to strike a pose. "Fits me perfectly, thank you very much."

"There's a sparkly butterfly on it."

"That's a hawk."

"Mmm. Want me to give you a few pointers?"

I lift my chin proudly. "I have my own special method."

Said method mainly involves having no method at all. Poor Ben's really going to have to carry our team. For my first turn, I attempt to look like a pro. I stride smoothly to take my spot at the lane, wind up, aim, and then drop the ball so it lands with a heavy *thunk* two feet in front of me. It doesn't even officially make it into the *lane*.

"Not bad, not bad," Andy chants with some overzealous claps.

Eli whistles.

Everyone agrees I can try a do-over, and this time, instead of trying to look cool, I spread my legs wide, wind the bowling ball back between them, and let her fly. The bright pink ball clunks down the lane, successfully nudging two pins off balance.

"Two!" I shout, whirling around, hands in the air.

"Actually, only one fell. The other just wobbled," Kevin says, pointing behind me.

I groan as I walk back to my seat.

"Just so you know, your goal is to knock them *all* down," Eli teases, patting my shoulder as I brush past him.

Thankfully, Kevin is even worse than I am, but Arianna is shockingly good—like what the hell, did she spend her summers at bowling camp or what? Andy isn't bad either. Together, they've formed a team that can't be beat. They high-five each other and bump chests, really getting into the

154

spirit. Eli and Kevin are too. They're talking strategy and cracking up together, their heads bent close. They look as adorable as ever.

Meanwhile, Ben has chosen to sit as far away from me as possible. I'd have to yell if I wanted to say something to him.

I try not to read too much into it and when it's his turn, I sigh, secretly happy to have an excuse to ogle him without it seeming strange. I *have* to watch my team member during his turn, right?

He's taken off his jacket and his gray crewneck t-shirt isn't tight, but I'm still very aware of his muscular build, as is the group of old women to our left. They've paused their game to watch him take his turn.

He winds up and releases the ball. It cuts right down the center of the lane and smashes into the pins with a loud *whack*. Every single pin gets knocked down and then he turns, just in time to see me staring at him with a tinge too much hero worship in my gaze.

This is getting a little pathetic.

I leap to my feet and wipe my sweaty palms on my jeans. "Beer, anyone?"

There's a chorus of resounding yeses, along with a few shouts for nachos.

My boyfriend—sign boy—is working the snack register. When I request two orders of nachos and six beers, he tells me the nachos are on the house and then winks before motioning down at the candy.

"Care for anything sweet? My treat."

I'm about to take him up on his offer of some free Skittles when Ben cuts in and lays cash down on the counter.

"You can keep the change," he says, starting to gather beers. I swear he nearly growls at the kid.

He won't even look at me.

I take the last two bottles and the nachos, placing them on a tray.

"You really cramped my style back there," I say as we walk back.

"Oh yeah? Is that the guy you have in mind for your first time? He weighs 75 pounds."

I grin. "I could have sweet-talked him into giving me a chocolate bar if you hadn't come along."

"If you're still hungry after all this, *I'll* get you a chocolate bar," he says, glancing down at my tray, which is loaded down with our stuff. "Can you carry that?"

"Yup," I say before stuffing a whole nacho into my mouth and smiling proudly.

When we make it back to the group, I expect him to reclaim his old spot and go right on ignoring me. Instead, he tells me to scoot over and sits beside me, stealing a nacho. His hip is touching mine on the orange plastic bench. I take a long swig of beer, realizing I need it.

"You look different tonight," he says as Andy hops up to take his second turn.

"Oh?" I ask, very cool, very confused. *Me? Different? How so?* "Good different or bad different?"

"Just…different." He leans back to assess me then reaches for a strand of hair. "I've never seen your hair straight."

I shrug. "Well, don't get used to it. It took a woman at the mall like an hour to style it like this. I'd never have the patience to do it myself."

His brows tug together. "You got your hair done for tonight?"

Shit. What? No! What kind of loser gets her hair done for bowling?

156

I shake my head. "Just needed a haircut," I lie, and for once I'm grateful it's biologically impossible for men to tell when a woman has cut her hair. I swear my dad and brother never notice.

"It looks good."

Three words, not even all that flowery, but he might as well have declared his love with the way my heart is beating.

I smile as I bring my beer back to my lips. He watches me take a sip, and are we the only ones in this bowling alley or does it just feel that way now? I swear he's about to lean in and tell me something, but then Eli nudges me in the shoulder, announcing it's my turn.

"Clear the area," Andy shouts, hands forming a megaphone around his mouth.

"Ha ha ha," I say, playing along with his joke. "Just watch—I'll get it this time."

I do not get it this time. I somehow manage to miss every single pin even though the gutter guards ensure my ball makes it all the way down to the end.

When I retake my seat, Ben nudges me. "That's impressive. I think it might be harder to not hit a single pin than it is to get a strike."

His sly smirk all but seals my fate. I spend the precious minutes between my second and third turn sharing nachos with him and praying he'll say more things that make my stomach dip. Suddenly, I'm up again.

"Ugh, do I have to go?"

It really is embarrassing.

Ben stands and hooks his hands under my arms, forcing me. "C'mon, I'll help you."

We all know what that means. We've seen the movies. Ben's going to stand behind me a little too close, touch me a little inappropriately, all in the name of sport. And, of course, because our friends are all mature adults, they whistle and catcall us as Ben moves up behind me.

"Oh yeah, Ben, show her how it's done," Andy says.

Ben flips him off.

"*Oh*, I'm not sure, Ben—do I stand like *this*?" Arianna mocks and okay, she's funny, and I like her. Also, how dare she?

"Don't listen to them," Ben says, shuffling us toward the lane.

"This *is* a little cliché, you have to admit." I smile and glance at him over my shoulder. Whoa—I didn't realize he was *right* behind me. His lips are in danger of touching mine. Sure, I'd kind of have to go up on my tiptoes and crane my neck, but still. *Someone crank the air in here ASAP.*

"I know," he says with a shrug. "But you really suck and I can't allow things to continue like this or there's no hope of us winning."

He leans down to arrange my feet so one's staggered in front of the other. Then he loops one arm tightly around my waist so I'm forced to stay right there, pressed against him. His other hand wraps around my forearm so he can guide my arm back, showing me how to take aim before I let go of the ball.

"Got it?" he asks, breath on my neck.

"Show me again."

"Oh my god." Kevin laughs. "Did she really just say that?!"

Joke's on them. When I do eventually roll the ball down the lane, I manage to sink five pins. I turn around and Ben's there, smiling. I walk toward him to accept his double high fives. His fingers lace through mine and we stay like that for a few seconds longer than necessary. Eyes locked. Hearts pounding.

"Nice job."

"Thanks. It was all in my form."

He smiles. "You have really good form."

Suddenly, we're not talking about bowling.

Eli whistles. "Okay, just to be clear, that one totally doesn't count. Ben basically bowled that turn for you."

One game turns into two, then three. I have a second beer and my technique really improves. In one turn, I manage to knock down six pins. It's a personal record. Kevin and Eli buy us all another round of nachos and some pepperoni pizza that looks barely edible. Of course, we all attack it like vultures.

"Not fair," I groan, trying to steal the last slice from Ben. "I barely got any. I had to share mine with Kevin."

He arches a brow and takes a massive bite. Half the slice is gone.

When he chews, he wears a little smirk.

I narrow my eyes. "Evil."

He holds it out to me and the gesture is clear: take a bite. *It's nothing*, I tell myself. *Don't read into it.* I lean forward, eyes locked with his, and take a bite, ensuring I steal the last pepperoni. There's a little sauce on my bottom lip and I lick it off. He's wearing an expression I don't quite recognize, one that makes my spine tingle, so I reach out for our beers and force his into his hand. We both take hefty swigs.

It's my final turn and I jump to my feet, eager to prove my skills. The game's tied. We're neck and neck with Arianna and Andy. They've won two games, though, and they're getting cocky. They're talking about joining a bowling league, asking the manager to put their signed headshots up on the wall. It's time someone taught them a lesson.

"Ben, hold my beer," I say, wiping my mouth with the back of my hand and then walking over to retrieve my pink sparkly bowling ball. Earlier, a twelve-year-old tried to steal it. Eli had to tell her to scram.

I'm less steady on my feet than I was an hour ago. The lane looks ridiculously long. I'll never be able to get the ball all the way down there, but I want victory more than I have all night. I start to walk forward, gaining momentum, rear back, and let the ball go. It rolls fast, not hitting the bumpers once. When it's close to the pins, it's still centered perfectly in the lane.

No way. *NO WAY!*

My hands shoot to my mouth. The ball connects and every single pin goes flying.

"OH MY GOD! I DID IT! *I DID IT!*"

I'm jumping up and down. If I could cartwheel, I'd do one. Big hands spin me around and Ben lifts me up.

"Did you see it?!" I ask as the room whirls around me. My smile is so big it hurts.

He laughs. "Yeah, I was right here."

Of course.

My feet dangle off the ground as my body slides against him. Our hips are aligned perfectly. We sizzle.

"It was a really good strike," I conclude, my voice breathy. "Best one all night, if you ask me."

His gaze is on my lips as his arms tighten around me. "Agreed."

"I want to rub everyone's faces in our victory."

"We can hear you." Eli laughs.

"Also, you haven't won yet," Andy points out, bitter. "Ben still has to go."

"Right. Don't botch this for us," I say as he sets me back down. My tone is full of mock solemnity. I brush a hand over my clothes as if to straighten them. Clear my throat. Try to affect a more serious manner. "This is important. It all comes down to you."

As he prepares to take his shot, I walk back over to our group. Eli bumps my hip and I glance over. He straightens his glasses then lifts his chin toward Ben.

"You two are really cute."

I frown. "What do you mean?"

"Maddie, c'mon—it's obvious you two have feelings for each other. You've been flirting all night."

My cheeks redden with the realization that everyone has likely seen me drooling over him all night.

"Earlier, you were warning me to stay away from him," I point out.

"Yeah, well, maybe I was wrong."

I hear Ben's ball roll down the lane and the tell-tale *smack* of it colliding with the pins. My eyes are still on Eli as Arianna and Andy groan in defeat.

"He wants you—*bad*."

"What'll you have, Chief?"

"Double bacon cheeseburger—"

I clear my throat forcefully.

"*Single* bacon cheeseburger," my dad amends, glowering at me.

"No bacon and no cheese, Dad."

He throws up his hands. "Are you trying to make me depressed? What's the point of living if you can't enjoy the taste of melted cheese on a burger?"

His theatrics won't work on me. I yank the menu out of his hand, stack it on top of mine, and pass them to the waitress with a sweet smile. "He'll have a turkey burger on a whole grain bun with a side of steamed vegetables. I'll have the garden salad with grilled chicken, please."

She jots down our orders then winks at my dad as she takes the menus and slides them up under her arm. "How about I accidentally spill a few French fries onto your plate on my way out of the kitchen?"

My dad beams. "I always knew you were a good egg, Sally."

When she walks away, my dad gloats. His big mustached smile gleams at me from across the table.

"Proud of yourself?" I ask, tacking on a what-am-I-going-to-do-with-you smile.

"*Very.*"

My phone vibrates on the seat beside me, but I don't reach for it right away. I wait until one of my dad's friends walks by our booth and they strike up a conversation. There are a lot of claps on shoulders and hearty laughs between old buddies. Once he's good and distracted, I reach for my phone, hold it underneath the table, and nearly explode with excitement when I see I have a new text from Ben. Seeing his name on my screen is exhilarating. It doesn't matter that we've been texting pretty consistently over the last week, ever since bowling; each time feels as wonderful as the last.

Ben: Andy and I watched that true crime documentary you recommended last night. It was good. I need more recs. I'm addicted.

I smile, proud. He liked my recommendation! He thinks I have good taste!

Madison: There's another good one, but I can't remember the name. I'll check when I get home.

Ben: Oh...you aren't home?

Madison: It's Friday night, of course I'm not home. I'm very cool, Ben. Or haven't you realized?

The waitress returns with our drinks and I glance up to ensure my dad is still chatting with his friend.

My phone vibrates again.

Ben: So what are you up to then?

164

I nibble on my lip while considering my options. I can't very well tell him the truth—it's too pathetic. I decide to be coy instead, throw him off my scent.

Madison: Bad things.

Ben: Gone rogue on me?

Madison: Oh yes. I'm stealing money out of a bank vault as we speak. All black attire, getaway car, the works.

Ben: Huh. From what I can see, it looks like you're about to eat dinner...

My eyes widen and I jerk my gaze up, scanning the diner.

The place is packed with a mix of old folks and a few young families. It's the type of crowd who enjoys early bird specials, just like my dad and me. Ben isn't in here. I would have spotted him immediately. It's like my brain has a homing beacon on him.

Then movement draws my attention out past the window and sure enough, there he is, standing out on the sidewalk with Andy. They're both in suits, looking as if they just left work. My stomach clenches tight and I drop my phone on my lap.

Our gazes lock through the glass, and I'm worried when I see mischief lurking in his. It's clear he's up to no good even before he mutters something to Andy. They both pivot and change course.

Oh no. Surely he's not going to...

The door opens and in walks the subject of all my fantasies, tall and intimidating in his navy suit. My stomach drops. My worlds are colliding. He's not actually going to stay, right? My dad doesn't know we're friends.

But, of course, Ben does stay, and worse, while he's talking to the hostess, he points to the empty booth just two down from ours. She smiles wide and leads them over. Andy shoots me a wave and waggles his eyebrows before he slides into the side of the booth facing away from me. Ben claims the other side, right smack dab in my line of sight.

His smirk is barely hidden.

I'm shaking.

Good thing a rambunctious family of five sits in the booth between us or I'd immediately bolt. One of the kids screams that he doesn't like spaghetti *noodles*, just spaghetti *sauce*. I want to high-five him for the distraction.

"Maddie, you remember Nolan, right?" my dad asks, drawing my attention to his friend. "He and I went to high school together."

I glance up, my attention stays on Ben. I couldn't tell you if Nolan was white, black, purple, green, if he had one head or five.

"I haven't seen you since you were yea high," he says, holding out his hand just below his hip.

I nod. "I'm good. Thanks for asking. How are you?"

They stare at me like I'm from another planet. *Oh shoot. What did he just say?*

My dad laughs and shakes his head, making excuses for me that I don't care to hear. Their conversation drifts into the ether as Ben takes off his suit jacket and rolls up his sleeves. I swear to God, the scent of his body wash carries over to me.

I'm dying here.

I reach for my water and guzzle half of it down as Nolan walks away.

My dad frowns. "You okay?"

I nod and my phone vibrates on my lap. I can't check it. I know it's Ben. I know it will be a taunting, teasing, make-me-bad text, and I cannot for the life of me survive this meal if I let him get into my head. I force my attention onto my dad and smile.

"I'm fine, just really hungry."

He snorts. "I would be too if all I ate was rabbit food. You should have ordered a double cheeseburger for yourself. Could use a little meat on those bones."

Of course. My dad wants nothing more than to fatten me up like a stuffed pig. If he had it his way, we'd be slathering cheese on every one of our meals.

The way Ben positions himself, he makes it so I can't look at my dad without seeing him. He's there, filling up the entire restaurant, his presence so impossible to ignore that I start to sweat.

My phone vibrates again and my dad frowns.

"You need to take that?"

I reach down to turn my phone off, but before I do, Ben's words catch my eye.

Ben: I have a challenge for you.

I suck in a breath.

"Maddie?" my dad asks.

I clear my throat. "It's nothing. The bank."

Clearly my taunt about a bank heist is still on my mind.

"The bank?" he asks skeptically. "Since when do they send texts?"

"I'm sorry." I shake my head and turn off my phone. *Get it together.* "Not the bank, just some spam thing. Oh look, they turned the game on."

I point to the small TV mounted over the bar. Some sports team is on there, running around a sports field catching sports balls of one sort or another. I am so distracted. I need to talk to Ben, now. *What does he think he's doing?!*

My dad turns to see what I'm talking about and I glare at Ben over his shoulder, hoping to send him a whole slew of warnings with just one glance.

It's no use. My scowl is met with bold indifference. Those amber eyes are locked on me as he throws an arm across the top of the booth. The cherry on top of the sundae is his barely contained smirk. He's thinks he's untouchable. He thinks this is all fun and games. He likes how nervous I am, how uneasy I feel.

I watch as the waitress walks by their table, and if she was putty with my dad, she's completely helpless when Ben aims a handsome smile her way. He's pointing at my booth, saying something, and she nods, grinning.

My scowl only deepens as I watch her walk away and disappear into the kitchen only to reappear a few moments later with a big ol' chocolate milkshake.

Ice cream confections are meant to be innocent little things, but this one is lethal. She waltzes right over to our table and starts to set it down.

"This is from that—"

"Oh! Thank you!" I reach up to yank it out of her hand, and I can tell she's annoyed that I cut her off.

She tries again. "That gentlema—"

"Gentle machine makes the best milkshakes," I finish for her. "I know. Thank you for bringing this over. I've been craving one all day."

Her eyes narrow and it's obvious she thinks I have a few screws loose.

My dad watches the exchange with equal amounts of confusion. When she walks away, he tilts his head, studying me. "Did you order that?"

"No. She must have just sensed that I needed one. Here, have a sip."

I don't have to tell him twice. It's perfect, really. My dad has a bigger sweet tooth than I do, and this chocolate milkshake is the just the diversion I needed.

Thank you, Ben.

I stand and explain I'm going to the bathroom. As I pass Ben's table with my chin raised and my shoulders pushed back, I completely ignore him.

It doesn't matter. I know he'll follow me anyway.

I barely take two steps down the side hallway where the bathrooms are located before I sense him behind me. I pick up my pace as if I'm trying to outrun him. I reach the door of the first bathroom and am about to twist the handle when his hand covers mine, keeping me from opening it.

His mouth hits the shell of my ear as his chest hits my back. His body blocks out the hallway light, casting me in shadow.

"Don't you want to know what my challenge is?" he taunts.

I squeeze my eyes closed, trying to stay steady on my feet.

Isn't this already a challenge? Having to stand here in this hallway with his skin on my skin and his body on mine?

Keeping the truth from slipping out, burying my true desires—*it's all a challenge*.

"Madison…"

Has he always seemed this intimidating or is it worse right now when my heart is stumbling over itself and my hand is shaking? We can't do this—whatever *this* is.

We're in a busy diner. This bathroom probably isn't empty. In a second, someone's going to try to turn the handle and exit but they won't be able to because we're keeping it closed from the outside.

"Ben," I whisper. "My dad is going to find us."

"He doesn't have to know."

His voice is low and menacing. He's playing the villain I cast him as. Eli's words filter through my mind: *He wants you—bad.*

"Did you try the milkshake?"

I hear the amusement in his tone and squeeze my eyes closed.

"That was reckless. You nearly got me caught."

"And yet here you are."

Voices carry down the hallway. Conversations seem to close in on us. *Is that my dad? Is he still at our table?*

Ben's free hand squeezes my shoulder, and he applies just enough pressure that I'm forced to spin around and look up at him. When his gaze catches on my expression, his brows furrow in frustration. He looks devastatingly handsome…handsome and *mad*.

"Are you scared?" he asks, hands falling away from me.

Our eyes lock and my heart pounds.

"*Terrified*," I say, my voice barely above a whisper.

Then I look away, embarrassed by my honesty.

He steps closer and our hips brush. The contact makes me lose my breath and he must enjoy it too because he reaches out to grip my waist, pulling me closer. "Worried your dad will find you back here with me?"

That's nothing, *nothing* compared to my real fears: the falling sensation I felt when Ben walked into the diner, my excitement every time his name appears on my phone, the easy banter, the give and take. We're building something. Can't he feel it? Is that why he's leaning closer? His chest brushing mine...

"Honey?" A voice carries down the hallway and I try to jerk away from Ben, but he doesn't let me.

It's our waitress carrying two plates of food: my salad and my dad's hamburger.

If she thinks it's weird that Ben and I are pressed up against the bathroom door, sharing an intimate moment, she doesn't let on. She just tilts her head back toward our booth with a knowing look in her eyes. "Food's ready."

She disappears and Ben finally steps back. I take full advantage, bolting down that hallway as fast as my feet can take me, and I don't even get my feelings hurt when Ben walks out a few minutes after me and doesn't look in my direction. He throws some cash down onto his table, yanks his jacket on, and then he and Andy head outside.

My dad finally catches sight of him as they walk past us on the sidewalk.

His eyes narrow, but he doesn't say a word. I pray he doesn't realize Ben and Andy were in the restaurant. To him, it should look like they're just walking by after work, like they would have done if Ben hadn't spotted me in here and come inside to taunt me.

———

That night, I lie in bed, staring at my phone, analyzing the last text Ben sent. *I have a challenge for you.*

I never texted him back—even after we finished eating and left the diner—and I'm too chicken to text him back now. I'll just ask him about it in the morning when we both show up at the library for story time.

I'll be the one in charge then, the one calling the shots. I won't have him cornering me in hallways and making me sweat.

In fact, the next morning, I'm back to my chipper self, more confident than ever that I can deal with my all-consuming crush on Ben Rosenberg and live to tell the tale. I act like yesterday never happened, like we didn't almost kiss in that diner hallway and my feelings aren't in danger of boiling over. I've been doing it for weeks, feigning disinterest. Today should be no different, except for the fact that Ben didn't get the memo. He doesn't want to play along.

He walks in with an air about him, like he's just won the race and he's doing a victory lap. He's wearing a black shirt, and I decide that color should be erased from his wardrobe because I just can't take it. He must like the way I ogle him, though, because he's clearly gloating as he passes me a surprise latte.

"I had them add a little hazelnut. That's how you like it, right?"

"Oh." I glance down at the to-go cup, a little shocked. "Yes, thank you."

"No problem. How was the rest of your dinner?"

I clear my throat. "Fine. Better than fine, in fact. I ate all of my salad."

I glance up in time to catch his very subtle smirk. "Like a good little girl."

My stomach ties itself into a knot—a double knot.

"You think you really got me yesterday, don't you? That show in the hallway? Very daring. If my dad had found us, you'd be six feet under right now."

He shrugs, unperturbed. "Maybe, but it would have been worth it. You should have seen yourself. You really thought I was going to take advantage of you right there, in the middle of the diner."

My eyes go wide. My cheeks burn hot.

"What?! *No I didn't!*"

He chuckles. "Come on, Madison. It was all in good fun—part of your plan, remember?"

Of course. All part of my plan.

What's my plan again?

"So even if that waitress hadn't interrupted, nothing would have happened?"

"What kind of man do you take me for?"

A dangerously tempting one.

He smiles, and *ah, yes.* He knows exactly how I feel. I'm sure of it.

He's not fooling me.

This friendship is starting to get messy. You can't flirt and text and touch as much as we do without crossing some lines. Doesn't he realize that?

I decide to put a stop to this conversation by sending him over to the ladder I asked Lenny to bring down. We have work to do. Today's story time is winter wonderland themed. My dress is ice blue and I have a snowman clip in my hair.

I want to hang paper snowflakes from the ceiling for the kids. They'll flip, and fortunately, Ben is game. He takes off his jacket and sets down his coffee before he climbs right on up. I hand him a couple of snowflakes connected to strings and then step back to watch him work.

His shirt rides up as he stretches to attach the first one, and I catch a few inches of his toned torso. I nearly lick my chops. Good thing he's too busy to notice.

"Is that good?" he asks, in reference to the snowflake.

I mumble something inaudible then scurry back to my table. I'm glad I have a solid objective to get back to: arranging snowballs in a pile.

"Do you have plans later? Andy wants us all to watch a movie at his house."

"*Us?*"

"You, me, Arianna, Kevin, Eli."

It seems I have no choice. I'll be spending the evening in Ben's company, suffering, keeping my dirty thoughts to myself.

"And I told him to pick something scary," he continues.

I glance back over, glad to see his shirt has fixed itself. *Thank God.*

"Why?"

So I'll be forced to cower in fear? Sidle up close? Hide my face against his chest?

His brow arches. "Because you want to be bad, Hart. Blood and gore go hand in hand with that, don't you think?"

So it has nothing to do with us touching. Fine.

I turn around and return to my task. We work in silence and I wonder if I should bring up the boyfriend search again as a way to test the waters between us. It's an underhanded tactic, maybe even a little childish, but it's the only tool I've got, so I'll use it.

"I've been wondering," I start. "How has the search been going for my nice guy?" He grunts, but I trudge on. "You know, since Andy rejected me...I keep expecting you to find someone to take his place."

"I've been too busy at the firm to think much about it."

His tone sounds stiff.

"Oh?" I start to arrange the name tags. "That's understandable. You know what? Maybe you could find someone to invite to Andy's tonight," I suggest sweetly, as if getting my hopes up. "What better way to get to know someone than in a group setting?"

"Wouldn't work," he says brusquely, shutting the door on the subject.

I frown.

"Why?"

"The numbers would be all off. Andy has two couches and two chairs in his living room. With seven people, someone would have to sit on the floor."

"So we'll just bring in a chair from the kitchen."

"Hand me another snowflake, will you?"

Ah, so he's just going to ignore me then. Wonderful. It's as if the whole topic bores him, which makes sense. He's never been in my shoes. He's never had to go years starved for affection, yearning to know what it feels like to just…

I resist the urge to groan and yank my hair.

He was right earlier—I *did* think he was going to take advantage of me in that hallway. *I wanted him to!*

"Madison. Snowflake."

Right. I grab some off the table and walk over to the ladder so I can pass them off to him. My shoulders are sagged. My smile is wiped clean.

Even on my tiptoes, our hands barely touch. He stares down at me with a grim expression.

"Just…not tonight, okay?" he asks, his eyes imploring me to drop the subject. "Let's just hang out with the group and we can figure out that boyfriend stuff later."

I hate that he wants to shelve the topic. It might not be a big deal to him, but it is to me.

I thought we were getting somewhere. I thought I was going to back him into a corner so he'd be forced to come clean one way or the other. Instead, he chose a third route, one I didn't even see coming: total indifference.

CHAPTER FIFTEEN
BEN

A warm front is moving into Clifton Cove today, the first of the season. I've been tracking the weather a lot this week. I turn on the morning news and listen to the meteorologist droning on about the terrible storm headed our way. They weren't kidding. Last night, it rained cats and dogs, and it's still drizzling right now. I see it through my office window.

I don't mind though. With the rain comes the heat, not nearly as warm as it gets here in the middle of the summer, but it'll be warm enough for a plan I'm debating putting into action tonight.

It's been two months since I first started volunteering with Madison. I've endured two months of hanging out with our fledgling friend group, of forcing a distance between us and ensuring my hands stay to myself as much as possible. We text all the time. We're building a relationship that neither one of us is acknowledging.

Her family still doesn't know about us and other than the stunt I pulled in the diner, I've respected that fact. She never has to insist that I park around the block from her house when I drive her home. I do it because I don't want to make her life any harder. I do it because spending time with her is the best part of my week, because when she's in my car, I feel like…

I can't finish the thought.

I'm a mess.

Since the picnic when she asked me if I found her attractive (in a hypothetical sense), we haven't delved into feelings, no talk of romance and seduction and the urge I have to suppress every time I'm within ten feet of her. I want to kiss her, all the time—in that hallway at the diner, when she was curled up on the couch beside me at Andy's house for movie night, when she's reading a story aloud to the kids in the library, when she wears the green dress that matches her eyes.

I'm a man falling, though I've tried to convince myself otherwise.

For Christ's sake, I'm supposed to be finding her some other guy to date.

Andy finds the whole thing truly hilarious. He thinks I've really stepped in shit this time.

"It's so poetic, don't you see? The universe is finally setting things straight for guys like me. All these years, I've had to endure women throwing themselves at you. Now *you* want Madison and *she* doesn't want you. No, wait—she *can't* want you. There's a difference, and you're having to really mind your manners. Have you even kissed her?"

"Get out of my office."

"Oh man, no kiss? You've thought about it though, right?"

"I'm going to physically remove you."

"I'd like to see you try—I'm heavier than I look. So, what's your plan? Stay in the friend zone? Bet you've never been here before. It sucks, doesn't it? Suffering day in and day out and knowing there's nothing that can come from it."

I stand up from my desk then, prepared to make good on my promise to forcibly remove him.

He leaps to his feet and holds out his hands to fend me off. "Hey, hey. Okay, I hear you loud and clear. You're obviously a man possessed."

I stop short and prop my hands on my hips.

"So what are you going to do about it?" he prods.

"I don't know."

He shakes his head, all humor erased from his eyes. "I don't believe you. In our first year of law school, you'd already outlined our firm's five-year growth plan. You're always ten steps ahead of everyone around you. It's the way your brain operates. You want Madison—are you really not going to fight to get her?"

His words are a constant taunt through the remainder of my day.

Am I going to fight for her?

It's a tricky situation. Her family doesn't like me, and there's not much I can do about that. I can't shed my last name or make myself meek. I can't minimize who I am, and I won't, not even to gain their acceptance. In truth, half the things they assume are accurate. I did grow up privileged, and I've had the world at my fingertips. But, my mom's death ensured that I know what's most important in life. I want a family. I want a house that's a home, not an empty shell. I want to love someone the way my parents loved each other, through thick and thin, through sickness and health.

As to my initial reservations about whether or not I'm the right man for her…well, maybe I'm selfish enough not to care about that anymore. Madison said she wants a nice guy, but she's never been stripped down…seduced…*desired.* How does she know what she wants?

Maybe I'll just have to show her.

———

Later that night, I'm standing in front of her house with a rock in my hand. I honestly can't believe I'm doing this. Her dad could still be awake. A neighbor could spot me. I could misjudge my strength and shatter the glass.

A car turns the corner and I hit the deck, hiding behind the bushes until their taillights fade. This is ridiculous. If Madison lived on her own, I wouldn't feel like a teenager right now. As it is, I could just call her and tell her to come outside, but this feels like it fits better with her plan. She wants me to make her bad. What's worse than sneaking out of your parents' house?

I push back up to my feet and cup my hands around my mouth.

"Madison," I hiss, careful not to project too much.

Nothing.

Another car. Another few minutes hidden in the bushes. A wandering raccoon spots me and stares, judging.

I shoo it away and stand back up.

"Madison!" I shout, this time a little louder, and then I follow it up with a carefully tossed rock. I flinch, waiting for glass to break, but it pings right off. Such skill. Such mastery. I look back to see if the raccoon was watching.

A noise catches my attention overhead and I glance up to see her window slide open. A moment later, Madison's head pops out.

"Ben?" she whisper-shouts. "What the hell are you doing? You're crushing my dad's azaleas."

Whatever. Just one more reason for him to hate me.

I wave her down. "C'mon. You're sneaking out."

She laughs and then slaps a hand over her mouth, cautious of the noise. We both stay silent, waiting. A moment later, the house is still quiet. We didn't wake her dad up. *Yet*.

"My dad only went to bed a few minutes ago," she explains.

"So just be extra quiet when you climb down."

"Are you serious right now? I'm not sure I can handle another injury to the head. Why don't I just sneak out the front door?"

Sure, she could tiptoe downstairs and walk through the front door, but this night is not about playing it safe. Her window opens to a slanted roof. She can easily step out and then walk to the edge and lower herself down. I'll be underneath her, prepared to ease her fall.

Of course, when I explain this to her, she doesn't seem all that convinced.

I throw my hands up in defeat. "Do you want to be bad or not?"

She fists her hands then walks away from the window, and I think she's gone for good. I'll be standing out here alone all night. That raccoon's going to get the last laugh.

Then her head pops out a second later and she groans. "Okay I'll do it! Just let me change!"

"No need. Where we're going, it won't matter."

I don't hear the things she grumbles under her breath as she checks to make sure her dad is still asleep. A minute later, something hard falls out of the window and lands in the bushes.

"Oops! Sorry," she cries. "I meant to say heads up."

It must have been her phone. We'll get it later.

Her slender leg peeks out of the window and then she hoists herself up and over the ledge. Okay, maybe in hindsight, she could have worn something a little more practical than a flimsy nightgown. Her hair isn't even tied up. The long strands are blowing in every direction. She wraps her arms around her midsection and squeezes. It's not that cold, but then I'm wearing jeans and a jacket.

She stands up there gazing down at me. I shouldn't be thinking she's beautiful, but Madison has a way of looking incredible in the least convenient moments.

Her nightgown cuts off at mid-thigh. From where I stand, I have a dangerously tempting view. I force myself to be a gentleman as I tell her what I want her to do.

"Lower yourself down slowly and by the time you're hanging, I should be able to reach you. Got it?"

"Okay. I trust you, but I'm just wondering if I should go back in for some ice packs before we continue."

"Madison," I admonish. "C'mon, I've got you. I swear."

She does exactly as I say and soon enough, her calf is within reach. I lock my hand around it and like the good guy I'm pretending to be, I don't notice how silky smooth it is.

"Keep going. I can almost reach your thigh."

"Don't look up my dress!" she hisses.

"I'm not," I insist, sounding deeply affronted.

But just to be clear, she's wearing panties with a flower print on them—pink, if I'm not mistaken.

"Okay, lower yourself down a little more."

My other hand skims up her thigh. This is the most I've touched her. Sure, there've been a few fleeting moments like at the tattoo shop and diner, but normally we're on a strictly need-to-touch basis. Incidents include a game of leapfrog during story time (Her hands were on my shoulders. Her butt grazed my forehead as she jumped over me. Incidentally, I love that game now), and last week, I dragged her away from the library for lunch in the middle of the week. After our meals arrived, we both reached for the ketchup bottle at the same time. Our fingers accidently brushed and you would have thought I'd just slid my hand into her panties. She stumbled over her words. I jerked the bottle away and then thrust it toward her.

"Here, you go," I said.

"No. Go. You," she responded.

Neither of us could form whole sentences for a solid five minutes.

Now, my hand is sliding up her nightgown. I'm lost to the feel of her thighs. They're so smooth. I want them wrapped around my face.

"Ben! I'm going to let go now!"

Shit.

Reality slaps me across the face. Madison is dangling precariously from her roof. I'm the only thing between her and certain death, or at least a seriously rolled ankle.

"Not yet!" I hiss, trying to keep my voice down. "I need to get a better grip on you. Can you lower down a little more so I can get your waist?"

She tries and fails. "Ah! My hands are slipping!" she cries.

Everything happens at once. She lets go. I reach for her and…she lands daintily in my arms. It's so unexpected that we both blink at each other in silence, trying to discern if there are any serious injuries we've yet to realize. Does she still have all her limbs?

"Are you hurt?" I ask hesitantly.

"I'm fine," she says, wetting her bottom lip.

I'm not the only one here with their mind in the gutter.

"You weren't a very soft thing to land on, though. Your chest feels like a rock," she whispers, gaze on my mouth. "Am I heavy?"

I shake my head. Her eyes are two Jumbotrons blaring the kiss cam. She wants me to lean in and put my mouth on hers so bad, it's a wonder she doesn't scream.

But, we're on a mission, so I set her down and lead her to my car.

We're halfway across the lawn when she remembers something and doubles back. *Oh, right, her phone.* Except the thing she picks up and dusts off isn't a phone. It's a half-full bottle of whiskey.

She holds it up proudly as I open the door for her. "I have no idea where you're taking me, but I figure this can't hurt."

Our destination is very close by and just as deserted as I hoped it would be.

Not many people want to be on the beach at night in early April. There's still a chill in the air. A full moon hangs heavy in the sky, and a few waves lap lazily against the shore.

"Swimming at night? That's dangerous," she says, cradling the bottle of alcohol against her chest.

I didn't take her for much of a drinker, much less hard liquor.

"Sure you need that?" I ask, watching her uncork the bottle and brace herself for a shot.

"Oh yes. *Positive.* I have a feeling I know what you're going to suggest we do."

We lean against my car as she takes short, shallow sips followed by howls of disgust. She wipes aggressively at her mouth and emits a passionate *blergh* sound any time the alcohol passes across her tongue.

"Think you've had enough?" I ask, tempted to reach out and take the bottle from her. She's small. A little of that stuff can go a long way.

"Hold on. One more sip," she says, bracing her shoulders and steeling her spine. I watch as she uses her right hand to run through the sign of the cross and then she tips that bottle back for a nice long swig.

When she's done, she shudders. I cork the whiskey, set it in my car, and close the door.

"Okay. I'm ready," she says, shaking out her hands. "I feel like there's a fire burning in my belly now. Say the dare."

"Skinny dipping."

The two words make her mouth form a perfect O.

"Wait, I thought we were just going to go swimming."

I arch a brow tauntingly. "Not bad enough, Hart."

She narrows her eyes, trying to find an escape route. "Did I say I wanted to be bad? No, no. I just want to be *less good*. There's a difference. I want to return my library books late, play hooky at work, sneak into a double feature at the movie theater."

I reach down for her hand as she lists off all the reasons why this is a bad idea.

"I'll catch a cold. I'll get stung by a jellyfish. I could swallow a whole bunch of salt water."

I tug her toward the stairs that lead down to the sand. We're a few yards from the water when I stop and turn to face her, starting to gather the material of her nightgown in my fist.

"I distinctly remember you saying you wanted to be bad. Skull and crossbones. Motorcycle rallies. Criminal on the run."

"Oh wow." She laughs prettily and pats my chest. "This is a giant misunderstanding. We better just go back to the car and crank that heater."

I'm tugging her along by her nightie, dragging her forward. When we're nearly at the water's edge, I stop.

She shakes her head and grips my hand with all her might as if I'm going to let go and push her in.

"I think you should go first," she says, eyes focused on the waves.

"Oh, I'm not going at all. This is your thing, remember? The whole 'live life to the fullest' mantra is something you want to do. I'm fine right where I am."

She sidles a bit closer. I wonder if she's meaning to tempt me or if it's just the way things are between us. "Oh c'mon, you can't do this to me! It's winter. *Freezing*."

"It's Texas," I say, deadpan. "At worst, it's 60 degrees."

"The water's probably colder…"

"You're right. No worries. We came—that counts for something. Let's just get you home and tucked right back in that bed you've slept in since you were five years old. Who needs—"

"Okay! Jeez, just hold on. Let me take off my shoes."

"And the nightgown."

She arches her brow. "This is just a big ploy to see me naked."

I don't deny it.

"Do you even have a towel for me to use when I'm done?"

"I have a jacket. You can wrap it around yourself."

She grumbles under her breath, just loudly enough for me to make out every single word. "Arrogant jerk" is said with the utmost clarity.

She leans down to yank off her shoes and then places them neatly in the sand away from the water. When it's time to remove her nightgown, she pointedly arches a brow in my direction.

I turn slightly to the side as she starts to lift it overhead. I can still see her in my periphery. Her bare skin glows in the moonlight and she has three seconds to get in that water before I turn and push her down into the sand.

"I'm leaving my panties on," she announces as she starts to tiptoe forward. I peek. Her arms are wrapped around her breasts, but the rest of her body is perfectly exposed. I spot her new ink on the side of her ribs. Her smooth, pale shoulders. Her toned legs and narrow waist. Her panties are cut high, revealing the bottom of her rounded butt cheeks.

She is…unimaginably beautiful.

"It's really not so bad," she says, glancing at me over her shoulder.

There's a vision if I've ever seen one: Madison with her long brown hair hanging untamed down her back, her legs disappearing into the water. Her eyes are on me as she rests her chin on her shoulder. She's watching me with a hint of amusement. That mouth proves it, her soft pink lips curled up in a knowing smile.

"You should have had some of that whiskey."

"Why?" I ask, embarrassed by how strained the word sounds.

"Because I feel great and you feel…"

Out of control.

She's right. If I had the bottle right now, I'd take the longest swig of my life. I'd probably keep going until the whole damn thing was empty.

"Sure you don't want to come in?"

She beckons me like a siren.

I told myself I wouldn't. It's not a good idea. That water is a barrier. My phone and keys are in my pocket and that means I have to stay here, on land.

She turns away with a shrug and takes a few more steps. The water slides up to cover her butt. Now she looks completely nude. Her hands release her chest and she dips forward, falling into the water slowly so she can start to swim away.

I don't consciously realize I'm removing my shoes until they're both gone. My jeans are off before I can even blink. I think I just shredded them. My shirt and jacket are tossed aside and I'm following her into the ocean for one reason: there are so few moments like this in a lifetime. I won't let this one pass me by.

I run and crash against the waves, swimming fast. I catch her without much effort and reach out to grab her foot. She jerks around, smiling, and I let go.

"See? It's not bad, is it?"

No, not at all. The water insulates us from the chilly air, and it's almost warm now that my body is used to it. We swim for a little, keeping our distance until I find a sandbank and wave her over. She stops in front of me and stands. Her shoulders just crest the top of the water, but most of my torso is exposed to the cold air. We're a few yards from shore and the waves are just strong enough to bob us back and forth in a constant rhythm. Our arms float at the surface of the water to keep us stable.

The water is dark enough that I can't really see anything below the surface. I know she's nearly naked though, and every now and then, the tide pulls out to build a wave and I catch dangerous, teasing glimpses of her pale curves cast in moonlight. The ocean is on my side. It wants me to see her. *Fuck.* I'm trying to keep my attention elsewhere, but just like Andy said earlier, I'm a man possessed.

We're hardly a foot away from each other now. I force a safe distance, but the waves are trying to bring us closer together, and if I'm not careful, we'll accidently touch.

The tide strengthens and pulls the water out to sea and her breasts crest the surface. She bends down quickly, lowering herself under the water more, then she laughs lightly and looks away, knowing what I just saw.

It's all so innocent and sweet. I need to scrub a hand down my face. I need this water to be forty degrees colder.

This is bullshit. My hands could be on her—I *know* she wants my hands on her—and yet I'm standing here, resisting.

Is she nervous being out here with me alone like this?

I want to ask her, but she breaks the silence first.

"Have you ever been skinny dipping before?" she asks, giving me her profile.

I want to lie to her, but I don't.

"We all did back in high school."

She frowns like I knew she would.

"I never did it alone like this, though…with just one other person."

"So in some ways, this is a first for you too," she says, finding comfort in that.

I know it bothers her, the idea that I've done more, *lived* more than she has. I've had girlfriends and intimate relationships, and she's had the company of her books.

"I'm not completely hopeless, you know," she says suddenly, eyes narrowing out toward the dark horizon. "Guys have been interested in me. Not a ton, one or two over the years…I don't know, maybe they would have taken me skinny dipping and sought me out more, but my dad was pretty strict and I was a rule follower."

"You don't have to explain."

She laughs and it sounds shrill, pained even. "Don't I?"

She shakes her head and makes a move to swim away, but I reach out for her, clamping my hand around her bicep. She's not going anywhere. A tidal wave could swell against us and we'd stay right here, rooted together.

"You're beautiful."

She puffs out air like I've just said something absolutely ludicrous.

"Fucking hell, Madison. You're drop-dead gorgeous. Every guy in this town would agree."

Again, her eyes roll and she yanks her arm, trying to get away from me so she doesn't have to face what I'm about to tell her. Compliments are hard to receive, especially if you're not used to hearing them. I want her to hear these.

"Can you tell how much I want you?"

Her gaze jerks up to me and her eyes narrow suspiciously. "Okay, Ben, you've made your point. You've made the loser girl feel very pretty and special. You can go back to your cool friends now and tell them you did your good deed for the year."

I want to shake her. In fact, I do. I grab each of her shoulders and haul her right up against me. It wasn't intentional, but now we're skin to skin, and I feel her breasts brush against my chest, soft and full and slippery from the water. It's so intimate, I can't breathe. I'm surviving on dredges of oxygen as she tilts her head back and looks up at me. There's fear there.

I've never been forceful with her—I've never been forceful with any woman—but like I said, this night is a first for me too.

I can't let her go. My hands stay right there on her shoulders even though they ache to move lower. I want to feel the weight of her breasts, to knead them and tease them and show her why I'm the man for her. Not Andy. Not some nice guy. *Me*.

"Would you just listen to me?" I plead. "You think I'm lying to you?" I bend to her eye level. "You have eyes so green, sometimes I can't look right at them. Your hair is never brushed. I'm not fully convinced you even own a brush, and yet your hair is all I can think about. I want to fist it in my hands and tug on it so you're forced to look up at me just like you are right now."

She swallows and blinks, completely and utterly frozen. She looks like an innocent animal caught in my trap.

"You're funny and kind. You take such good care of everyone in your life. You have a heart the size of the moon."

There are tears collecting in her lashes and I feel bad now. Maybe she wasn't ready for the truth. Maybe I should have eased into this nice and slow, written her a note with one letter on it and sent it to the library. Each day, I'd send another, until one day, finally, she'd have a full sentence:

M-A-D-I-S-O-N H-A-R-T, I-M F-A-L-L-I-N-G F-O-R Y-O-U.

"Sorry, I'm hurting you," I say, and I'm not just referring to my hands on her shoulders.

She shakes her head and sniffles. "I'm only crying because I'm a little drunk," she says, wiping her nose on her shoulder.

Right. Jeez. I've picked the worst possible time to be honest with her. I tell myself I need to release her and give her space, but then her palm hits my chest, flat against my heart.

"Did you mean all that or are you just being nice?"

"I'm not that nice."

She laughs and shakes her head, letting her hand wander down my torso. Her finger dips past my navel and I squeeze her shoulders in warning.

"I really want you to kiss me right now," she says, gaze on my mouth. "Is that crazy?"

"No."

"Because you could kiss me and I wouldn't turn away. It would be another life experience I could cross off my list. Kiss Ben Rosenberg in the ocean: check."

"Madison?"

"Yeah?"

"Be quiet so I can kiss you."

CHAPTER SIXTEEN
MADISON

This kiss is going to ruin me. I will have this kiss up on a pedestal for the rest of my life, encased in glass. On my wedding day, when I stand across from an ordinary man who makes me feel ordinary things and the pastor announces "You may now kiss the bride," I'll think of Ben and the time when he held me in the ocean and told me I was beautiful.

I'll think of the way he looked: cast in moonlight, tapered muscles, hard lines. I notice the smallest details: the little freckles on the bridge of his nose, his amber eyes backlit by the fire burning inside him, his wet hair sending water dripping down the hard planes of his face.

There's a terrible feeling buried deep inside me that keeps me from completely giving in to this moment. This is a gift, I remind myself, a memory to keep forever. Not to be confused with a beginning—this is not the first of many.

One of his hands curves under my jaw and the other loops around my waist, hauling me against him even more. We're touching like we're lovers, like every bit of his skin is mine for the taking and vice versa. I'm a live wire, the result of too many weeks pining.

Everywhere we touch, our skin sparks. My hips meet his and I feel his hard length beneath his briefs. It's close, but not close enough. I bring one leg up around his waist. He helps me with the other and now I'm connected to him, coiled like a snake. Waves lap against our bodies and his hands are cradling my face. His lips brush against mine, but it's not a kiss. It's an impatient touch, a hint of what's to come. Another wave builds and it's bigger than before, crashing against us hard enough that I think Ben will lose his footing, but he stays right where he is.

"Please," I whisper against his mouth.

My breasts drag across his chest with every wave.

"*Please*."

Put us out of our misery. Kiss me. Drown me. *Something.*

His hands bring my face against his again. His nose brushes mine and I smile. We're two Eskimos. Then his mouth trails over to my cheek and he whispers something I can't hear. I *wish* I had heard.

I'm impatient. I turn and steal a peck, but then I jerk away before he can deepen it. Why? I don't know. I want this kiss, but I'm so scared of what it'll do to me.

I'm shaking and I'm glad I had that whiskey. I feel just free enough to let this happen, just free enough to let Ben finally turn my face back to his and let his lips fall to mine again, for real this time. I breathe deeply as his mouth presses firmly, slanting, seducing.

His head tilts and the kiss deepens. This is what I've been longing for. My arms lock around his neck and my breasts graze his chest. They're so sensitive, and I'm so anxious to be touched there that a moan escapes me as Ben breaks the kiss and gulps in air.

He brushes hair out of my face, finding my eyes. He's searching for something. Consent?

I lean in and give it to him with my lips. I kiss him first this time. I take his bottom lip between my teeth and tug and then he returns full force, his fingers digging into my waist. Our tongues touch and we're creating magic. We're starting to grind together, and the water adds the most intoxicating element. We're wet and slippery, but Ben has a rock-solid hold on me. Even still, my heart must think I'm in danger with how quickly it's beating, how quickly it's sending blood through my veins.

We kiss long enough that my lips start to ache and my fingers turn to prunes. Long enough for him to carry me closer to shore so we're only halfway underwater. Long enough for his hands to find their way to my breasts, to curve gently around them. I'm braced for the impact, but he does the most tortuous thing: he doesn't actually touch where I want him to. His fingers drag along my skin slowly. He trails along my ribs and then his thumb grazes the side of my breast and the shadow just beneath. Each time he moves, my chest caves as I exhale in preparation, and each time, I'm left wanting.

I know a first kiss shouldn't be more than that. I know we've gone from zero to a hundred, but he can't deprive me of this. He can't give me his hands, so big and so rough, and not show me exactly how they'll feel when he touches me *there*.

I'm losing my head. I'm losing… That's just it: I'm losing, and Ben is winning. Ben is convincing me that this kiss *could* be a beginning and that even though he's from a world of polished silver and trust funds and expectations, I could meet those expectations. I could be the girl he wants, the girl who gets the guy.

Please fall in love with me, I beg with my mouth as our kisses turn hungrier, more savage. My nails are digging into skin and he's cursing under his breath. I need the moon to hang right where it is and for him to keep ahold of me.

His hand finally drags up and takes my breast and I arch into him, *ache* for him. His palm covers me, rolling back and forth, skimming across the tip. My thighs clench around him and his grip turns possessive. Hot. Needy. My breast fills his hand and it feels so good to have him touch me there. My flushed skin is sensitive and he knows just how to work me up.

I'm so turned on. I didn't know *this* is what I've been missing all these years. I've touched myself. I've felt my own hands on my own skin, but this feeling is nothing like that. Ben has an impatient grip on me. His hips are grinding with mine. His mouth is hungry and impatient. His body is so big and warm. He was waiting for me and my head was in a book. How could I have lived in that library day in and day out and not realized Ben was out here talking with these lips and using these hands for things far less important than this?

Lights flash behind my eyelids and I think I've gone too long without air. I break free and heave a breath. I blink, forcing another deep inhale. There, again—red and blue lights swirl in my periphery.

I might have had some whiskey, but I know those lights, and they aren't a result of our kiss.

———

"I'm sorry."

I've said the phrase so many times, it sounds distorted. I can't keep saying it. Besides, I don't think Ben's listening anyway. His attention is on my dad's approaching figure.

Oh yes, that's right: D-A-D, as in my father, as in the last person I want to see at this moment.

Let me rewind.

Ben was seconds away from tossing me down onto the sand and devouring me whole and I was seconds away from demanding he do just that when a police officer who was patrolling the seawall saw Ben and me in the ocean. Hence the swirling red and blue lights.

It's not illegal to swim at night. However, it is considered indecent exposure to swim in the buff. Even at night. Even on a deserted beach.

Everything happened so fast once he parked his cruiser and shouted at us to get out of the water and cover ourselves. Ben reverted into lawyer mode, telling me I didn't have to answer when the officer asked if I'd been drinking. Apparently, he thought I was drunk because I was stumbling around for my clothes. I might have been a little tipsy, but I was only stumbling because I was in such a rush to cover myself. *Hello!* It's one thing to work up the courage to go topless around Ben, quite another to have one of my father's police officers see me in that state!

Once we gave our names, the officer's tone changed. He reared back in shock.

I should have lied and said the first thing that came to mind. *Oh, my name? Sand. Sandy Palmtree.* We could have laughed. *Yes, ha ha. My parents are big hippies.*

Instead, he looked at me with new, fresh concern.

"Hart?" he asked. "As in the chief's daughter?"

I nodded as I tugged Ben's jacket tighter around my front.

Then he nodded and stepped away, his hand hitting the radio on his shoulder.

My stomach dropped.

"Wait! Do you have to, y'know, call this in?" I asked with an air of hope. "Can't we just keep this between us?"

Ben's hand hit my arm—a warning to stay quiet—but I couldn't just let this happen. In any other city, a cop would find the humor in the situation, tell us to get our clothes on, and move along.

In Clifton Cove, apparently every police officer is given strict orders to contact my father if I ever have a run-in with the law. It's his way of protecting me, I suppose. As I watched his cruiser pull up to the beach, it didn't exactly feel that way.

This whole thing is ridiculous.

I'm not going to accept the charges, and I tell that to Ben.

He has the audacity to smirk and rub his jaw. "Yeah, that's not really how it works."

I turn back to watch my dad walking toward us. I can feel his angry energy from a mile away. Every sea creature in the ocean behind us is probably swimming for its life in the exact opposite direction.

When he gets within earshot, I step forward.

"Dad, hi," I say, trying for a genial tone just to see how far it will get me.

His eyes slice me in two. Okay. Right. He's going for bad cop.

"James, thank you for the help. I can handle it from here."

The other officer nods and heads for his car, leaving me alone with my dad and Ben. I guess his work here is done. *Fine. Go! Get. Good riddance.* I want to kick his tires.

"Dad…I think this has all been a misunderstanding."

He ignores me and impales Ben with a searing glare. When he speaks, his finger is pointed at Ben like it's a loaded gun.

"I told you to stay away from my daughter. In fact, I recall shouting those exact words at you a few months ago when you were on my front lawn."

Ben stands quiet. Stoic. Pissed. In his black t-shirt and jeans, he has a few inches on my dad. His eyes are fierce. His chin is lifted.

When it's clear he's not going to reply, my dad shakes his head with disdain. "I should throw your ass in jail."

Ben's eyes narrow imperceptibly and I take the opportunity to jump between them. My hands hit my dad's chest and I try in vain to push him back a few inches.

"Truly, this isn't so bad."

His eyes slide to me. "You reek of whiskey."

"First of all, thank you. Second of all, you have to stop. This is not what it looks like."

His eyes widen. "Not what it looks like? *Madison*, I just got a call in the middle of the night from an officer telling me my daughter was stumbling drunk on the beach, completely nude. You tell me how that sounds."

I cringe. "Okay, yes, that's…not ideal, but—"

He shakes his head and reaches out for my arm, yanking me toward him. "C'mon, we're going home."

I try and fail to pull myself out of his grasp. He can't do this. He can't turn the best night of my life into the absolute worst.

"Dad, let go," I hiss, trying to keep the hysteria out of my voice.

Ben steps forward then. "You heard her."

No. No. *Shit.*

My dad's nostrils flare and I know we're seconds away from going down a road there's no coming back from. If Ben touches my dad, my dad will press charges. Ben will be in jail and maybe one misdemeanor didn't matter, but I'm pretty sure assaulting a police officer—even one who's off duty—won't be brushed aside so easily.

Even still, I can't blame Ben for thinking I need his protection. My dad is trying to physically drag me off the beach, and I'm resisting. It doesn't look good, but my dad isn't a bad guy, and neither is Ben. Everything just looks…bad.

"Shit!" I shout suddenly, finally finding enough strength to break free. My arms flail as I speak. "Both of you stand down. *Jesus*. I don't need either of you getting into a fight over me. This is ridiculous." I turn to my dad, my finger poking his chest with every word I speak. "Ben isn't a bad guy. You think he's an entitled rich asshole, but he might be the kindest man I've ever met outside of my own family. Pull your head out of your ass and stop with all this 'stay away from him' bullshit! And you," I say, whirling around to face Ben. "Just…"

Please don't give up on us.

Please don't let this ruin what we have.

Please answer the phone when I call you in the morning.

Those are all the things I want to say, but instead, I settle on, "Please don't punch my dad. He means well."

His eyes soften a smidge, but not nearly as much as I would like.

They're still acting like two dogs circling around each other, hackles raised. Neither one of them is going to back down. My dad's not going to toss up his hands and say, *You know what? You're right. Ben, you have my blessing to date my daughter.* And Ben isn't going to beg my father to see reason and give him a chance. He has too much pride.

Ben's eyes turn to me, and I see his anger boiling there. I feel so bad for dragging him into this situation. I don't want to be the reason he suffers. My dad has it wrong. Ben is a good man, and he doesn't deserve to be yelled at like this.

"I want you to leave my daughter alone."

I cringe at the request, hating how mean my dad sounds, how fiercely protective he's being. Any other man would do exactly as he says and walk—no, *run* from the beach, but Ben stands immobile, his amber eyes on me. Steam rolls off his broad shoulders. He won't leave me here, and my heart is breaking for him.

There's no good option. I could leave with Ben—my heart is screaming at me to leave with Ben—but I can't do that to my dad. My dad, the man who sacrificed so much to raise me, who's stood by my side my whole life.

No matter what I decide, I'm going to hurt one of them, so I do the only thing I can do. I throw up my hands and turn to walk away by myself.

Now no one needs to be my protector. No one needs to drag me away.

I'll go all by myself.

Ben shouts at me to slow down. My dad does too, but I don't listen to either one of them. I walk and I continue walking until I hit the sidewalk. I cross the street, lock my arms over my chest, and head in the direction of my dad's house. Sure, Ben's jacket and my nightgown are both soaked, but the anger burning in my belly makes it so I can barely feel the cold night air.

God, I'm sick of this town. I'm sick of being the police chief's daughter and Colten's little sister. I'm sick of being treated like a teenager with a curfew. I'm a grown woman. It's time to start acting like one.

I'm so mad I could keep walking straight to Canada, just Forrest Gump it all the way up the coast. *Run, Madison, run.*

A car follows behind me slowly. I know one of them is trailing me to make sure I make it home okay, but I can't turn around to see who it is. If it's my dad, I'll be upset it's not Ben. If it's Ben, what would I tell him? *Sorry you'll never have a normal life if you date me? Sorry my dad is overbearing? Sorry I nearly got you arrested? Sorry I'm twenty-five years old and still don't have the strength to stand on my own two feet?*

Clarity sinks in during that trek to the house, and not just a little thought like, *Hmm, I should eat my vegetables if I want to live to 100.* This is a meteor-sized realization that drops down right on top of my head.

If I want to change my life, I'm going to have to initiate that change. I can't use Ben as a crutch. I have to move my life along, and not just in this superficial bullshit way where I get little rose tattoos and sneak around with Ben. *Oh, yeah, wow—real exciting stuff there, Madison.* How about I grow up? How about I muster the courage to move out of my childhood bedroom? How about I finally stand up to my dad and Colten and tell them life is going to change? No more nice Madison. No more pleasing everyone and pushing my wants and desires aside. I wanted real change when I blew out that birthday candle and now, finally, I've found the strength to make it happen. I don't need Ben to make me bad.

I can be bad all on my own.

If this were a movie, a sick beat would drop at this exact moment.

———

When I get home, I head straight up to my room to start packing a bag. I'm not going anywhere tonight. It's late. I don't own a car, and I'm not asking my dad to drive me. The notion is laughable. *Hi, Dad. Yes, I'm leaving. Could you perchance give me a lift?* Not to mention the fact that there's still a little whiskey working its way through my system. I should probably stay put until morning.

202

I want to call Ben and talk about what just happened. I can't believe I just left him on the beach. I feel terrible. What if he thinks I didn't like what we were doing?! *No*. Not possible. Before the police officer reached us, while we were yanking our clothes on and kicking up sand, our gazes locked and I knew—whatever had just happened in that ocean wasn't just because of the dare. He meant those words. He wanted me.

I reach for my phone and dial, but he doesn't answer.

Shit.

I try again, pacing my room, and this time, I leave a message. "Hey Ben, it's me…*Madison*. If you could give me a call back, that would be great. Okay. Um, also, thank you for…that, for…whatever just happened. Okay, bye! Also, oh! Sorry about my dad!"

I cringe and toss my phone onto my bed then turn for my closet so I can start grabbing clothes. First thing in the morning, I'm going to move out. I'm going to hunt for an apartment until I find something that works for me. Hopefully I can find some place to lease in one day. If not, I'll stay at a hotel. I will not spend another night in this house.

I can't.

My poor dad is just going to have to deal with it. I cringe. No doubt there'll be a guilt trip. I'm sure he'll try to persuade me to stay here with promises of change and more freedom, but the fact is, it's time.

I have to spread my wings and fly.

Sorry. I'm sorry. I had to say it.

Anyway, I barely sleep. I stay up all night, scrolling websites for places to rent and not so subtly checking my phone to see if Ben is ever going to call me back. I've never actually looked at real estate in Clifton Cove before. There aren't many apartments nearby and absolutely none in my price range. The city council has strict zoning laws, making it nearly impossible for large apartment complexes to be built in the desirable parts of town. Mostly, they're relegated to the outskirts, near the insane asylums and hazardous waste dump sites and outlet malls. My commute to the library would be quadruple what it is now. I'd rather stay within walking distance. I just need to figure out how.

Eventually, I do sleep. I'm not sure when it happens, but I wake up the next morning with my iPad covering my face and a thin layer of drool coating the screen.

I jerk up and see the bag at the foot of the bed with clothes spilling out. A ball of anxiety forms in the pit of my stomach.

Can I really do this?

I love this house. I love my dad. Sure, he kind of ruined the best moment of my life last night, but he's a really nice dad and he did the best he could all on his own. He never forced me into Girl Scouts when all the neighborhood moms were pressuring him to. Also, he let me eat ice cream whenever I wanted, and he let me stay up extra late on the weekends to watch movies with him and Colten. These are important things. These are the reasons my heart is heavy as I pad downstairs.

He's in his usual spot, crossword in hand, glasses perched on his nose.

He glances up at me and I can see the remorse in his eyes.

I should handle this gently. I should come up with a very strategic way of leading into the subject…

"Dad, I'm moving out."

CHAPTER SEVENTEEN
BEN

I acted like a fool last night. When I look at the situation from Madison's dad's perspective, I hate myself. Madison had a few shots and might not have been the best swimmer to begin with. I had ahold of her in the water, but what if something had happened? What if a wave had come that was a little too big? Too powerful? It's not like I was looking. I was completely possessed by her. What if she'd fallen under and the tide had swept her out of my reach? It was too dark to see more than a few yards away. I wouldn't have been able to find her. She wouldn't have been able to tell which way was up or down.

Fuck.

Sharks—what if there was a shark?

Stingrays.

Jellyfish.

Whatever. I'm going into a tailspin. The point is, I'm an idiot for taking her there, for daring her to strip and pushing her when she didn't really want to go in. I should have never let her drink that whiskey. I could have taken it from her. I should have fought harder for her when her dad showed up. I stayed silent, thinking it was more respectful to let him get his anger out than to speak up and contradict him, but by not defending myself, was it just as bad as admitting guilt?

Oh god, I *am* guilty. Of taking her there. Of putting her in that situation.

Maybe I'm as bad as her dad thinks I am.

I say all of this to Andy. I'm at his house the next morning, tearing my hair out, pacing, refusing food.

"You're in a bit of a pickle, huh, bud?" he says, propping his feet up on his coffee table and sipping his coffee.

He's wearing flannel pants and slippers. What man owns and proudly wears slippers?

"What do you think I should do?"

"Oh, you have quite a few options, right? You can give up all hope and move on, find some other willing female to warm your bed. That wouldn't be too hard. My birthday is next month, and Arianna and I have already started planning a party—there'll be plenty of women there for you to meet."

I shoot him a deadly glare and he shrugs, unperturbed.

"Or you could fight for her? Go talk to her dad? See if you can't change his mind about you?"

"And say what exactly? I didn't mean to endanger her life last night? I didn't mean to sneak her out of your house? It was all an accident? I just happened to be standing under the window, in your azaleas when she fell out?"

His eyes narrow as if he actually thinks that's a possibility.

"Andy, no. Fuck. You're right—I should move on. Why am I hung up on this one girl? There are a million others."

"*More*, even." Andy nods.

"She's wrong for me in so many ways."

"Really?"

"Yes. I mean, she's so goddamn naive. She let me lure her into the ocean last night. She stripped when I barely taunted her!"

He hums. "Sounds terrible. Go on."

"She's twenty-five and still living at home. I don't even think she has a driver's license."

"Ugh, horrible," he mocks. I'm too busy conjuring up ticks against Madison to notice.

"And her family! Jesus, her brother probably wants to murder me right now."

"I think you've already mentioned the family—"

"Worst of all," I say, sitting on the edge of his couch and dropping my head into my hands. "I think I'm already half in love with her. No, more—three-quarters of the way in love with her."

Andy's hand hits my shoulder and he pats twice before pushing to his feet. "Well, sounds like you know exactly what to do."

I jerk my gaze up to him. "What? What do you mean?"

"Oh you know, just follow your heart. Listen to your gut. Let the winds of fate guide you to your destiny."

"What the fuck are you saying?"

"I don't know. I'm just trying to wrap this up. I'm hungry and you don't seem to be anywhere near the end of this existential crisis. Do you want a donut? I think I'm gonna make a run."

Andy is absolutely no help.

I spend the remainder of my weekend stuck in a vortex of guilt and anger and indecision. I replay her voicemail and contemplate calling her back, but I can't. She texts me Saturday night with two words: I'M SORRY. I feel so bad, I don't reply. Why is she sorry? Why is she the one apologizing?

I don't know what to say and Andy won't come up with a reply for me, so I just don't answer.

Sunday, she texts me again.

Madison: I really am. Y'know...sorry.

I want to shout at her to stop. The apologies are only making me feel guiltier. Her heart, the one so big it could fill a football stadium, is not something I deserve. Have I been playing with her feelings? Manipulating her for my own amusement? No. That's what her dad thinks, but that's not who I am. I have to keep repeating this to myself, especially after her brother visits me at work on Monday.

I'm in the middle of returning emails when one of my junior associates rushes in, eyes wide, lip quivering.

"There's a police officer outside asking to speak to you. He says his name is Colten Hart. Are you under arrest or something? Will I have to find a new job?"

I wave away his concerns and push to stand, not at all surprised that Colten has come to talk to me.

Of course he's wearing his police uniform, all black. Is he purposely fidgeting with the gun in his holster or am I imagining things?

The second I push open the door, he squares his shoulders, juts out his chin, eyes me like he wants to skewer me on a stick.

I have no idea how I should approach him. Guns blazing? Respectful and meek? That one nearly makes me chuckle. *Yeah right.* I settle on stuffing my hands in my pockets, narrowing my eyes, and waiting for him to speak first. It's a power move in its own right.

"You have some nerve," he says, spitting at the ground.

It's like we're in an old western and he's about to challenge me to a duel.

"What can I do for you, Colt? I have a lot of shit to do."

His upper lip curls and he steps toward me, finger pointing. Then he shakes his head and pivots to the side, cooling his jets.

"I'm not here to fight with you."

That's a surprise.

"I'm here because I want to talk to you about Madison."

My stomach tightens at the mention of her name.

It's been two days since I've seen her, two days since I've heard her voice or seen her in one of her colorful dresses. I wonder how angry she is with me for going radio silent. I wonder if she'll understand when I explain my reasoning to her.

Colten keeps his gaze out on the parking lot as he continues, his tone is calm now, nearly civil. "You and your friends think this town belongs to you. You're the gods and we're just your playthings, here for your amusement."

"That's bullshit and you know it."

"Yeah? I seem to remember you being quite the asshole back in high school. You're telling me you've really changed since then? That you're not the same rich punk who used people however he liked?"

I throw my hands up, indignant. "Jesus, that was more than a decade ago. You think I'm still running around doing the same old shit?"

I used to think Sum 41 was the pinnacle of music. I thought long surfer hair and puka shell necklaces were going to be around forever. He can't be serious right now. I was eighteen and stupid.

"I'm not the same person I was then."

"Why are you messing with her?" he asks, gaze turning back to me.

"I'm not."

"To you, people like Madison don't matter. Not really."

A trigger flips inside me and I'm in front of him, right in his face before I realize what I'm doing. I can smell the fucking coffee on his breath. I'm seconds away from grabbing hold of his collar and escalating this to a level neither of us want it to go to.

"She matters," I say, so convincingly it's like I've just chiseled the words into his chest.

He snorts derisively. "Yeah? Until when? Until another pretty girl catches your eye?"

I turn away to cool down, to regain some semblance of control.

I'm staring out at a tree in the parking lot. I stare so long my vision blurs and the leaves blend together into a mess of green, the exact color of Madison's eyes.

"You think you deserve her?" he asks, voice nearly breaking. He sounds desperate. "What have you ever done in your life to deserve a girl like Madison? She's good, Ben, better than you and me, and I won't let you hurt her."

When his car door slams and he peels out of the parking lot, I'm still staring out at that goddamn beautiful tree.

———

We accept the love we think we deserve. I've heard that before. Maybe I read it on the inside of a crinkled chocolate wrapper, I don't know, but it's stuck in my brain the rest of the day. In a sense, it's true. It's how I've operated in the past. This time, with Madison, I'm reaching. Colten asked what I've done to deserve her—what do any of us do to deserve love? Love should be given freely. I want Madison, and I think she wants me. I don't know. Two days with no communication means a lot could have changed. Maybe her family finally convinced her to leave me in the dust.

Maybe she realized she could do much better than me. She could turn heads and break hearts if only she put herself out there.

The idea kills me.

I go by the library later that day prepared for two scenarios. I have a document waiting for Madison's signature, outlining that I'll be switching my volunteer location from the library to the soup kitchen. If things don't go the way I want them to, I won't keep forcing myself into her life. I'll give her space.

I purposely wait to go see her until it's nearly closing time. I hate having to go to her work at all for something like this, but I can't show up at her dad's house, so this is really my only option.

She's not at her desk when I walk in. I ring the bell but there's still no sign of her. I hear a heavy *thunk*, like a box of books getting shuffled around, and I head toward the hallway that leads to the storage room. That's where she is, tidying up.

She doesn't notice me at first. Her hands are on her hips as she surveys the space, deciding what to do next. She's wearing the white sweater dress I love, the same boots she wore to the beach. Her hair hangs in dark undone curls and when I knock on the doorframe, she jerks around to face me and pushes some of it behind her ear.

She's as perfect and angelic as I've ever seen her. Her skin is the exact shade of the cream I pour into my coffee.

She's a goddess and I'm undeserving of her.

That's what everyone thinks.

Her eyes light up when she sees me. She doesn't know what this is about. Right now, she just thinks I'm here to see her.

Without a word, she turns and walks toward me. She doesn't stop until she's right in front of me, her boots hitting the toes of my dress shoes. Her hands slide underneath my suit jacket and she wraps her arms around my middle. Then she lets her forehead fall to rest against my chest. I haven't felt so much comfort from a hug since before my mom died.

"Hello," she says softly.

"Hi."

"My brother said he went to see you at work today."

My only view is the top of her head.

"He did."

"Was it terrible?"

"Wasn't great," I concede, careful to keep my hands off her.

She's gripping me with everything she's got and I'm holding her at arm's length.

She must realize it because she steps back and nods.

"So then do it already. Say it."

I frown.

She laughs like I disgust her. "You think by staying silent, you're not speaking, but I hear it all loud and clear, Ben. So do it." She whirls around and tosses her hands in the air. "God, it's so predictable. *You're* so predictable."

I can't lie to her. I can't tell her I don't want her or say I'm not falling in love with her. So, I settle for the simple truth. We have to get it all out if there's any hope of moving forward. "I'm not the man you should be with."

She fists her hands. "Of course you're not! I'm sure my father said that. Colten too, yeah? I bet I can recite the whole conversation word for word and get most of it right. They warned you to stay away from me? Not to break my heart? Big deal! They've said that to every guy who's ever walked into my life. You're not special. You're not any more 'bad' than the rest. You…you're—"

She rears back and shoves me with everything she's got, her hands pushing against my chest until I hit the wall behind me.

"You're a coward," she says, spitting venom. "You're scared."

She's a ball of rage.

I grip hold of her biceps to keep her fists from pounding on my chest. "*Of course I'm scared!* I care about you," I say, voice booming. "I want life to be easy for you. I want you to be happy. You said yourself you want to be with a man your family approves of."

"Well guess what?! I fell for you instead!" She groans with everything she's got and then flings my arms off her. "I'm so mad I can't even think straight."

"Tell me the way forward then," I say, coming up behind her, turning her around so she has to look up at me. I want her looking in my eyes as she lays out her master plan. "Tell me how this works. You defy your father and keep sneaking out of your house to see me? I want more than that, Madison. I want—"

Before I can even finish that sentence, she's on me, pushing me up against the wall, crashing her mouth against mine. I'm so angry I could shred her clothes, pull her hair, bite that lip. Clearly, so is she. I've had enough with the games and the silly shit. No more pushing her out of her comfort zone under the guise of a birthday resolution. No more pretending what we have is just a friendship.

She fists my shirt and kisses me back with an angry vengeance. Our mouths slant together and our tongues touch and I'm grinding into her, gripping her ass, pulling up her legs so they wrap around me.

The gloves are off. The time for indecision is over. I came here with two options: fight for her or give her an easy out, a chance to leave me behind. It seems we've made up our minds.

I'm not going to walk away from Madison. She'll have to find a new family—*I'll* be her family. I'll take care of her and shelter her and if her dad doesn't like that, tough shit.

She melts against me, gripping, writhing, moaning. Her hands are unbuttoning my shirt and my hands are up under dress, pushing beneath her panties. I have her ass in my hands and I grip it like I'm as angry with it as I am with the last few days. We've been in hell and this is our reward, our light at the end of the tunnel.

"Ben," she moans as my mouth trails down her cheek, her neck, her chest. I spin us around so she's up against the wall. I use it to my advantage, leaning back and gaining better access. Her sweater dress is just stretchy enough that I can tug the neck to the side and expose one of her shoulders. If she's wearing a bra, it's strapless. On Friday night, in the ocean, I didn't appreciate what I had. I felt like she hadn't given me permission to touch her, not really.

Now…

Now I'm going to make up for that.

"Are there cameras in here?" I ask, breathless. If so, I'll find a gun and shoot out the lenses. We're not stopping.

"No. Wait—I don't know. Who cares? Lenny is old and probably needs some excitement in his life."

She's saying this as she works my jacket off my shoulders. It falls to the floor. My shirt gaps open.

"What are we doing?" I ask, wanting to get everything out in the open. If this is some foreplay bullshit, I need to know now.

"What are we doing?" she mocks. "I thought you'd done this before…" She leans forward and takes my earlobe between her teeth. "I'm supposed to be the innocent one."

Of course when she says that, in that tone, while dragging her tongue across my skin, I am gone. I'm the evil version of Ben everyone seems to want me to be. Poor Madison. For her first time, she deserves candles and rose petals and a Phil Collins playlist. I tell her that. I give her the out.

"I'll take you to a fancy bed right now. I'll make it special, memorable—scrapbook-worthy," I promise as I hold her against the wall and start to bend to my knees.

Her eyes watch me as her head falls back. Her hand fists my hair. She knows where I'm headed and there's a little blush on her cheeks that I want to kiss off.

"Madison?" I ask with a raised brow just as my lips touch her inner thigh. "Should we—"

"NO! We're staying! This wall is really soft—cloud-like, even," she says as I tug her dress up to her waist to expose her panties.

Lilac.

I let my face fall against them and the silky material tickles my nose. I want to die in this spot.

"Ben?" she asks, concerned.

"Who's Ben?"

She laughs and yanks my hair, pulling me back just far enough that she can see my eyes.

"I've spent a lot of hours in this library, a lot of time with my nose stuck in a book. I want a memory that will make me blush every time I walk into this room. I want to do something bad…something very, very naughty."

The edge of my mouth hitches up. "Naughty?"

Her laugh is cut short when my fingers catch on either side of her panties. Her stomach quivers as I give the first little tug. They slide down an inch and more of her creamy skin is exposed. Another inch and I can't wait. I'm not a patient man. The panties can stay. I drag my middle finger down the very center of them, right over the silkiest part. Her resulting shudder is gas to a flame. I do it once more and her eyes flutter closed.

"Has a man ever touched you like this before?"

"No."

I do it again, slower this time, making sure I hit the most tender spot.

"But I've touched myself before."

My heart lurches in my chest. My dick strains against my zipper.

I stand back up and cover her body with mine, finding her mouth, kissing her at the exact moment my hand slides down into the top of her panties and I find her wet, wanting.

One finger glides inside smoothly, and Madison has never known the meaning of naughty before today. Her fingers dig into my forearms as I taunt her, running one finger up and down her seam. I drag that wetness up, up, up and swirl the pad of my middle finger while she loses brain cells.

My lips touch her neck, and the contact is too gentle to douse the flames. No, I'm fanning them. With my tongue. With my finger as it spins circles just slow enough to make her arch her back. I drag my hand up her over stomach and then back down. I'm talking to her, teaching her.

Do you want me to keep going lower? my fingers ask as they still on her hipbone.

Her skin is so flushed it's a wonder she isn't feverish.

She's rolling her hips against me. Her body is telling me all the things she's too shy to say.

She's growing impatient.

She wants a release.

Friction.

Heat.

It's only been a few seconds since I touched her there, but it must feel like forever.

I brush her hair off her forehead and cradle her face. She looks at me like she's about to swoon.

"More," she demands with a lusty, choked voice, and I smile, happy to oblige.

This time, I use my mouth.

I bend back down on my knees, and there's no more tiptoeing around this. My fingers hook on either side of her panties and I yank them down her thighs. They pool on the floor and she steps out of them. Her dress covers her, barely. One of my hands pushes up the thick sweater material and the other wraps around her thigh, tugging, goading her legs apart.

I expect her to protest, and she does try to push her dress down a little.

"I've never…" she says, letting the sentence hang.

I glance up so my gaze locks with hers and I kiss the inside of her knee. Then I peel her dress up and follow its path with my mouth. The material drags across her skin, goose bumps bloom, and I kiss them away, lapping her up until I reach the spot between her legs. I'm too tall for this angle. Her legs are long for her height, but still, I need more room. I wrap my hand around her calf and lift it up so her foot perches on my shoulder.

Her hand flies up to cover her eyes, like if she doesn't look at what's happening, she doesn't have to be embarrassed by it.

I smirk.

It's cute. All of it—the idea that she would turn this down because it's out of her comfort zone, the idea that when my mouth connects with her soft, wet flesh she won't crumble into a million pieces.

My tongue slides across her and I watch that hand curl up into a fist and fall away. Her eyes stay closed though. Her mouth drops open. So does mine. I lean in and her legs spread wider. My hands were keeping them apart, but there's no danger of her closing them now. I let go of her thigh and bring one hand between her legs to compliment my mouth.

If I had a timer, I'd start it.

She won't last another minute.

My middle finger slides into her and I start to pump slowly.

Madison's eyes squeeze tightly. Her hand fists against her mouth like she's scared of what will fly out. My tongue swirls faster and my finger matches its rhythm. That timer is counting down and Madison is grinding against me, rocking her hips, taking it and taking it, trying to stave it off as long as possible, but I'm better at this than she is. I pump faster and my tongue speeds up and the first shudder I feel is followed by a second one that's even more powerful. Her orgasm rocks through her and she cries out, fisting my hair, keeping me there, ensuring that I help her milk every last drop of pleasure.

I kiss her and soothe her as she comes back down to earth. Her eyes blink open slowly and I'm smirking, very pleased with myself.

Her sweater dress falls back into place, the rest of her still in complete disarray. Light-socket hair. Flushed cheeks. Wide, crazy eyes.

She opens her mouth to say something and a giggle escapes instead. She presses the back of her hand to her mouth, shakes her head, looks away. Apparently, she's having a hard time piecing herself together, so I decide to help her. I pick up her panties and slide them back up her legs. When they cover her again, I pat her butt and step back.

"You've done that before," she says, impressed.

I laugh.

Her brow arches. "I could return the favor, you know. I'm not opposed."

My dick says yes, but my brain thankfully wins out.

"It's probably best we don't stay down here. Besides, it's late—I'm sure your dad is wondering where you are."

"Oh, about that…I moved out."

She's biting down on her lip to contain her smile.

I blink in shock. "What do you mean?"

She's innocent now, playing with her dress, acting as if this isn't monumental information. "Mrs. Allen has a garage apartment. She's letting me stay there and pay rent. Well, technically, I haven't convinced her to take my money, but I will. It's nice. I mean, it definitely hasn't been lived in since like the 70s. There's green shag carpet and a smell I can't quite seem to locate the source of, but it's my own place, at least."

"You moved out."

She smiles. "I moved out."

I'm in the bathroom of the library, freshening up before we leave. I try, very hard, to remove the blush from my cheeks. I fan my face, splash some cold water on it, shove my head down under the hand dryer. It's no use.

It seems it's permanent.

I can't believe we just did that. In the storage room. Where I store books. Books are stored there and Ben did that and I have to get out of this bathroom. The redness is getting worse.

He's waiting for me by the library exit with my bag in hand, checking his phone. He's beautiful in his suit. His hair is only slightly mussed from my hands. He looks composed, nearly bored. I try to mimic his expression and probably come across looking as though I've had bad Taco Bell.

"All set?" he asks.

I take my bag with a little meek smile and then lead him through the door.

Mrs. Allen lives a few blocks from the library, which is the main reason I worked out the living arrangement with her. It's not the ideal scenario. Like I told Ben, the garage apartment is not exactly the lap of luxury, but it'll do the trick for now.

He guides me to his car and then I direct him to her house. Thankfully, the apartment has its own entrance and exit in the back alley, so I can come and go as I please.

We park and Ben sits quietly for a second. It's an ominous silence, the kind that leads into bad conversations I don't want to have.

I prepare myself for the following possibilities:

"Madison, that was fun, but I want to keep this casual."

"Madison, now that I've sampled the milk, I don't really care to purchase the cow."

"Madison, bye."

Instead, he turns to me, eyes narrowed in frustration. "That's the entrance to the apartment?"

I turn to see where he's pointing. The staircase off the alley leads straight to the front door. The light overhead flickers like we're in a horror film. It's charming, right?

"Yup. Just up the stairs."

"And the apartment doesn't connect to Mrs. Allen's house?"

"No, thank God."

His frown intensifies. "Has your dad been here?"

I'm confused. What's he getting at?

"Not yet."

My dad took the news of me moving out surprisingly well—so well, in fact, that I suspect he's been waiting for me to be ready to leave the nest for a while now. I truly thought he needed me there. I thought I was doing him a favor by staying and looking after him, cooking him meals and keeping tabs on his health, but as it turns out, it might have been the other way around.

I'm wondering about the hilarity of that when Ben leans forward.

"Madison, this alley has no security cameras. Nothing. That door doesn't even have a deadbolt."

I frown, not quite seeing his point. Clifton Cove is safe. There's nothing to worry about.

"You were held up at gunpoint a few blocks over from here—what makes you think that couldn't happen again? Or worse?"

"So…you don't want to come up and see it?"

He emits a low grumble—more like a growl, really—and then follows me up the stairs. Looking at it from his perspective, I can see his point.

"I was so eager to get out of my dad's house, I didn't really have many options," I say, turning my key and pushing the door open. "The rent here is cheap, and it's just supposed to be temporary."

I step inside and the room seems even smaller than when I left this morning. I didn't want to move any of my furniture over here since it's not technically mine. My dad bought that stuff. I need new, adult stuff that I purchase with my own money, so I'm currently sleeping on a futon. The other furniture is all stuff that was already up here collecting dust. There's a funky gold floor lamp beside the futon. A card table is currently covered with my two duffel bags full of clothes. Behind a door on the right, there's a toilet and a shower. The toilet only flushes when it feels like it and I haven't figured out how to get hot water in the shower, but I'm sure if I keep at it, I'll figure it out. Easy peasy.

"Madison," Ben says, his tone just as hard as it was down in his car. He doesn't see the same charm that I do.

"What? It's homey!" I say, pointing to the Bob Ross-style landscape painting covering most of one wall.

"Come stay with me," he says, as if it's the simplest idea in the world.

"For a night?"

"Yeah, sure, or for…longer."

223

For a second there, I thought he was going to say forever. My eyes bug out of my head. "No. Way too soon. I can't believe you'd even suggest it."

"Is it too soon? I'm thirty-one. I've dated a lot of women."

"Well I haven't dated a lot of women, or men, for that matter. I've been living with my dad and I don't want to jump from his house to yours. I'd like to stand on my own two feet, at least for a while."

"How long?"

"What?"

"How long is a while?"

"I don't know." I turn and walk away from him, pretending I have some important task I need to take care of. I refold a shirt on the card table before I shrug. "A month…two months. I've never thought about it." I'm annoyed that he's forcing me to put a specific timeline on my figurative goal. "I just don't want to look back at my life and feel like I was never confident enough to pave my own way."

"I admire that, but I'd also like to point out that your dad wasn't supporting you. You work full-time. You take care of yourself. I understand what you're saying and I'll let you do what you need to do, but I'd just like to point out that you've been standing on your own two feet for a while now—you just don't realize it."

With that, he walks out the door.

My heart drops.

"Hey, wait! Where are you going!? Did we just break up?"

He laughs and shakes his head, continuing down the stairs. "I'm going to the hardware store. It should still be open for a few more minutes. Also, no, we didn't break up, but I would like to take this opportunity to ask you to be my girlfriend."

He's back on the ground now, looking up at me. Bugs the size of my fist swirl near the light at my head, but they cannot ruin this moment.

"Okay. Great." I shrug. "That'd be fine. I guess."

He smiles smugly and then turns to head for his SUV.

Thank God he left because I definitely need a few minutes to compose myself.

GIRLFRIEND.

GIRLFRIEND!

I step back into my apartment and my gaze leaps from one inanimate object to the next. None of them seem all that excited for me except for the snazzy gold lamp. Lamp is excited for me.

"Girlfriend," I say to it in disbelief.

About an hour later, I've settled into my new role in Ben's life very well. While he was gone, I reenacted some very lifelike scenarios in my head. *What's that? Oh yes, I am Ben's girlfriend. Thanks for asking. Oh, sorry, I can't come to your party tonight because my boyfriend, Ben, wants to have sex with me.*

It's probably good he can't read my thoughts.

Now, I'm heating us up a Cup of Noodles and he's drilling through my door, adding a deadbolt. He ran to the hardware store and then to his house to get some tools. He changed out of his suit. He's Ben Rosenberg, trusty contractor, and his flannel shirt and jeans are making it difficult to get the noodles to my mouth without some major spillage.

I sit crisscross nearby, watching him work. "Did you happen to ask Mrs. Allen if this was okay before you started doing construction on her property?"

225

He aims a pointed brow in my direction and keeps right on working. "First of all, it's a door—I'll buy her a new one if she has a problem with it. Second of all, this is about your safety. She should be glad I'm doing this."

I smile. "Plus, isn't it better to ask for forgiveness than permission?"

He smirks. "Spoken like the true bad girl you've always wanted to be."

I laugh and shake my head. "Oh god, can we please forget that whole thing ever happened? It was silly."

He pauses and glances down at me, studying my features. "Was it? Seems like a lot of things have happened in your life in the last two months, things you might not have had the courage to take on if you hadn't set that goal, silly or not."

I stir my noodles. "True. I finally stood up to my dad and laid down the law. I told him I wanted him and Colten to give me room to grow. He didn't even protest when I asked to move out—did I tell you that? I was really relieved. And now, I have these snazzy new digs, not to mention"—I tilt my Cup of Noodles in his direction—"you."

He opens his mouth for a bite and I oblige, grinning like a fool.

"It's like I've evolved into my final form: a big, bad butterfly."

He chuckles and returns to his work. I watch him change the drill bit on his power tool and my heart thunders in my chest.

I have to keep talking to distract myself from the overwhelming urge I have to tackle him to the ground and force him to continue what we started earlier.

"So, does being your girlfriend come with any perks?"

He sends me a smoldering glare over his shoulder. "What do you mean? Outside of the bedroom?"

Oh Jesus, I am going to die.

I clear my throat and look anywhere but at him. "No, I mean, like…you're Ben Rosenberg—surely dating you comes with free admission to amusement parks, float privileges in the Fourth of July parade, etc."

"You're ridiculous."

"I just want to know if I get some kind of airline miles or rewards points when I dine out at the restaurants your family owns."

"So it's true, you're only dating me for the power and privilege it provides?"

I shrug and add a little frown for emphasis. "'Fraid so."

Then, I hold up another bite of noodles and he accepts eagerly, fully aware that I'm kidding.

A few minutes later, he's all done installing the deadbolt. He stands and brushes his jeans off then leans down to help me up too.

"How did you learn how to do this stuff?"

"My dad and I would do little things around the house when I was growing up. The old Victorian homes around here need a lot of upkeep."

I test out the lock and it slides perfectly into place. We're both locked in here. My evil plan has worked. I twist around and aim a pretty smile his way. If I knew how to bat my lashes without looking like an idiot, I would.

"Stay the night?"

He laughs as he heads to the bathroom sink to wash his hands. "You're kidding. That futon is barely big enough for you. I have work in the morning. I need actual sleep."

I try not to let his rejection go to heart. He's not turning *me* down, he's just saying no to my slightly underwhelming abode.

"Besides, I'm trying to force you to see reason and come stay with me. I have a king-sized bed, two guest rooms, a really comfortable couch—all of those are better options than that futon."

I scrunch my nose, annoyed at myself for wanting to cave. Does sleeping on a futon in this apartment make me any more independent than if I was sleeping with him in his big, comfy bed? Ugh.

He walks out of the bathroom and finishes collecting his tools.

"If you insist on staying here for a while, I'll see about putting up a camera outside and maybe replacing that door. The deadbolt isn't much more secure than the previous lock. If someone wanted to, they could still just kick the door down. It's flimsy."

I nod and walk toward him, wrapping my arms around his middle. My ear is against his chest and I can hear his heart hammering. I close my eyes for a moment.

"Thanks for the lock and for sharing this very fancy dinner with me."

He kisses my hair and then I lift my chin to receive a second kiss on my lips. We both keep it short and chaste, but there's an underlying hunger that nearly splits me in two. I wish he were staying the night.

He groans, runs a hand through his hair, and then makes his way to the door. I shoo him out with plans to see him tomorrow and then steal one last quick kiss. I close the door and lock it behind him.

This sucks.

For some inane reason, I want to cry.

I have to listen to his feet carry him down the stairs, his car's engine rev to life, his tires kicking up gravel as he drives away, and then…his car pulling back up to my apartment, engine dying, car door slamming, feet thundering up the stairs. I undo the lock and he's there, laughing and kicking the door closed behind him.

"I guess one night won't kill me, right?" he asks, wrapping an arm around my waist and lifting me up off the floor.

Oh my god, I'm going to attack him. My arms are around his neck and I'm kissing his jaw, his forehead, the sharp edge of his cheekbone.

My mouth finally finds his, and it's just like before, in the storage room. We're so anxious and starved, we're not so much kissing as we are *consuming*. His tongue sweeps into my mouth and I moan, tilting my head, somehow still wanting more.

My feet dangle above the ground as he carries me deeper into the room.

The backs of my legs hit the card table and he sets me on top, not realizing my weight will throw it off balance. It's made to hold five pounds, tops. One of the legs creaks and then gives out. I go crashing to the floor right along with it and I'm laughing so hard, tears gather in my eyes.

"I'm sorry, I'm sorry," he murmurs, trying hard to fight off his own laughter.

He lifts me back up and kisses the smile off my face.

"My butt hurts," I groan.

He reaches down under the guise of soothing it, but his touch is hot, needy. He fists my dress and tugs it up. My hips roll against his jeans and I feel how hard he is. I can't do it any longer. Twenty-five years of going without is too damn long.

"Please please please tell me you have a condom."

"I grabbed one when I went to my house earlier."

"Oh my god, yes." I nearly say *I love you* jokingly, but I stifle the urge—mostly because at this point, it's not a joke.

It's so fitting that my first time will be on an old dingy futon. I don't want calm, quiet sex on a perfectly made bed with a lamp on across the room for soothing ambient light. In here, we're a mess. The gold lamp gets knocked over as I tug Ben toward the futon. It clatters to the ground right along with the card table, and I'm not fully convinced the rickety excuse for a couch-slash-bed will make it through this either.

There's a good chance we'll end up on the floor. I'll be picking shag carpet fibers out of my hair for days.

"Let's slow down," Ben says, yanking my sweater dress over my head and throwing it across the room. In the process, he nearly dislocates my shoulder.

I shudder and nod. "Yes, jeez, let's take a breath and relax." Then I yank his shirt apart and one of the buttons flies off and pings against the wall.

We're not very good at heeding our own advice.

My hands tug impatiently on the zipper of his jeans. It's only halfway down when I give up and yank the denim down with all the strength I've got. He kicks them the rest of the way off and in the process of removing his pants, I nearly took off his briefs too. The tight black material hangs low on his hips. More of him is exposed than ever before, the hard edges of his abdominal muscles pulling tight with each inhale he takes. I'm crouching down in front of him before I fully realize what I'm initiating.

I want to see him. God, I just need him in my hands, and the groan that slips past my lips is only half as lust-filled as it should be. I tug his briefs down his legs and my eyes go wide. Without a thought, I reach out to grip his hard length and run my hand up and down it. Ben bucks his hips forward. I grow courageous and empowered. I do it twice more, pumping, fisting, bringing my mouth closer but not quite touching him there…yet. My lips are a whisper against him.

"Madison," he says, his voice full of longing.

He seems big, but then I don't really have much to compare him to. All I know is that when I look at it from this angle, I'm not totally sure how he's going to fit. The thought sends a spiral of panic through me, but I brush it aside. This is natural, meant to be. It will fit. Hopefully.

I lean forward and drag my tongue across the tip and he fists my hair, a little nonverbal plea for more. I oblige, taking him in my mouth and sucking deep. How did we get here? How did our night turn from innocent construction to clothes-shredding passion?

I take him deeper and suck again and again. I want him so wound up, coiled tight, tight, tight like a spring. My name passes through his lips again and it's more ragged than the first time, desperate, depraved.

I will keep going until he gives in, until his hips thrust uncontrolled and he releases everything. Before this moment, I'd have turned my nose up at the idea. Now, I don't want to waste a single drop.

I can feel him at the back of my throat and my breaths come shallow, pained. *This is where I die*, I think as he starts thrusting faster. *Goodbye sweet, sweet world.*

I barely finish the thought before he hooks his hands underneath my arms and hauls me to my feet. My mouth hangs open.

"I'm not finished," I say, sounding deprived. I'm a child whose lollipop has just been ripped from her mouth.

Ben doesn't care about my disappointment, and he apparently doesn't care about taking care of himself either.

He's spreading his hands over my body, edging me back step by step. My legs hit the futon as his hands unclasp my bra. The soft material slides off my skin and it's immediately replaced by impatient hands and greedy touches. His palms roll across the tips of my breasts and my head falls back. He bends and his mouth takes over. He closes his lips and sucks. I'm thrust from one heady sensation to another, rough to soft. The juxtaposition is enough to jumble my thoughts. I'm no longer in control here. Oh right—I never was.

Ben's a master at this: his mouth, his tongue, the flick of it across my delicate skin. I have tingles between my thighs, wetness that feels naughty. When I glance down, my fair skin is a map of where he's been. His hands leave marks across my body—it's the curse of being pale, though in this moment, it seems more like a blessing.

His mouth moves to my other breast and his hand slides down my stomach, down farther past my navel, and then his finger curls beneath my underwear. A shiver racks through me.

"Should we talk about what we're doing?" I ask, suddenly nervous.

He pulls back and the self-assured smile he's wearing makes me want to punch myself in the face for asking such a silly question.

His brow arches. "You want the play-by-play?"

Oh Jesus.

He looks like the devil.

His hair is dark brown in this light. I'm surprised I ever thought his eyes were the color of amber. In here, right now, they're black as night.

"I'm kissing my way down your body," he says just before he fulfills his promise.

I wish my stomach would quiver a little less, wish my heart would slow its pace or my hands would stop reaching for him. I want to touch him everywhere I can, the bulge of his biceps, the hard ridges of his abs.

"I'm going to slide your panties off."

I cover my eyes. "Oh my gosh. Stop."

"This?" he asks, nudging my panties down an inch. I'm barely concealed.

"No, the words. Your narration—it's making me blush."

A low chuckle escapes him and then he pushes me back onto the futon like I'm a stuffed animal. I flop down, legs splayed, and he crawls on top of me. I'm trapped.

This stupid excuse for a piece of furniture was not made for this. It's wobbly and small. There's hardly enough room for one person, let alone two. Ben keeps one of his feet planted on the ground and leans down over me, mouth taking mine in a soul-stealing kiss. I arch up to meet him when it seems like he's going to pull away and he returns full force, tongue meeting mine. My hands cradle his neck and he peels my panties down my legs. I'm completely bared.

I'd have time to freak out about being naked in front of him if he didn't reach down and cover me with his palm. He rubs the heel of his hand up and down, right between my thighs. Right. There. Again. Once more and my nails dig into skin. I'm wounding him because he's wounding me. My heart will never be the same.

"Do you want to feel more?" he asks right before his middle finger slides inside me.

"Yes."

"Like this?" He pumps in deep.

"Jee-zus."

"You're more than ready for me. God, you feel so good." He sounds mad as he adds a second finger. My toes

233

curl. "I'll make you come like this. I'll give you the play-by-play, yeah? You're so tight. I'm seconds away from losing…" He groans. "Spread your legs."

My legs fall apart as if they belong to him now.

I pinch my eyes closed and his fingers pump faster.

"It's going to hurt, Madison. Look. Open your eyes."

I do and he's wiping hair from my face, tilting my chin so I have to meet his heavy gaze. He kisses me quickly and then leans back again.

"This can be over now. I can make you come just like this. It feels good, right?"

He swirls his thumb and, "Yes." I let out the word on an exhale.

"We don't have to keep going. We don't have to have sex."

If I had a condom in hand, I'd tear it open and throw it at him.

"Please, Ben."

He doesn't give in to my demands. He keeps going, keeps pumping, keeps turning me on. I know he's ensuring that I'm ready, that I'm as wet as I could ever be, but I'm dying a slow death here. He's kissing me seductively and his tongue is so convincing, I nearly give in. I'm so close to orgasming just from this—

No. I break off our kiss and cradle his face in my hands, staring pleadingly into his eyes.

"Please."

Our gazes stay locked and I brush my thumb across his cheek.

"*Please.*"

He stands then, depriving me of his touch. He turns to find his pants and tugs a condom out of the back pocket.

I sit up a little, watching him. Suddenly, I feel very naked with him halfway across the room.

I feel silly and small and what does he think of this ridiculous apartment? What does he think of me? I hate that I'm even thinking about that right now, but this is all new to me. Not to him, though—he's been here before. Other women have come before me, and maybe this moment doesn't meet his expectations. Maybe I don't meet his expectations.

Then he turns back and he halts as his gaze catches on me. I'm completely naked, lying there, waiting for him. His eyes light a fire across my skin, he starts between my thighs, then he moves up across my taught stomach and my full, heavy breasts. When our gazes lock, he looks wild, *feral*. I might not know everything about this, but I know one thing: the way Ben's looking at me, it's like there's no other woman on earth. This place might as well be a penthouse suite. I might as well be lying on a bed of silk and rose petals instead of scratchy black cotton.

He comes back to the futon, condom in hand, and reaches down to arrange me so there's more room for him to wedge his knee between my thigh and the cushion.

Foil tears and I watch, attention riveted, as he unrolls the condom onto himself, pumping up and down twice before he positions himself on top of me.

"Wrap your legs around my hips," he says, grabbing the backs of my thighs. When I comply, he nods. "Yeah, like that."

He fists his length and brushes it up and down between my thighs, coaxing me, drawing this out just a little bit more. When my nails bite into his skin, he starts to push himself inside slowly. His upper body falls over me, blanketing me from the world.

His lips hit my cheek and he whispers, "Just try to relax."

I take a deep breath and he pushes in another inch. It burns in such a unique way, a way that seems unbearable. My first instinct is to tell him to stop. I fist my hands and push against him. *No, you can't keep going. It doesn't feel right.* He slides in another inch. The pain intensifies and I must make a sound because Ben kisses me hard on the mouth, assuring me, promising me, soothing me. He continues until he's all the way in and the fire is eating me up from the inside out. Instead of shoving him away, my hands are on his back now, gripping him and ensuring he stays right where he is. I'm scared of movement, of the potential for more pain.

"Breathe," he begs, lifting up just enough to trace his hand along my body. He finds my rose tattoo and his palm flattens over it reverently.

I move my hand to cover his and I squeeze, hard. His eyes lock with mine and an invisible string knots us together. Right now, with him buried deep inside me, he can see straight into me, and maybe, for once, I can see straight into him too.

Emotions overwhelm me and I lift my head to kiss him, hoping I can keep him from noticing. His hand moves from my tattoo, dragging down my stomach, inciting lust in its wake. There's a point at which the pain starts to slink away, beaten back by the promise of pleasure. My jaw slowly unclenches and my legs start to ease apart. His thumb brushes between my thighs and I clench around him. It's like my body knows just what to do. His lips move over mine and his kisses turn demanding and hot. His reassuring touch is gone. Now, he's pouring fire over me and stoking the flames I thought the pain had doused.

He drags himself out a little and then thrusts back in. The sensation is otherworldly, and what I think starts out as pretty damn good turns into something extraordinary.

I moan and then demand he continue.

"Like that. *Yes*."

He pulls out a little more and then pushes back, rocking his hips back and forth. His sinful smile is back and a lock of brown hair falls over his forehead. I brush it back in place, but it's futile. He's moving too much now, thrusting and rolling his hips against me. His pace is impossible to match, so I let him have his way with me. *Oh yes, don't mind me.* I'm little more than a limp body and I'm truly sorry about not doing my part, except not really, because holy hell he's good.

His hand covers my hip, keeping me right where he wants me, and he looks down at where our bodies meet, thrust for thrust. My back arches and his finger finds the sweet spot, the spot where, when he makes contact with it, I'm prepared to sacrifice my life if only he would continue.

Like that.

The barest brush.

The constant building need.

I know what's coming. The chain reaction has already gripped hold of my body.

"I'm going to—"

There are tingles in my toes.

There's no chance for me to finish my sentence as his pace picks up.

His ab muscles ripple as he thrusts in and out of me. I want to hold off as long as possible, to grip hold of this feeling that seems so beautiful and fleeting. I'll only have this moment once in my life and if it passes me by, then what?

Then…I'll…

I clench tightly as I cry out, body racked with waves of pleasure.

I didn't realize how starkly different it would feel to orgasm with him inside me. There should almost be a new word for it. It's an experience unto itself. He fills me up and I clench, and that perfect sensation is what I'm made for.

There's no space between us. Our chests are flush. Our mouths are sealed together. He's grinding inside me so deep, milking, dragging, clawing out every last bit of pleasure I have to give, and when I'm drained, when there's no way I'll be able to move or breathe or continue living, his body shakes and a low rumble releases from his chest. It sounds like I've split him right down the middle. He jerks into me, filling me, and now our roles are reversed.

I'm soothing him, running my hand down his back, helping him come down from the high. I'm kissing his cheek and keeping him close. We stay on that futon wrapped around one another. The silence blares around us. Our hearts beat on, trying to give us back all the oxygen we've just burned up with blazing passion.

I want to lean back and meet his eyes and speak the truth. I love you.

Simply that. I love you and maybe that's silly. I love you and this was supposed to be a fun adventure, a daring departure from my normal life. I love you and that love comes with no strings and no assumptions, no requirements for you to say it back. Just love, given.

And because this is the year I'm living my life without safety nets, I do exactly that. I say those exact words. I shoot myself right in the foot.

"I've fallen into the cliché," I lament. "My first time and here I am pouring my heart out." I laugh and move away. "Ignore me."

"Don't do that," he says, grabbing hold of my wrist. "Don't say those things and then erase them as if they don't matter."

I blink, shocked.

"Falling quickly isn't wrong. My dad fell for my mom the first day they met."

My heart flutters. "You don't talk about her much, or about them, really."

He looks down at me, eyes narrowed. It's like I've just shared a revelation. *Did he not realize how closed off he is about her?*

I think he's about to slam the door closed on the subject but instead, he asks simply, "What do you want to know?"

"Everything."

"I'm not still grinning, am I?"

Eli rolls his eyes. "Yes. Tone it down. I can see every one of your teeth."

"Really?!"

I could have sworn my face was back to normal.

"Why are you so happy? Just because you and Ben are dating and he's a wild animal in the sack, now you're just going to walk around smiling all the time?"

"Maybe."

Arianna and Kevin make fake gagging sounds, but I don't care. I'm floating. Permanently. Life continues on below me, but I'm on a cloud, and my happiness is untouchable. It's glorious.

"We might not be able to be friends anymore," Eli quips.

I poke him in the ribs and steal one of his chips. Then I adjust Ben's baseball hat on my head and try very, very hard to seem appropriately happy. It doesn't work. They all groan and throw chips at me. Joke's on them though because I'm hungry.

It's Saturday and we're all at the park together. Andy and Ben are out tossing a football around. The rest of us are under an oak tree lying on blankets, enjoying the good weather.

Oh, and don't worry, a few guys showed up with a frisbee a few minutes ago and Ben forced them to go to the other side of the park.

"My hero!" I shouted, making everyone laugh.

Ben and I are still in the beginning stage of our relationship, working out all the kinks, like do we want to have sex eighty times a week or ninety? It's been a real challenge.

Joking aside, I've had to be careful with my time. I don't want to get so involved with Ben that I neglect my dad and brother. In the last week, I've gone to see my dad twice after work. I cooked him dinner and played cards, even helped him with particularly stump-worthy crossword clues. Last night, Colten was there too, and it was a little awkward. I could tell neither of them was quite ready to put the beach incident behind them. They were tiptoeing around it, asking about my apartment and work.

If they'd had it their way, I wouldn't have brought Ben into the conversation at all, but I had to address it. Ben is here to stay (*hopefully!*), so my dad and Colten are just going to have to get over it.

I told them, very plainly, that I had no plans to end my relationship with him.

We subsequently ate the rest of dinner in silence.

I wince just thinking about it, which is the reason I *have* to do something. Life can't continue like this. I have a plan. I'm going to host a breakfast at my apartment and everyone will be invited: Ben, Colten, and my dad.

In my head, I envision it playing out like a United Nations round-table discussion with the addition of freshly-baked pastries and orange juice. We're all going to leave our weapons at the door and put on our most diplomatic smiles. Everything will work out and we'll be singing Kumbaya by the end of it.

This is all well and good, but I don't work up the courage to actually initiate the breakfast for another month.

I'm scared. *Honestly*. What if the relationship between Ben and my family is irreparable? What if I have to choose sides? *No*. I refuse to dwell in those negative thoughts. Instead, I focus on the things I can control, like how to whip up some freaking stellar scrambled eggs. Potentially laced with some kind of feel-good drug.

———

Saturday—a month into my relationship with Ben—I wake up bright and early in my apartment and get to work fixing a feast using my microwave and recently purchased hotplate, and when that turns out abysmally, I run to the donut shop down the street and order two dozen glazed donuts fresh out of the fryer. My cheap coffee pot doesn't produce the best cup of joe, so I have Ben stop to grab a carafe from Starbucks.

Now we all sit around the cheap card table in my apartment with the gold lamp adding harsh lighting to an already tense situation.

We have enough coffee and donuts to stuff our mouths for a week and thus far, that's exactly what we've done.

Conversation has been limited. I've tried and failed to initiate all sorts of bonding moments. I casually laid out a newspaper highlighting the Astros' win over the Cubs last night. Boys like baseball. It's simple. They should all be discussing it ad nauseum. Unfortunately, they don't bite.

I have music playing on my phone, my dad's favorite: George Strait. He should be tapping his foot under the table and swaying side to side. Instead, nothing. His face is stone cold.

Colten keeps glancing over at Ben, shaking his head, and then forcing down another sip of coffee.

Ben, to his credit, isn't necessarily antagonizing them, but he's not being friendly either. Also, I know he doesn't *mean* to be, but he's a force to be reckoned with. His presence takes up a lot of room. I keep trying to get his attention so I can tell him to sink down in his chair a little. I don't know…maybe if he affects worse posture, he won't seem so intimidating?

There's a lot of testosterone and ego in this room. I haven't managed to eat a single bite of my donut, and if I drink any more coffee, I won't be able to sleep for a month.

"So, did you guys see the score from the baseball game last night?" I ask, pointing to the newspaper.

They offer nonverbal grunts.

Right.

Okay, this isn't just awkward—it's full-on cringe-worthy. I want to disappear into thin air.

I truly didn't think this whole feud of theirs would last this long. It's been weeks since Ben and I…you know…on the futon. I blush thinking about it. I can't even look in the direction of said piece of furniture or I'll start sweating.

Since then, we've spent almost every waking moment together. It's pathetic. My heart might still beat in my body, but it's now inscribed with the initials B.R.

Every day, when the clock strikes 5:30 PM, I sprint right out the front door of the library, shouting goodbye to Eli as he heads for his car. I proceed down to Main Street and am at Ben's firm, in his office, kissing his face at exactly 5:35 PM. Sometimes he's on a phone call and sometimes he's in there with Andy, but I don't care. I kiss him no matter what. Andy always covers his eyes and tells us to get a room. Ben always kicks him out soon after.

Then I sit patiently on his couch, reading while he wraps up whatever he has going on. If he has to work late, we eat dinner at his office and then I head home, but more often than not, he drives us back to his house so we can spend the evening together and make dinner at his house. During the drive, his hand usually finds a spot on my body he can torture me with: the nape of my neck, the inside of my thigh, my forearm, hand, *anything*.

We make it into his driveway, he throws that puppy into park, and we race to the front door. Dinner prep is long forgotten as we tear at each other's clothes. *Oh, Chinese food? Sounds great. Take off your pants.* I know we're in the honeymoon phase. I know we won't always be rabid like this, but that's okay. For right now, I'm enjoying it. My clothes, however, are not. I've lost about forty-five buttons, and half my panties are torn!

At the end of the night, I have him drive me home. In fact, I insist upon it. I've yet to stay over at his house. It'd be too easy to give in. Believe me, I've tested his bed, and that mattress is made from some kind of NASA-engineered bullshit. It's out of this world (*heh heh.*) I will not let it tempt me. I'm standing on my own two feet, dammit! Or at least that's what I'm telling myself.

Still, even without giving in to the urge to stay at his house and sleep on his luxurious bed, I know this thing between us is magical and I'm starting to wonder if he's the real deal. The one. The yin to my yang. I'm fairly confident he is, which is why we're here, enduring this hellacious breakfast.

The three of them *have* to get along.

This silent game has got to end.

I tilt my head toward the door.

"Did you see the new deadbolt Ben installed?"

It's the perfect bridge to connect the three of them: they all care about me and my safety! I will talk about deadbolts and locks and security measures for forty days straight if it means they'll actually converse with one another.

"Doesn't really help the fact that the door is made of particle board," Colten grunts.

Ben's eyes narrow and I lean forward to grip his forearm. "I know, Ben hates the door too."

Look! Let's bond over doors! This is fun!

Ben puts his coffee cup down and turns to my dad. "I'd like to know the progress of the investigation concerning the man who held Madison up at gunpoint a few months ago."

Oh god, not this again. He's obsessed, brings it up every chance he gets. Just last week, he made me go through every single detail of that night again as if he was Nancy Drew, looking for some overlooked clue. I'm thinking of buying him an oversized magnifying glass as a joke. I don't think it'd go over well, though.

It's silly that he's this worried about it, and it's partly my fault. I never should have told him I thought someone was following me the other night after work. I was walking to Ben's firm from the library and that feeling overcame me, the same one I felt that night I was held at gunpoint. I could have sworn someone was watching me and it freaked me out, so I told Ben about it as soon I saw him. Now, I regret that. He thinks the same guy was following me, and he wouldn't listen when I tried to convince him it was just the wind playing tricks on me.

He thinks it's something more serious.

Even now, he's in full lawyer mode. I've seen him like this before at his office. I've stumbled in on him while he's on the phone with a client or wrapping up a meeting, and it's like he's Ben the Hard-Ass. Business Ben. I like it. I want Business Ben to bend me over his business desk.

Not the time, Madison.

My dad crosses his arms over his chest and his brows scrunch together to form one thick line. "That's not really your concern."

CHAPTER TWENTY
BEN

Not my concern?

Is he kidding?

I glance over at Madison, and she's ten seconds from crumbling. Her gaze is on her untouched donut. Her hand is shaking as she reaches for her coffee. She tried so hard to get us all here this morning and force us to get along, and none of us is really putting forward much effort. We're all too stubborn. I'm surprised our egos haven't blown the roof off yet.

"Madison *is* my concern," I say, turning to meet her father's gaze head-on.

He wants me to kowtow to him, or better yet, he wants me to fulfill all the expectations he has for me. They want me to be heartless, to use her and leave her. Colten already said I'm not good enough for Madison, and it's clear her father agrees. They both want to be right about me so badly they'd choose it over Madison's happiness. I'd point that out to them now if it wouldn't cause a scene.

Madison jumps to her feet. "Why don't I top off everyone's coffee?"

She's already grabbing cups, but I won't let her take mine. She doesn't need to wait on us hand and foot. "I'll get some in a second. Thank you."

She nods and turns away. I glance back to her father in time to see him exchange a glance with Colten. I have no idea how long they're planning on holding out. A year from now, will it still be like this? Two years?

No. That would tear Madison apart. She deserves better. She deserves to have us try, at least.

So I'll go first.

"Mr. Hart, I'd like to apologize for anything I might have done as a teenager to ruin your perception of me. I'm sure we did some pretty stupid stuff back then and—"

"No apology necessary."

What he means to say is, *I don't accept.*

Fine. Let's all just sit here and make Madison suffer. Pass the fuckin' donuts.

The second half of breakfast goes as dismally as the first. When her dad and brother stand to leave, I hang back, giving Madison space to say goodbye to them without me hovering nearby, but then I'm shocked when her dad tilts his head out past the door.

"Ben, let me talk to you for a second."

Oh good, I bet this is the part where he holds up a shotgun and threatens my life if I don't leave his daughter alone. I prepare for the worst, but at the bottom of the stairs outside, he shoos Colten along and turns to me. His eyes are less hard than they've been all morning. He props his hands on his hips and turns to me. Madison tells me he's a big softy. I'm wondering if that's really the case.

"We don't want Madison to worry. That's why I didn't want to answer your question in there." I instantly bristle. Withholding information from Madison isn't the way to keep her safe. She's not a child. "Madison and you both gave statements about that incident, but it wasn't enough to go on. The perp was wearing a mask. His height and build weren't all that unique, and there was no physical evidence left at the scene when my guys swept it later that night. We've increased the police presence around the library as much as

250

possible, but the fact is, the guy will likely get away with what he did to her."

My gut clenches.

That's the last thing I wanted him to say.

"My fear isn't so much that he'll get away with it, but rather that it'll happen again. What happens next time when I'm not there to intervene?"

My question seems to stump him for a second. "You seem to be taking this relationship with my daughter pretty seriously."

I lift my chin and reply with one word: "Yes."

His eyes narrow as he studies me in an unusually intense manner. It's like he's trying to read my thoughts. Then he shrugs and sort of chuckles—I swear the man *chuckles*—before he turns and unlocks his police cruiser.

That's all.

I guess it's a start.

———

Today is Andy's birthday, the big 3-2. He's having people over to his house later and I know Madison's excited to go. She thinks she has the best gift ever for him. Now that he and Arianna are a couple—believe me, it's all I hear about at work—Madison got them matching bowling league shirts with their names embroidered on the back.

She also ordered some for us, Kevin, and Eli, but she doesn't think I know that. She's pretty bad at keeping secrets.

We're at her apartment, spending the afternoon together like we usually do, and I've just basically broken a hip trying to have sex with her on this damn futon. It was worth every second, mind you, but I'm about done with this place. The second I think she'll actually accept, I'm asking her to move in with me. A part of me knows she wants to give in. That cold shower she's taking right now can't be enjoyable. She's in there hissing under an icy stream.

I'm on my laptop, researching anything I can about her case. I know odds are I won't find anything. I know the incident might have been a one-off thing, a complete coincidence, but I can't seem to squelch the idea burning in my head that Madison might have been targeted on purpose. I got her talking about it again after her dad left this morning, though she hates when I bring it up.

"I can't live in fear my whole life, Ben. Besides, I was probably just being paranoid when I thought someone was following me."

I don't think she was being paranoid at all. If anything, she needs to be more concerned.

Another news article on the Clifton Cove Times website leads me to a dead end. There's nothing. No write-up about the incident. No mention of Madison or a suspect on the loose. It's probably for the best. There's no point in worrying everyone, and there's such little crime in this area of town. I'd understand it if Madison was walking over where Mac and his friends hang out, over near Murphy's. They probably—

My brain stops short on that thought.

It's stupid, really. Just a whim.

Shit. I'm already on my feet, stuffing my phone in my back pocket and finding my keys.

"Hey Madison!"

"Yeah?" she calls from the bathroom.

"I just remembered I've got to go run an errand. Is it okay if I meet you at Andy's party?"

The shower cuts off and a second later, her head pops out of the bathroom. "What do you mean, an errand?"

"It's something for work."

She frowns in disbelief. "Um…okay, I guess. You're definitely lying to me right now, though."

I nod. "Yeah."

"Why?"

Because if I tell you where I'm going, you'll ask me to stay, but I have to try.

"I'll tell you at the party," I say, stepping over to her and kissing her forehead. Then I think better of it and kiss her lips. She's warm and wet. It'd be a better use of my time to push her right back into that shower, but then I remember it only gets freezing cold water and that idea pops like a bubble.

"I'll meet you at Andy's. I won't be late, I swear!"

Ten minutes later, I'm outside Andy's house insisting he get in my car.

He's hanging out the window, shaking his head. "I've got party setup to do, man—streamers to hang, balloons to fill. Arianna wants to give me my birthday present before the party starts and I'm pretty sure it's a blowjob."

His eyebrows dance with the possibility.

"That's cool, man, really. No one wants you to get that birthday blowjob more than me. I just need you to get into the car and help me with this one little thing. I'll have you back here in a jiffy."

His eyes are skeptical. "You've never once used the word jiffy. You're not a 'jiffy' kind of guy."

I lean over and push the door open, forcing his hand.

"You really aren't going to tell me where we're going?" he asks as we start pull out of his neighborhood.

I smile, big and wide. "It's a birthday surprise."

He fully believes me until we cross the highway.

"You aren't taking me to Chuck E. Cheese's, right? Because Arianna already took me and—"

"Shockingly, no."

"Okay, well, you just crossed under the highway." He points out the window for proof. "Did you take a wrong turn?"

I don't reply.

"Are you taking me to that seedy strip club in the bad part of town? Because while I appreciate the gesture, bro, I'm not really looking to spend my birthday at Solid Platinum. That place is haunted."

I turn off the main road and down another side street. My hand is gripping the steering wheel hard enough that my knuckles are turning white. I might be a little nervous. Down another side street, the neon sign for Murphy's glows in the distance. Motorcycles and trucks are parked out front. A few guys smoke near the door. They're probably the ones who "witnessed" my fight with Mac and came to his defense. I swear they're all wearing leather jackets with mean expressions. I can't be certain, but one of them looks as if he's sharpening a knife.

Ben jerks forward in his seat.

"Murphy's?! Seriously?"

He tries to reach over to grab the steering wheel and I fend off his tepid attack.

"Hey! Cool it! I'm about to drive off the road!"

"Good! I'd rather end up in a ditch than in that bar again."

"I have a reason, and it doesn't involve fighting anyone!" I say, holding his arms at bay. "I just want to talk to Mac."

"Talk? There is no talking to Mac! He used to be a normal kid, but now he's an angry psycho, and sorry to say, I know you've been working out a lot, but he's bigger than you." He holds his hands out around his waist. "Just rounder, you know, from all the fast food. C'mon, I'd really prefer to not have my best friend get killed on my birthday."

I pull into the parking lot and turn to him. "I have this idea, and it's not a good one, I'll admit that—"

"All right, I'm glad you see reason. Put 'er in reverse and let's head back to the party. I bet Arianna's all done inflating the balloons which means she can move on to blowing something else."

Instead of doing as he asks, I unlock the doors. Andy reaches over and frantically relocks his like monsters are about to break in. Hell, maybe they are. The guys near the door watched us pull in and park. My SUV doesn't exactly blend in out here. I should have parked down the street or something.

"This is stupid. They're going to kill you and dump your body. I'm going to have to run our damn firm all by myself."

"No they won't. They're not murderers. Just—"

"Look!" Andy shouts, pointing out my window. "The cops are already here arresting someone else! Probably for murder!"

I jerk my attention to where he's pointing and sure enough, three police officers are escorting a guy out the front door in handcuffs. The light's not great out here, so it takes me a second to realize one of the officers is Madison's brother.

Oh good. We can continue what we started this morning, round two of Hart vs. Rosenberg.

"Look, see? That'll be you. If you go in there, you're going to get arrested again. Mark my words."

255

I ignore him and watch as Colten steers the guy toward the waiting police cruiser. I'm wondering if I should wait until Colten's gone before I get out. I don't really want to get into it with him right now, but then I take another look at the guy they're arresting and my attention snags on his shoes.

My breath stops short.

I know those shoes.

I've *seen* those shoes.

I yank my car door open and slam it closed behind me before I fully realize what I'm doing.

Andy's yelling at me to get back in, but my pace only picks up.

"Don't be stupid! What are you doing?!"

This is the guy.

This is Madison's attacker. Those faded red sneakers with the black laces—they're the same pair I described to the police that night.

He's here now, slightly shorter than I remember and younger, a punk making a scene as the police try to haul him toward the cruiser. He kicks and jerks around, calling them every name under the sun and trying to break out of their hold. They're having a hell of a time getting him into the back of the vehicle and I think, *Good, let him cause trouble.* Hell, they should just let him go. I have a bone to pick with him.

Colten sees me walking over and nods his head to the officer beside him, making sure he has control of the situation. Then he breaks off and makes his way toward me, hand outstretched as if to stop me from going any farther.

I realize then I must have murder in my eyes.

"What the hell are you doing here?" he asks brusquely.

256

"That's him," I say, trying to swerve around him. What's my plan? I don't know. Let me get my hands around that guy's neck and we'll see.

Colten sidesteps in front of me and presses his hand to my chest. "Yes, it's him. Don't be stupid."

Don't be stupid?

"I'm not, just—here, let me have your gun for a second."

He laughs and the sound is so shocking that I blink, my rage-filled cloud starting to dissipate.

"Jesus. Remind me not to piss you off," Colten says, shaking his head.

I chuckle, just once, but it feels good. Oh shit. Oh fucking *shit*. I was so close to walking into that bar and doing something stupid. My adrenaline was already pumping. My heart was prepping me for the fight. I wasn't even thinking.

I lean forward, drop my hands to my knees, and laugh. I'm near tears. I think I'm delirious with relief. I really didn't want to have to go in there and face Mac. I had no plan. I sort of hoped he'd feel bad for the whole talking-shit-about-my-mom thing and getting me arrested, bad enough that maybe he'd be willing to give me information about his friend here.

All in all, I was going to end tonight with another black eye, at least.

"So…what are you doing here?" Colten asks again. "I take it you're not just here for a drink."

I stand back up and face him. "Turns out, the same thing you are."

He furrows his brow.

I shrug. "After your dad said there wasn't much hope of solving the case, I thought I'd take matters into my own hands. So you got him?"

Colten nods. "We've been looking into people who might have had a motive for hurting Madison. Turns out, I arrested this guy's brother a year ago on a grand theft auto charge." He tilts his head toward the cruiser. "He thought he'd get revenge by scaring Madison, but then he bragged about it to some friends, friends who had no problem throwing him under the bus when we pushed them on it. Pretty stupid if you ask me."

Any ill will I might have harbored toward Colten is gone, just like that, with the snap of a finger. He just made sure Madison won't get hurt again. He's arresting the guy. I kind of want to high-five him, but I don't get the feeling that we're there yet.

"If you'd shown up and we weren't here," Colten continues, eyes narrowing on me. "What were you going to do? Just march in there and—what? Shout out to the bar and ask if anyone's held up a girl at gunpoint lately?"

I smirk. "Basically."

He laughs then. "Idiot."

I shrug. "I love her. What would you do if you were me?"

His laughter dies suddenly and, much the way his dad looked at me outside her apartment, Colten assesses me like he doesn't quite recognize me.

Then he nods, a look of resigned understanding on his face. "Yeah. I guess I'd have done the same thing."

His partner calls out to him, asking how long he'll be. Colten holds up his hand before turning back to me.

"Listen, about the other day at your office…the stuff I said to you…"

I shake my head. "Don't worry about it."

I know all the wrongs haven't been rewritten for us. We still have a long way to go, but I don't need him to apologize for looking out for Madison. If I had a sister, I know I'd act the same way.

I hold out my hand and he shakes it. Before he walks away, I continue, "Hey, I'm not sure what time your shift ends, but Andy's birthday is tonight. He's having a few people over to his house for a party."

Meanwhile, said birthday boy is still sitting in my car, safe and sound with the doors locked. When we look over, he waves excitedly.

Colten nods, a ghost of a smile on his lips. "Yeah, okay. I'll see. This'll take a while."

———

"Do you want me to tell everyone you beat the guy up and then the police had to pull you off him?"

"No."

"Okay. I'll just say you had a knife and you were waving it around like a wild man."

"Andy."

"You're right—no weapons. Instead, you unlaced your shoes and tied his hands behind his back with the laces. The police commended you for your hard work. Hometown hero, they called you. On Monday, you're being presented with a medal."

We're in my car, at DQ, drinking milkshakes. Andy's party has already started, but he said he was so "shaken up" from the events of the last hour that he needed to cool off. I remind him that we didn't actually do anything.

"We were close to doing something, and that fear was real, my friend. I was worried I was going to have a little accident and ruin your nice leather seat here. You going to finish that?" he asks, grabbing for my half-finished milkshake.

"No."

"Cool."

"Happy birthday," I say with a smile.

"Thanks. If it's okay with you, I'm going to tell Arianna I helped the police detain him. She beat me at foosball the other day and I'm still trying to regain some ground in the manly man department."

I smirk, leaning back against the headrest. "Andy, have you ever thought that maybe you're not a manly man? You're wearing a pink gingham shirt."

He looks down and runs his hand across the button-down. "Arianna says it brings out my eyes."

His eyes are brown. I don't tell him she's full of it.

"Ready to go to your party?"

"Give me another ten," he says, sucking down the frozen chocolate treat. "I want to make an entrance. Think word will have spread about our good deed yet? I really want people to clap when I walk in."

I don't have the heart to burst his bubble.

If pressed, I'll lie and tell Arianna he saved the day. It is his birthday after all.

CHAPTER TWENTY-ONE
MADISON

Ben lied.

First, when he wouldn't tell me where he was going. Second, when he told me he'd be on time for this party.

I've been at Andy's house for half an hour now and Ben still hasn't showed. Andy isn't here either.

"Bet they went to a strip club," someone jokes. A group of people snicker near the drink table and I pour myself an extra inch of wine before heading right back to where Kevin and Eli are sitting with Arianna.

She's madder than I am. Apparently, Andy just disappeared too. We have no idea where they ran off to.

"I planned this whole freaking party for him and then he bails? I'm about to pop all these balloons and kick everyone out."

I hand her the extra glass of wine I poured. Honestly, I was going to double-fist it, but she needs it more than I do.

"If it helps, you look really pretty."

She's wearing a leather miniskirt. Combined with her short blonde hair, she looks like a kickass Tinkerbell.

She offers a small smile as she accepts the wine. "Thanks."

There are a ton of people here, cool kids, people I recognize from around town, and people who would have paid me absolutely no attention before I started dating Ben. It's not like we've announced our relationship on a billboard or anything, but we didn't have to. Ben is...*Ben*. Everything he does is newsworthy in this town, and I suppose I'm just as intriguing now too.

"…what designer is she wearing…"

Ah, yes, the illustrious TJ Maxx.

"…do you think she got those shoes in Paris…"

I've had them for three years. I honestly think they just appeared in the back of my closet one day.

"…she really is pretty, but maybe it's just the makeup? Do you think she's had some work done…"

Do people not realize their voices carry?!

I get it, though. They're all curious about how the dopey librarian won over the unattainable king of Clifton Cove.

When I find out, I'll be sure to let them know.

I take another hefty sip of wine as a cute guy cuts through the crowd and makes his way over to us. His shaggy blond hair makes him boyishly handsome. I don't recognize him immediately, which is rare for Clifton Cove.

"Hey sis, is the beer in the fridge free game or—"

His question is cut off by the tell-tale sound of glass shattering somewhere in the house.

Arianna groans and jumps to her feet, running toward the noise. I hear her murmuring obscenities under her breath as she goes. Andy better get here soon or she's going to lose it.

I meet her brother's gaze and shrug, holding back a laugh. This whole night is truly a bust. Where the hell are those guys?

"Guess that's a no on the beer," her brother says, scratching the back of his head.

I stand up, taking pity on the guy. "C'mon, there are some coolers out back—I'm pretty sure that's where the beer is."

He holds open the door to the patio and I point him in the right direction. I'm about to go back inside when his hand juts out in greeting. "I'm Pete, by the way."

I smile. "Madison."

He nods and reaches for a beer. "Want one? I saw you double-fisting earlier."

"Oh, yeah, about that…"

I could have sworn no one was watching me.

He laughs and breaks the awkward moment. "I'm kidding."

Now that he has his beer, he should leave me alone, but he doesn't. I'm wearing the jeans from my "bad girl" day at the bowling alley. They hug my butt. I had a cardigan on over my silky white tank top, but with all the people crammed inside, I got hot. Now, I feel like I should probably run back and get it.

I'm beginning to realize that the superhero mantra "With great power comes great responsibility" might apply to sex appeal too. We've hit the crucial point in our conversation where I either need to turn and head back to Eli and Kevin or somehow work in that I have a boyfriend. It feels very much like Pete is hitting on me, and when he not so subtly checks me out, that point is made even more clear.

No. Don't be silly.

Not every man wants you. Just Ben. Just Ben who is now lying to you and disappearing into the night…

With that thought, I turn back to Pete and smile.

"So, do you live around here?"

Apparently, he's Arianna's younger brother and he's visiting from Dallas. He's just down for the weekend, and we talk about the places he should visit while he's in town.

"You've been to the beach already, right?"

He laughs. "Yeah, you know, Clifton Cove being a beach town and all…"

I wave away his sarcasm. "Right, okay. Ignore that suggestion. There's a cool farmers market on Saturday mornings. This time of year, I bet they have some good produce."

He looks at me like he doesn't quite understand what I'm saying.

"How old are you?" I ask.

He grins. "22."

I nod. "Right. Okay, so no farmers market. Probably forget about the train museum too. Unless—wait, are you into that kind of thing?"

His eyes narrow playfully. "Y'know, not really. It's weird, but I'm not a big train guy."

I chuckle. "Right, well, probably just stick to the beach then. Women in bikinis, sun, waves—you can't go wrong."

"Do *you* like going to the beach?" he asks, taking a step closer.

WHOA.

This dude wants to see me in a bikini!

I've officially crossed into the red zone. I feel bad now. *Am I cheating?! Is this cheating!?*

I open my mouth to quickly blurt out an apology followed by *I have a boyfriend whom I very much love please stop looking at me like you want to kiss me because I will throw my drink in your face*, but I never get the chance.

There's a commotion near the front door. People are yelling, "Surprise!", which is odd, because this is definitely not a surprise party. I think people got confused when they arrived and Andy wasn't here.

Through the large back window, I watch as Andy steps into the living room and laps up the attention, more than happy to have everyone focused on him.

"No way! Guys, I'm totally shocked!" he shouts, accepting hugs and felicitations.

Apparently, he's also forgotten this isn't a surprise party.

I stand rooted to my spot as Ben walks through the door behind him. If everyone rushed in to greet Andy, they do the opposite for Ben. The crowd parts and stares. The special guest has arrived.

It's like he's stealing the spotlight without even trying. It's his own damn fault, really. He shouldn't wear that black shirt. With his brown hair and tan skin, it's just too much. Jesus, wear pink or purple or just go without clothes altogether. At least then we'd all pass out and be put out of our misery.

Ben nods to a few friends but brushes past the people who step into his path, trying to stop him for conversations. His eyes are sweeping the room, looking, searching. My heart thunders in my chest and I nearly use Pete to block myself from his view, but it wouldn't do any good. This is my life. Ben is my boyfriend. I'll just have to get used to the overwhelming emotional grenade he sets off inside me by simply walking into a room.

When it's clear that I'm not in the living room, he turns for the kitchen then pauses and glances out the window. The invisible rope tied between us pulls taut when he glances my way. We're half a back yard apart and it feels like he just ran a finger down my spine.

"Do you know him?" Pete asks, turning to look between Ben and me.

I forget to answer him as Ben winds his way through the party and steps outside.

I forget to blink. I don't think I've taken a breath since he walked in the front door.

He walks straight to me, confidently, boldly, and bends low, kissing my cheek, whispering next to my ear. "Sorry I'm late."

I squeeze my eyes closed and nod.

When he steps back, it's only far enough for him to loop his arm around my waist and tug me close.

"I'm mad," I say quietly.

He glances at me. "Yeah?"

I have a frog in my throat that prevents me from continuing, so I nod. Yes, mad. Why again…? Ben's shirt is so black and his arm is so strong.

"Because I lied to you?" he offers.

YES.

I jerk my gaze to his amber eyes and he can't hide his smile. He's not even pretending to look worried about my supposed anger.

"I'll tell you all about it."

Then his gaze flicks to my mouth and I think he wants to kiss me, but Pete's still standing there, staring at us. "So, I take it you're not single?" he asks, laughing good-naturedly.

Ben arcs an eyebrow at me as if to ask, *Well?*

"No," I say, keeping my attention on him. "I'm not."

Pete shrugs. "Figures."

When he walks away, Ben turns and steps in front of me, pushing me back. The garage is behind us. The door is closed, but Ben clearly isn't going to let that stop him. People are definitely watching us. If I looked up, I'd find faces pressed to the windowpanes in curiosity, noses flattened like pigs.

"Where are we going?" I ask nervously.

He reaches behind me to open the door and then he pushes me backward. "Step up. There's a stair."

He mostly lifts me up and into the cold, dark space.

A light flickers on and the door closes behind him. There's a car parked inside and a bike leaning against the wall beside some tools.

Our footsteps echo against the concrete floor as he pushes me deeper inside.

"I'd like to apologize for my absence," he says, his finger looping through my jeans so he can pull me close.

"Where'd you go?" I ask, arms crossing over my chest.

The skin around his eyes crinkles, but he doesn't smile. "I'll tell you after you say you forgive me."

I shake my head and lift my chin. "No."

He hums and reaches for my silky tank top, twisting the material in his hand. "It appears we're at a stalemate."

"Guess so. Maybe I should go back out there and chat with Arianna's brother."

I don't mean the threat. There's not enough heat behind it. He glances down to the floor, smiles, and then his eyes meet mine again. He's not jealous. He's amused. He thinks I'm cute. He wants to bop me on the tip of my nose.

"That's it, huh? Now that I've turned you into the real Madison—the *bad* Madison—you're just going to up and leave me?"

I have to bite down on my smile. I shrug and look away. I even manage to look at my nails as if I'm bored. It's only half convincing at best.

I arch a brow. "Maybe so. I'm a hot commodity now, Ben. That guy wanted to take me to the beach. I think he was picturing me in a bikini."

He steps forward and grips my waist, brushing his hands up under my tank top. His thumb drags across my bare navel. My stomach dips in anticipation and there's no fooling him now. He just revved my engine and he knows it.

"Are you going to tell him about all the bad things you like to do?" he asks, dipping low and whispering the next words against the shell of my ear. "Taking your panties off at parties? Leaving them behind for anyone to find…"

If I were standing in front of glass, my breath would fog it twice over.

He pops me up onto the workbench behind me. I'm blinking over and over, trying to keep up. How does he do it? Seduce me? Slay me? There's no point in even trying to fight it.

"Speaking of bad things," I say, wrapping my arms around his neck as he slowly pushes his hands higher. Big, rough palms glide across my skin. When he grazes the edge of my bra, I shudder and lose my train of thought.

"Madison," he says, urging me to continue.

Huh? What day is it?

He kisses the edge of my mouth and then pulls back, waiting for me to continue.

"Right, yes. I was just going to say that I haven't done anything bad in weeks, really, not since the skinny dipping…"

"So you want to make up for it?"

He gets me. We're soul mates.

I reach down for his jeans as I ask, "How long do you think we have before Andy realizes we're gone?"

"Did you see him when we walked in? He's in heaven. Everyone wants to talk to him. He'll be busy all night."

So this is happening then—dirty garage sex. I imagine what I'll look like after: oil-smudged face, hair covered in sawdust. Maybe we'll get crafty and use the bicycle seat. I'm imagining that exact scenario just as Ben finds the zipper on my jeans. We can't strip down all the way. There's no time. We're rushing. His hand brushes past the hem of my panties and my stomach dips. I unbutton his jeans and stroke his length inside his briefs. He's silky smooth and rock hard.

Then his finger slides into me and it's my undoing. I cry out and his mouth comes down hard on mine in a passionate kiss. It's hot, mesmerizing, *sensual*. He's so good, so giving. And when he tugs me to the edge of the workbench and thrusts into me moments later, his skill is only further demonstrated. Each hard thrust in and each slow drag out brings me closer...and closer. His finger circles around and around and my nails leave half-moons on his shoulders. We're in a frenzy. My moans and gasps would be heard through the entire party if his mouth wasn't silencing me.

We're getting so close to falling apart—*together*. Pleasure builds inside me just as he buries himself to the hilt, rolling his hips and when he moans deep against my lips, I moan too, coming with him. Completely lost.

The last wave of pleasure is still wracking through me right before a hand starts pounding against the garage door.

"Is someone in here?" a voice calls out.

Ben and I freeze. It's Arianna.

Shit!

She turns the door handle and I shove Ben away from me. We fly apart. By the time she walks in, my pants are zipped up and I'm holding a power tool up in the air while striking a pose that says I definitely know what I'm doing: hand on hip, hip thrust to the side, legs spread apart.

"Yup, so that's how you change a tire," I say coolly, pressing the trigger for emphasis.

The drill whirs to life and I yelp and drop it.

"What the hell are you two doing in here?"

She's laughing, but she shouldn't be.

"Tire stuff."

We should have hung a sock on the door or something. Ben would still be inside me at this very moment if only we'd planned ahead.

"The real question is, what are *you* doing here?" I ask, turning to her and giving her my most accusatory glare. I point a finger too, for emphasis.

It doesn't work. She laughs and shakes her head, walking over to open the spare fridge.

"We needed more soda."

Ben steps forward and takes the cases from her. "Here, I got it."

Then he just walks out! With the soda! Without me!

What about pounding me on top of Andy's bicycle?! I thought we'd do that next!

"So you really held out there for a while, huh?" Arianna taunts as we walk back into the house side by side.

"He's very convincing!" I cry. "Have you seen his hands? They were touching my *boobs*. What did you want me to do?"

She throws her arm over my shoulder as she leads me toward the bathroom so I can clean myself up a little. When I'm finished, we commiserate together on our way to the kitchen. Apparently, Andy hasn't told her why they were late either, but as it turns out, we're about to get the full story.

270

"Babe, I've been looking for you everywhere!" Andy cries as soon as he spots Arianna and me chatting in the kitchen. He sounds relieved and immediately walks up for a kiss, but she stiff-arms him.

"Uh huh. I've just been here," Arianna continues, "at *your* party, talking to *your* guests."

Andy presses his hands together in prayer. His brows are pleading with her to understand. "Arianna, sweet Arianna—don't you know what I was doing?" He points to me suddenly and theatrically. "I was saving Madison from certain doom! Tell them, Ben!" he says, eyes wide, tone dramatic. "Tell them what we were doing!"

Ben's behind him now, holding up two drinks. I left mine in the garage so I happily accept his spare as he comes around to pass it off and tug me against him. Apparently, Ben's into PDA. I'm all too happy to oblige. His finger hooks in my belt loop just as Andy prods him again.

"Ben! Help me out here, man!"

I glance up to him. "You were saving me from certain doom, huh?"

He shakes his head. "It wasn't like that."

"Don't listen to him. He's being modest! Ben was going to confront hardened criminals to get facts about that guy who nearly shot you a few months ago, Madison!" He's talking animatedly now, his hands flying everywhere.

"I don't think he was going to shoot me—"

My interruption goes ignored as Andy continues, "Arianna, Ben dragged me out of this house and forced me to participate in this wild mission! I wanted to be here with you! I can't stand to be away from you for a single second. You know that."

Oh my god. I can barely believe what I'm hearing. I want to burst out laughing, but when I glance over, Arianna's

271

eyes are melting pools of love. Wow. She's buying this. They're perfect for each other.

I look up at Ben, tone hard and unaffected. "What really happened?"

He sips his drink and shrugs. "I wanted to go see if anyone at Murphy's had information about the incident. Turns out, there was no need. Your brother had already found the guy."

I nearly drop my drink. "What? Are you serious?"

He tightens his grip on me. "They arrested him."

It's a staggering feeling, truly. I'm thrust right back to that night, one I've tried hard to pretend never happened. In some ways, my life continued on as normal. I didn't stop walking home from the library. I brushed aside my family's concerns on the matter, but sometimes, in bed at night, I'd still find myself YouTubing self-defense moves. I bought a can of pepper spray off Amazon and connected it to my keys. I looked over my shoulder more often than I did before, always aware that the person who attacked me might have the urge to do it again.

In some ways, I felt silly and paranoid. I didn't want to wave the victim card and make the whole thing seem more dramatic than it was. I didn't get hurt. He didn't do anything to me, *really*. Now, I realize I was completely deluding myself. He did hurt me. Just because that trigger wasn't pulled doesn't mean his attack didn't affect me. Now, I realize just how much relief comes with the knowledge that they caught him.

I need to sit down.

I turn for the dining room behind the kitchen and pull out a chair. Ben follows, concerned. I wave him off as I take a seat, unsure what words will come out if I speak.

"They'll probably have you go down to the station."

I nod, eyes focused on the woodgrain of the table.

"I'll go with you."

"Okay."

"Madison? What's wrong?"

"I'm relieved. I just don't think I want to go down there. I don't want to have to see him."

Ben sits down in the chair beside mine, leans over, and takes my hands. "He won't hurt you again."

I sit quietly for a few moments, working through all the conflicting emotions starting to bubble up inside me. "Is it strange that I kind of feel bad for him?"

"What do you mean?"

"I don't know. I don't want to go down there and identify him and put him in jail. I don't want to be the reason he's there."

"He did something wrong. You're in no way to blame."

To Ben, this is black and white.

"Right, but why'd he do it? Do we know yet? Maybe he really needed money. Maybe he was—"

"Colten arrested his brother last year. Apparently, this guy wanted to get revenge. You were an easy target."

"Oh…"

I don't have to look over to know his eyebrows are furrowed, his mouth tugged in a hard line. "You still feel guilty, don't you? Why?"

"It's hard to explain."

He murmurs under his breath and I know I'm making him angry. It's a hard concept to explain to someone.

Suddenly, he stands, taking me with him. "Let's go down to the station now. I bet Colten's still there."

"What about Andy's party?"

When we look over, Andy and Arianna are hardcore making out against the kitchen island. Andy is moaning against her mouth. Cups are clattering to the floor behind them.

"Baby, I'm so sorry I upset you," he says hungrily.

Arianna is fisting his shirt.

Oh jeez. I cover my eyes.

They're about to do it right there, in the middle of the party. I really hope her brother is still in the back yard.

Ben laughs. "Yeah, they won't miss us. C'mon."

I don't fully understand Ben's motives as we arrive at the police station and an officer directs us back to Colten's desk. We find my brother sitting there with a day's worth of stubble and three cups of coffee spread out across a mountain of paperwork. He looks exhausted.

"Madison," he says, relieved when he glances up and sees us approaching. "I was just about to call you."

I nod and glance over at Ben. *What are we doing here?* I don't want to see the guy. I definitely don't want to have to speak to him or anything. I know that makes me a wimp, but I'd rather go my entire life without having to confront him.

"I told Madison what happened," Ben explains to Colten. "And I think she should see this guy's criminal history."

My stomach drops.

"What? Why?" I ask.

"Because you feel guilty that he'll be put away for this one thing he did to you, like it's not bad enough, but what if that's not all he's done?"

Colten snorts and shakes his head. "Give me a second."

He types something on his computer, clicks around, types some more, and then swivels his monitor so we can see it. Scrolling fast, it still takes him a while to make it through this guy's entire criminal history. Random words jump out at me: grand larceny, second degree felony, aggravated assault and battery.

Good lord.

It's hard to catch my breath.

I really thought he wouldn't hurt me! I really thought he had just fallen on hard times or…Jesus! I'm so naive!

What if Ben hadn't been there?!

"Feel better now?" Colten asks. "This guy's been causing trouble for years, Maddie. You don't have to feel bad. Hell, we've had a warrant out for his arrest for the last few months, just haven't been able to track him down. The bartender at Murphy's tipped us off. If he hadn't, your guy would still probably be out there."

I'm fired up. Any guilt I felt before has now been set to flames. The ashes have formed a war paint I'll use beneath my eyes.

"Where is he?" I ask, determined. "I'm going to punch him! How dare he put a gun to my head?!"

Colten smiles. "He's back in the holding cell."

I cross my arms. "Great, well you just go get him so I can give him a piece of my mind."

Ben and Colten exchange an amused look. "Yeah, that's not really how it works."

"Well it does now. Where are your keys? I'll do it myself."

Colten turns back to Ben. "You got this?"

"Yeah. We'll be back when you need us. Tomorrow?"

"Yeah, that'd be great."

They're talking and blabbering on, meanwhile I'm searching high and low on Colten's desk for his keys. I shuffle papers. *Where does he keep the damn things? On his holster? I'll just take that too. Oh, look, there's his gun—even better.*

Big hands wrap around my waist and I'm hauled up and over Ben's shoulder like a sack of potatoes.

"Hey! Wait! No!"

"See ya, Colt."

"Bye, Ben."

"Oh, okay, I see, you two are best friends now?" I ask, dangling upside down. Ben's beautiful butt is right in front of my face. I poke it to be sure he's listening to me. "Hey, you, put me down."

He doesn't put me down.

He carries me right to his car and plops me down on the seat. Then he buckles me in nice and safe.

"I hate you."

He bends low to give me a kiss. "I love you. Should we go back to the party now?"

CHAPTER TWENTY-TWO
BEN

Two months later

Today's a big day for me.

A day I've been counting down to with mixed emotions.

A day I'm not sure Madison is aware of.

This morning, she seemed perfectly happy. We ate first and second breakfast in my bed. I checked work emails on my laptop, propped up against pillows while she watched an episode of a PBS miniseries. She records a bunch of stuff at my house since she doesn't have a TV at her apartment. It's all stuff I'd never even heard of before her: *Downton Abbey*, *Poldark*. If it doesn't take place at least a hundred years ago, she's not into it. I watched a little of the show this morning, but mostly I watched her watching it. She smiled whenever the handsome guy walked on screen. She really has a thing for men in old-timey outfits.

She caught me staring and held up her mug, waving it as if to say, *Refill this for me, would you?*

When I refused to get out of the warm bed, she just stole mine, sipping it slowly as she leaned against my chest. When I tried to get it back, she tsked and pulled it out of my reach. So, I guess things are getting pretty comfortable with us. She's been staying over a few nights a week, when I can persuade her. I had to start slow, compromising with just one night. That slowly morphed into two, then three. I can't believe she ever wants to sleep in that apartment on that futon—which, by the way, is broken now. We had sex on it last weekend and one of the screws came loose. Seconds into her losing herself to a toe-curling orgasm, we both tumbled to the ground in a heap of writhing, naked limbs. I found the screw, but I lied and said I didn't. It's part of my master plan to get her to move in with me. On my way out that day, I also stole her coffee pot. The less amenities she has, the sooner she'll come crawling to me, begging to move in. It's a pretty solid plan, if you ask me.

After her show ended this morning, we finally decided to get out of bed, but then I caught a little glimpse of her butt sticking out of her pajama shorts. Just one peek at her curves and I yanked her right back down, throwing the covers over us so there was no possible hope for her to escape.

"We'll be late!" she protested as I slid down her body, taking her shorts and panties off on my descent.

Turns out, she was wrong. I can be very efficient when I need to be.

Now, we're up at the library in the storage room grabbing a few last-minute things for story time.

Madison's partially hidden behind a row of boxes, digging for a stuffed penguin she says the kids will love, when I finally announce why today is so important.

"This is my last day volunteering here."

"I can't hear you."

I smirk. It's dead quiet in this room. She heard me just fine.

"Madison…"

She pokes her head around the edge of the box and narrows her eyes. "What?"

"I've completed all my mandated hours."

"Oh." She looks down at the floor. "That's great, Ben."

"You sound sad."

Her bright green eyes jump back to me. "I do? How's this?" She forces a smile and raises her voice a few octaves with her second try. *"That's great, Ben!"*

"Madison...you knew this was coming. You've been signing off on my volunteer hours every week."

"I know, but..." Her finger traces the edge of the box. Guilt laces her next few words. "I've been shaving off hours here and there as a way to keep you here longer." I already know this. I look at the form she signs and it's blatantly obvious. I should have finished volunteering over a month ago. "I was even thinking of telling Judge Mathers I didn't think you had really reformed yourself. I was going to ask that another 100 hours be added to your sentence."

She's crazy. I love her.

I tilt my head, studying her. She has that damn stuffed penguin in her hand now. She's toying with it, flapping its wings. She looks so sad, and my heart breaks a little.

"Eli is going to take over for me, right? And he's probably much better at this stuff than I am. Most of the time I just linger in the back of the room while you lead everything."

"Yeah, but Eli doesn't make out with me in here before the toddlers show up."

At this, her bottom lip juts out.

"Well, if you ask him, I bet he would," I say, deadpan. "He seems like an understanding guy."

She throws her hands up in annoyance. The penguin hits the ceiling. "Okay, fine. If you must know, it just felt like this was one reason you had to spend time with me every week. I knew no matter what, you'd have to show up here on Saturdays to volunteer with me."

"Right, but we're dating now. I see you nearly every day."

"Yeah, but we're probably only together because I'm your hot volunteer coordinator. You get off on the fact that it's forbidden."

"It is in no way forbidden for me to date you."

"Then if it isn't that, it's the hot librarian thing. Look at me! I'm sex on a stick!"

She's wearing a sunflower yellow dress. No makeup. Her rich brown hair is nothing short of wild.

She's fucking gorgeous.

I decide to push something I've been tiptoeing around for weeks.

"You're right. It's not enough, what we have right now. I want more."

Her eyes light up. "So you'll keep volunteering here?"

No. I need to carve out some time on Saturday mornings to get stuff done at the office, but it should work out well. I'll work while she's here, doing story time, then I'll swing by to pick her up when I'm done. We'll spend our afternoons at the park, making out, scarring the children.

"Move in with me." I say it solidly. It's like I've just plucked up all her stuff and dumped it in my house then wiped my hands clean.

"Move in with you," she repeats with no inflection.

"Yes."

Her eyes narrow shrewdly. "And what would that entail, exactly?"

"Oh, a key to the place, TV privileges, half the bed— maybe a little less 'cause you know I get cold at night. Some drawers in the closet, I don't know, however many you want. You can rearrange the kitchen, too, if you don't like how everything is set up. It definitely could use a woman's touch."

She rears back like she's offended. "So you're saying my place is in the kitchen?"

"This feels like a trick question."

She shrugs and drops the act. "You're right. I'm stalling. Moving in is a big deal. I'll get mail with my name on it at your house."

Seems trivial…

"Sure."

She's using her hands now as if trying to outline a complicated equation. "Items I purchase online will show up at your door. For me. There."

"Yes, that's how the postal system works."

She shakes her head in disbelief. "Wild."

I tilt my head, amused. "Is it just about the mail? 'Cause you could just get a PO box if a change of address is freaking you out this much."

"I don't know…probably 50% about the mail and 50% about how this is a really big step in our relationship."

"Seems completely reasonable. Do you want me to stop the mailman today and see if he can walk us through the procedure? Change of address, that sort of thing?"

"What?!" Her eyes are huge. "Oh my god, you can't just initiate something like that. I haven't even said yes. No, don't—and don't smile at me like you think I'm funny."

She's striding toward me now, finger wagging.

"I'm not."

"You're grinning. It's ear to ear. Any bigger and your cheeks will split."

"I'd wipe it away if I could."

Truly, I can't.

She's right in front of me now, hands on hips. "Try."

"There. Is it gone?"

"No, and now with your dimple, I'm going to faint. I've got to cover it up. There." Her hand covers my right cheek. "You're not even remotely as handsome as you were just a second ago."

I stare down at her big green eyes and wonder how I managed to find such a weirdo to fall in love with. "The children are waiting for us," I say, reminding us both.

"Is it already time to start?"

"Yes."

Her eyes rove down my outfit. Ah yes, she wasn't going to let me off easy on my last day.

"I feel so bad forcing you into this Darcy costume again. Believe me, I don't like seeing you in it any more than you like wearing it."

I'd believe her if her eyes weren't gleaming. "You organize the story time," I point out. "You rented the costume."

"No, no," she says, shaking her head, letting her fingers drag along the buttons on the shirt. She shivers as if just the sight of them turns her on. "It's done by the city council." She waves a hand in the air. "Years in advance."

"Wow. I had no idea it was such a serious undertaking."

I reach up to wrap my hands around her neck and tilt her head back. I want a good look at her. I want those lips against mine. There are screaming toddlers in the multipurpose room, but in here, it's just us.

"Madison, move in with me," I say, staring at her mouth.

I love when she wets her bottom lip in anticipation. She knows I want to kiss her, but I'm holding back. I need an answer first.

"Fine, if only because I know you stole my coffee pot and I'd like it back."

"Done. Today, after story time, we'll thank Mrs. Allen for taking you in during your time of need and then we'll pack up your stuff. I'll make you a cup of coffee as soon as we get to my place."

"I'll miss that apartment, truly."

I laugh. "It has no hot water, no windows. Last week you called me in the middle of the night because you found a rat under the futon."

She gags at the memory then catches herself and smooths out her face. She's the picture of serenity as she continues, "Yes. Obviously, it had its faults, but it's where I became a woman."

"Oh?"

"Yes. I blossomed into the mature adult you now see standing before you, flapping my wings of independence, owning my worth and conquering the world."

"Inspiring, truly."

"Thank you. Now that I've said all that, I'd really like to move in with you and please still accept me—and do you think we can get my stuff packed in an hour? I haven't even taken my clothes out of the duffle bags because there's a weird smell in that place and I'm worried it's contagious." She lifts her forearm to my nose. "Here, smell. I feel like it sticks to me even after I leave."

I sniff. "You smell like my body wash."

She blushes.

I can't help but grin as I bring her closer. "God you're so in love with me. It's written all over your face. You wanted to use me to make yourself into a bad girl, and now what? You're stuck with me, Hart."

"Ugh. You're squeezing me. I can't breathe."

"There. Better?"

"You just tightened your hold. I'm going to die."

"Say you love me and I'll let you go."

"I love you!" she groans, fake gasping for breath.

I grin and then plant one on her before we start our very last story time together.

EPILOGUE
MADISON

Three years later

A week shy of our first wedding anniversary, Ben surprised me with a trip. No details, no packing list, he just told me to be prepared for a long flight. After a little needling on my part, I did eventually get him to admit I wouldn't need a big winter coat or anything. I think his exact words were: "Just pack bikinis."

Oddly enough, I tacked on a few other items too: sundresses and sandals and big floppy hats. I had four paperbacks, but Ben thought that was excessive, so I compromised by bringing three paperbacks plus my Kindle. A girl has to be prepared.

He did a good job of keeping the secret from me. Even at the airport, he kept me from looking too closely at any of the monitors by pushing me along. When we were on the flight, he covered my ears when the pilot announced our final destination. I knew where I wanted him to take me, but I didn't dare hope that was where we were actually headed.

I forced myself to be practical. Maybe we were going to visit London or Paris. Those places are amazing! Great! Everyone says so! Still, I had my sights set on Vernazza, one of the five seaside villages in the Cinque Terre region of Italy, which Eli made me swear I'd visit at least once in my life. I wanted it to be our final destination so badly, I could hardly believe it when we actually stepped off the plane in

Rome with the sun blazing overhead and tourists everywhere.

I looked to Ben, mouth agape. "Are you serious? Are we really going to Vernazza?"

He looked at me like I was insane. "Don't you remember when you got your tattoo? How you rambled on about me taking you here?"

I kissed him, hard. "Yes, but that was all a lie! A *dream*! I was just rambling because I was scared of how much the tattoo was going to hurt. I didn't think you were actually *listening* to me."

Turns out, he was.

From Rome, we caught train after train, each one a little smaller than the last. My excitement grew. I don't think there was a single person in our path that I didn't smile at or try to drag into a conversation.

"We're going to Vernazza!" I said to the vendor who sold me a soda at the airport.

"Have you heard of Vernazza?! We're headed there now!" I said to the train attendant checking tickets.

"Hi! Where are you headed? We're going to Vernazza!" I said to the elderly woman sitting across from us on the second leg of our journey. She didn't speak a word of English, but I could tell she was happy for me. Maybe. She did get up and switch seats awfully quickly. Probably just didn't want me to see how jealous she was.

I never thought we'd actually arrive. The journey isn't for the faint of heart. It felt like we'd been traveling for seven days and seven nights before I finally got my first view of the ocean. I slapped my hand against Ben's chest.

"The ocean! Ben! THE OCEAN!"

You would have thought Clifton Cove was a mountain town with the way I droned on. It's like I'd never laid eyes on a wave before.

When the small regional train pulled up to our station and we rolled our suitcases out, I cried upon first seeing the village. Ben assumed it was mostly due to my hormones. I'm right in the middle of my second trimester and if I so much as see a sappy commercial, I cry for a solid fifteen minutes.

He was wrong, though—Vernazza's beauty would have made me cry with or without this baby girl in my belly.

"I can't believe I'm here. I CAN'T BELIEVE I'M HERE!" I repeated over and over again as we made our way down the cobblestone lane.

Ben had searched high and low for the bed and breakfast I'd mentioned to the tattoo artist.

"It wasn't easy," he said. "It's not as if these places have websites or anything. Everything here is a little old school. I only found the phone number after hounding Eli about it."

He found it, though, and it was just as I imagined. Small. Quaint. Tucked right in the heart of Vernazza's main town square. The view was split between the rolling waves hitting the breakers and the countryside sloping up behind the stacked buildings, each one a different pastel shade: blue, yellow, red, orange. Their facades were cracked and old, but their age only enhanced the beauty of the square. I wanted to cry again, but I kept it together.

Il Mare was painted on the plaster above the door.

When we strolled inside, a young woman with dark brown hair stood behind the main desk, arguing with the tall man beside her.

"Julianna loves kittens. You have to let her keep it! You'll crush her if you insist otherwise."

"She already has a cat. She doesn't need another."

"But it's Mopsie's child!"

He threw his hands up, defeated. "*Child*. Georgie, these are cats you're talking about!"

Just then, a large white cat hopped up onto the desk, wagging its tail tauntingly. The woman—Georgie, it seemed—pointed to it. "See, he knows we're talking about him." She reached out to pet him lovingly. "Don't worry, Mopsie, I won't let this old bugger win."

The woman's opponent shook his head before reaching down to whisper something in her ear. Her cheeks went bright red and she pressed her hand against his chest just as her gaze finally caught on us.

"Oh! Guests! Sorry about that," she said, pushing him aside and straightening her dress.

She was beautiful. They both were. Eli had described them perfectly, even down to their English accents.

"Luca, hurry—go get their bags. They look exhausted."

I felt a little self-conscious then. I probably did look a little haggard.

They helped us check in and chatted with us about the village and everything we had to see and eat while we were there. The following evening, we joined them for dinner out in the square, exchanging stories about Clifton Cove and how it compared to Vernazza.

"It sounds a bit similar," Georgie said, nodding. "Beachy town with loads of rich people. God, everyone here is pretty much just fancy Brits wanting to get away from it all."

"Like you two?" I asked, wondering if that was what had brought them there.

Georgie turned to Luca with a wink. "Our story's a little more complicated."

During that dinner, they recommended that we trek over to Monterosso, one of the other villages in Cinque Terre, to lay out on the beach since the weather was so nice and warm.

We're there now, lying under umbrellas, roasting and getting as warm as we can stand to be before we take another dip in the ocean. We're in no rush. This entire trip has been about slowing down, taking it easy, forgetting to check our phones. Our lives have been a little hectic lately. Ben's firm is growing, growing, growing. At a time when most people would buckle down, he's decided to take on less clients and shave off a little bit of the excess. *"It's not what life should be about,"* he told me the other night during dinner. I nodded and tried to hide my smile, glad he'd come to that conclusion all on his own.

In the last year, my programs at the library have grown too, and I've had to hire someone to assist me full-time, which means no more Intern Katy! HOORAY!

Our friends keep us busy as well. Arianna and Andy had a baby boy right around the time Kevin and Eli adopted twin girls. When we told the gang we were expecting, they screamed with excitement, Andy most of all.

This vacation away from everyone is good for us, though. We need time to wrap our heads around how much our lives will change in the next few months once our little girl arrives. I can't wait, but I'm appreciating every moment like this, just the two of us.

Ben's splayed out on the lounge chair beside me with his baseball hat covering his eyes. It's midafternoon and we just had a big lunch: fish caught just off shore, freshly baked bread, and vegetables grown right on the hillsides. By the end, I couldn't have eaten another bite if I'd tried, but then they brought out gelato and, well, somehow I managed to down that too. We're content right here, lounging and being as lazy as possible as the waves lap against the shore.

Ben's hand is running back and forth across my stomach slowly, lovingly. My bump is hardly showing, a fact I'm a tiny bit sad about. I'd wear my bikini proudly even if I was huge. As it is, it almost feels like a secret. No one else on the beach knows I'm pregnant, and there's something special about that.

"Think we should name her something Italian in honor of our trip? What was our waitress's name at lunch? Giada?"

Ben hums in amusement but keeps his eyes closed.

"No? What about Mopsie? Isn't that the cat's name at the bed and breakfast? The one that follows us everywhere?"

"Don't even think about it."

"Madison and Mopsie—you have to admit that's adorable."

"Adorable," he repeats sarcastically.

I turn back to the ocean and smile.

In truth, I have a list of names a mile long. Each day I wake up with a new favorite and I'm fully convinced that by the time this baby arrives, she'll have one of those long, rambling names like she's a British aristocrat. Katherine Marguerite Nicolette Rosenberg.

Ben shifts and sits up, dropping his hat on the lounge chair. It's the one he gave me after the frisbee incident, the one I let him borrow from time to time. We both know it rightfully belongs to me.

He stretches his arms overhead and his abs pull taut. I lower my sunglasses just a smidge to get a better view.

He spots me and smirks. "I'm going to get back in the water. You want to come?"

I shake my head. "You go. I'm comfy here."

"All right. Take care of our girl while I'm gone," he says before he turns, walking over the pebbled beach toward the waves. It's not so crowded that I lose sight of him as he dives forward and swims out toward the horizon. He's so beautiful, bronzed, and muscular. His brown hair has sun streaks. Even after years together, the butterflies in my stomach are alive and well.

I think part of that has to do with the fact that I haven't fully come to terms with reality. Ben Rosenberg is my husband. This giant rock on my finger is a real diamond, not a piece of costume jewelry. He tells me I'm beautiful and he laughs at my jokes. My wildest dreams have come true, and that's just it—all of this still sort of feels like a dream. I'm scared my dad will shake me awake and tell me I'm running late for work. I'll throw off my covers and slide right back into my old life, each day the same, each night spent wondering if there's something more waiting for me.

Then I press my hand to my stomach, and I know our child is growing there, our little girl who will be here before we know it.

This is real. This is what I wished for on my 25th birthday—well, not this *exact* thing. Wishing for Ben Rosenberg to impregnate me would have been kind of weird, but I like to think the universe extrapolated what I meant.

Ever since then, I've made some big birthday wishes. Why wouldn't I? The first one worked pretty damn well.

On my 26th birthday, I wished that Ben would propose.

Eight months later, he was down on one knee, sliding a ring on my finger while I did an absolutely abysmal job of keeping it together. In every photo from that night, I have snot running down my face. Eli has one framed in his house. He tells the twins, "That's your crazy aunt!"

On my 27th birthday, I wished that our wedding would go off without a hitch.

Cut to my dad and Ben's dad side by side on the dance floor, drunk as skunks, stumbling through the Macarena. They've been friends ever since.

On my 28th birthday, I wished we'd try for a baby.

And well, here I am, lying on the Ligurian Coast, knocked up.

It should come as no surprise that I've held on to that blue birthday candle, the one that first gave me the courage to change my life. In fact, it's tucked safely away inside a box in our closet, right on top of a stolen copy of *The Divine Comedy*, two souvenirs from my early days with Ben.

He suggested we give the book back to Jake. Never. Stolen or not, it's mine now.

I smile at the thought.

Maybe Ben really did make me bad.

Find other R.S. Grey Books on Amazon!

Hotshot Doc
Not So Nice Guy
Arrogant Devil
The Beau & the Belle
The Fortunate Ones
The Foxe & the Hound
Anything You Can Do
A Place in the Sun
The Summer Games: Out of Bounds
The Summer Games: Settling the Score
The Allure of Dean Harper
The Allure of Julian Lefray
The Design
The Duet
Scoring Wilder
Chasing Spring
With This Heart
Behind His Lens

Printed in Great Britain
by Amazon

56480395R00169